D. I. GHOST

By

LAUREN WHITE

A Detective Inspector Ghost Murder Investigation

Published by Tizz Publishing 2015
First published in paperback 2014
ISBN: 978-0-9930187-1-8

Tizz Publishing:
http://TizzPublishing.blogspot.co.uk
tizzpublishing@gmail.com

With thanks to: Lesley Dixon, Roman Ryczkowycz, Thecla
Geraghty, and Laetitia Rutherford.

For sisters and friends, dead and alive.

Other books by this author:

The Chalk Cliffs.

http://thechalkcliffsbylaurenwhite.blogspot.co.uk

Mirror, mirror...This is a modern fairy story as disturbing, enchanting, and humorous as any of the traditional ones we all know. Set in the recession of the 1980's a desperate young couple take their two daughters away on holiday with the intention of killing them. It is an act that flies in the face of everything they have done to nurture them, and they believe they are motivated by love, but over the course of a week they are forced to confront every assumption they have made about themselves, and each other. Damaged by the past and driven to breaking point, they have made a pact, but do they both want to go through with it, or does one of them have more influence, than the other. Some experiences are so traumatic, they cannot be resolved in one lifetime, but are passed on to the next generation. Seen through the eyes of the two girls, ultimately, this is a story about the nature of survival, the fragility of adulthood, the power of family relationships, and most of all, a child's determination to live.

ISBN: 978-0-9930187-3-2

SUMMER

I love to lie like this beside my sister watching her breathe. Why she fascinates me so much, I'm not sure. It must be because she's my mirror image. I look into her face and my sense of being quickens. Her olive-coloured skin, her brown eyes with mustard flecks, her thin fluted nose and burnt berry jam lips, so precisely replicate my own, my existence is confirmed by them. We are lying on our sides in the foetal position, facing each other. This is how we shared our mother's womb. We are indistinguishable but for one thing, my sister has a tiny cross on her forehead from the time, when as a small child, she fell and smashed her head against her bike. She needed three stitches and unbelievable to us both back then, I didn't. It was the first warning we had that looking the same would be no guarantee of life treating us the same.

I brush a silky black strand of hair away from her eyes. She's asleep but I feel it tickling for her.

You should leave him, I whisper in her ear.

I've been telling her this since the day before yesterday when she packed ten years of married life and motherhood into half a dozen suitcases, only to change her mind at the last minute. He - the creep - rewarded her loyalty by not coming home from work, until the early hours, and by the looks of it, he will do even better tonight. He has been keeping this up forever. He never explains where he's been. Poor Carrie thinks he's having an affair.

Why didn't you go through with it? When she's awake she does nothing but cry. *You worry me, Carrie. You really worry me.*

She should never have married him. This was our mother's mantra right up until the day she died and she was right. It was such an absurdly old fashioned thing for Carrie to do; getting married at only eighteen because she was pregnant. She has been giving birth to baby boys ever since – three of them – while I went to university without her, joined the police force and, during those same ten years, worked my way up the ranks to Detective

Inspector. By some miracle we stayed close. An identical twin is unavoidable. I can feel Carrie in my own soul. I know what she is thinking without her telling me. She is the same. That's the whole point of me lying here talking to her in her sleep. I know she'll be able to hear what I'm saying. Whether she will find the courage to act upon it is another matter.

There's a faint clicking sound downstairs. I lift my head from the pillow. He's back. That was his key in the front door. Sensing my withdrawal, Carrie rolls over away from me, breaking the symmetry of us. I ease myself off the bed to go out onto the landing to listen. He's gone straight to the kitchen. As I descend the stairs, I can see him by the light from the open fridge. His face is grimy. He can't have been fixing a car until this hour. Why would he bother? He employs five mechanics in that garage.

What time do you call this? She's been worried sick – as usual. Why didn't you phone?

He ignores me as he stands there picking at the chicken carcass on the top shelf of the fridge.

That's for the kids sandwiches, tomorrow.

He closes the door, but not before he's grabbed a bottle of beer. He caps this with his teeth. One of those tricks we used to think was clever in our teens. His only claim to fame, opening beer bottles with his teeth. What a loser. Swigging it down in one, he burps, loudly. Something else we thought endearing back then. Now, we have to warn the boys not to copy him.

Despite his disgusting habits, he's in good shape, Phil, good looking even, or he would be if the world were in black and white. In colour, there's something not quite healthy about him but you have to look past the blue eyes, wheat blonde hair, firm jaw, and fine boned nose to notice it. It takes practice. His handsomeness beguiles. By the time you find him out, it is almost too late.

He walks out of the kitchen and climbs the stairs two at a time, his long skinny legs racing each other, not out of eagerness but for the exercise. He likes to keep fit does the creep. Fit for nothing.

Don't go waking her up. She's only just got off.

6

Two seconds later, I know he hasn't taken my advice. I can hear Carrie crying and accusing but in a pleading, wheedling way because, although she refuses to admit this to me, she is frightened of him.

I don't have to answer to you, or anyone else, he yells at her.

Pack it in the pair of you, I mutter. *You'll wake the kids. You can discuss this in the morning.*

Caleb, my youngest nephew, is already out of bed. I can hear him padding across the floor. I don't want him to see this. It will only upset him. He doesn't understand why his parents row all the time. Their disappointment in each other is as passionate and selfish as sex. Lust, rather than love, turned sour. It crackles like static above the murmur of the city night.

I rush upstairs and slam their bedroom door shut to bring them to their senses and keep Caleb out. The noise shudders through the house.

What the hell did that?

Phil sounds startled. He pushes the door ajar to glower across the landing but I've retreated into the shadows where he can't see me.

The wind must have caught it, Carrie hurriedly reassures him. She doesn't want him to blame me. She knows I won't tolerate him having a go at me, the way he does with her.

What wind? There is no wind, he growls. *Loud enough to wake the dead, that was.*

My sister shrugs. *But, not the boys, luckily. Come on, Phil, let's get to bed. We can discuss this in the morning.*

Caleb is standing in the open doorway of his room, listening. I hold out my hand to him and he runs towards me, his gait lopsided, lurching slightly, in the uncoordinated way a three-year-old has.

Back to bed, Caleb.

I lead him inside his room, pop him under his covers, and sing him his duck song. He made this up himself several weeks ago. It is just a lot of quacks to the tune of London's Burning really but it seems to soothe him. He is asleep in seconds.

7

What time is it, Auntie Kate?

Jethro, his older brother, is awake on the top deck of their red, London, double-decker bus bunk beds. He has only recently learned to tell the time and he is obsessed with it, as though time itself were something meaningful.

Time you were asleep, young man.

He makes a face. Caleb is snoring his head off so I wedge myself between the bunks and the wall, where I can peer over Jethro's pillow and chat to him. I wouldn't admit this to my sister but he's my favourite nephew - only because six is a more interesting age than three and nine with boys, or so I tell myself to assuage my guilt for having a preference. Caleb is cute but he has the attention span of a gnat. And, Sam, who has his own room across the landing, has caught football fever already. Jethro has more space inside him somehow. He is a true philosopher. He runs deeper than imagination. He is the one I feel closest to.

Who's the lady downstairs, Auntie Kate?

What lady?

She sits in the rocker while I'm doing my piano practice.

The sweetness of his face moves me. He is going to be a heart breaker this child. I know that handsomeness doesn't always follow the milky skinned innocence of youth but Jethro has the kind of beautiful bones which will deliver a promise made. His eyes, chocolate pools in the half glow of the night light, are alert. I can tell he believes what he's just told me. I'm not sure what to say to him about it though. He's a bit old for imaginary friends, isn't he? Or did I awaken him from a dream when I put his brother back to bed?

What does she look like?

He considers this. *Blonde, pretty, except for her eyes.*

What's wrong with her eyes?

They're sort of glassy.

The word, hallucination, bounds unwanted into my mind. *Does she bother you? Do you want me to talk to her? I could tell her to go away, if you like.*

Can you see her too?

I don't want to commit myself, one way or the other. *I'm not sure. I'll take a look the next time you're practising. Okay?*

My relief at finding a full stop to this conversation soon breeds more anxiety. I wrestle with myself. It is no good. I am going to have to ask him. I've protected Carrie ever since she was dragged, kicking and screaming, into the world seven and a half minutes after me.

Have you told Mummy about this?

He shakes his head, his black fringe flopping over his eyes. It needs cutting.

Best not to for now, I advise him. *She has...She is a bit preoccupied with... well, you know, with mummy stuff.*

Which is probably the reason for all this, I decide. Yes, of course, that's it. Why didn't I realise it sooner? Jethro is feeling neglected. He's not getting enough attention from his warring parents so he has invented this woman who listens to him while he does his piano practice.

She must really like listening to you play. I know I do, I lie.

But who is she?

Ignoring the urgency in his voice, I shrug, playfully. *A big fan of yours, obviously.*

He smiles. The crooked grin of his father but I never hold this against him.

That's better. Now, go to sleep. You've got school in the morning, young man, I chide, pressing my lips to his forehead.

I sit in the same rocking chair as Jethro's glassy-eyed lady. How worried should I be about this? He doesn't seem to be upset in any other way. Not that I've noticed. But, he is the middle child. People say they get missed.

I sense Carrie standing beside me without having to look up at her.

Can't you sleep?

She answers me by going to the curtains and opening them. It's morning - watery beads of light spill into the room. I liked it better in darkness. I told her not to paint the walls this colour. Only trees look good in green. She calls this the family room because it's filled with comfort furniture. These are the old friends she inherited from our mother. The survivors of so many fights and spillages of hers and mine, the odd scratch and stain the boys manage to contribute doesn't much matter. A generous use of throws has replaced the worn dignity of their ancient admiral blue with yet another shade of yucky green.

We have to talk, Carrie. Are the kids still in bed?

I turn to listen for myself. The house is quiet.

She sits on the sofa, opposite me, pulling her knees up to her chest and hugging them to her. She is wearing my red plaid pyjamas. I don't mind but she should have asked me. She'd have a fit if I commandeered something of hers without mentioning it first. Her face is puffy. She has been crying again.

I'm concerned about, Jethro. He's invented a woman to listen to him play the piano. This can't go on, you know. You have to do something.

She sighs, deeply. She understands where this is heading. I'm offering her another reason why she should leave Phil.

I wish I had your strength, Kate.

I say nothing. I'm too angry. She's staying put. Not even the effect this is having on the boys makes a difference to her. I shall have to go on watching her fade from her life in silence. She's a good act, Carrie. During most of her marriage, her definition of pride has been pretence. It is no wonder she has a Green Room.

*I can't leave him. You do see that, don't you? Not now. I'm not even sure I can...go on...not without ...*She starts to sob.

For God's sake, Carrie, I can't bear it. What would you have me do?

She cries harder.

Okay, okay. You win. I'll investigate what he's up to before putting any more pressure on you to leave him but it might be nothing, you know. You might have to find the resolve to move on, without the excuse of him having an affair. I promise you I'll dig around though. I'll go to his garage and I'll try to discover why he is coming home so late.

It's the funeral tomorrow, isn't it?

I spin around. It is him. Did he hear me? No, he can't have. He hasn't even glanced in my direction. I'll say this for him. He looks

10

better on hardly any sleep than I feel.

I'm not sure I can face it, Phil. I can't believe...It doesn't seem real. I can't ...Carrie splutters the rest of the sentence into her hanky.

I get up from the chair. I've had enough of her gloominess. She can't leave him but she is miserable as hell with him. What sense does that make?

I'm going to get the kids their breakfast, I call over my shoulder to her.

Sam is already up. He's filling a bowl with cornflakes. He acts like I'm not there. It is the age, I tell myself: nine, going on plain rude.

Look at that!

I glance back through the open doorway into the room I've just left. My brother-in-law is staring at the rocking chair in astonishment.

It's moving by itself.

I roll my eyes to the ceiling. *What is it with this family and that chair?*

What does it mean, Auntie Kate?

Oh, you're up too, Jethro. Good, it saves me coming to wake you. It means your dad's brain is still asleep. I was sitting there. That's why it is moving.

He is standing transfixed by the front door, pouring over a photograph in the newspaper he has picked up off the mat.

I go to take a look. It's a picture of a young woman. *She is missing*, I read aloud over his shoulder.

Missing?

Mistake! I've been an aunt long enough to know that one careless little word like that can develop into an epidemic of sleepless nights and nightmares. I need to back pedal, and rapidly.

She'll turn up. She probably has already. There's no need to worry.

But, what does it mean?

Mean? What's he going on about?

Come on Jethro the time's getting on and you haven't had any breakfast yet. You don't want to be late for school, do you, I nag to change the subject.

He is still glued to the spot staring at the photograph.

It's the same lady who listens to me practising, Auntie Kate. The one with the glassy eyes.

My sister's house is an Edwardian semi situated on a wide, tree-lined avenue, which flows between a parade of commuter shops and a major roundabout, on the way out of London towards Kent. It comes with traffic, accordingly, which makes its upstairs view of Blackheath affordable.

A wreck when she and Phil first bought it, they've had to render over the settlement cracks and then paint it bitter-chocolate to make it look half way decent. It is still Carrie's private revenge over every raised eyebrow her rushed wedding provoked. It means to her that she has arrived - granted, via a different route than going to university as originally planned - but at least she's visibly comfortably off. Her boorish young husband comes from a prosperous family and, as soon as his father retired from the garage, he took over the running of it, and later when he died, he inherited it.

Carrie moves through this house like a ghost. It is a shock when I suddenly stumble upon her. It is as though she has materialised right in front of my eyes.

I didn't realise you were in here. I thought you'd gone out. She has slipped into the room where I usually sleep when I stay over. *Why are you dressed in black? You know it isn't our colour.*

She doesn't answer me.

There's no need to be pissy with me. I followed him about all day, yesterday, but I didn't find anything. Not really. The business isn't in brilliant shape but that's only because he has taken out a loan on the premises. Did he mention that to you?

Carrie is staring out of the window.

There isn't any sign of another woman, not at work anyway. I checked his desk and his mobile, and there was nothing remotely suspicious about either. He's a bit flirty with the female customers but that's probably good for business.

She crosses the room to the door and leaves without speaking one word to me. What's wrong with her? I hate it when she's like this.

I think he's just worried about keeping up the payments on that loan, I call after her. *That's why he's doing some of the mechanical work himself, at night. It has to be cheaper than employing another worker.*

When she doesn't return, I take up her position by the window. In the distance, I can see a paper dragon kite, brightly coloured, with a long thin tail, undulating on the air currents above Blackheath. I wouldn't have thought the wind was strong enough to get it airborne today. It is the first summery day we've had, though it is already half way through June. Where does the time go? The days bleed one into the other without me being able to keep track of them. I can no longer recall for how long my sister has been enveloped in this cloying sadness. I only know I'm sick of it. Her domestic situation is upsetting but resolvable so why is she bullying me with her ill humour? I haven't done anything to her; it's not my fault her life is crap and mine isn't. I wasn't exactly born with a genetic advantage.

Are you going to the funeral, Auntie Kate?

Damn! That's why Carrie is dressed in black. She must think me an idiot.

Will you sit next to me?

I smile down into Jethro's eager little face. *Of course, I will. Does it start soon? I'd better go and get ready.*

Is it me, or does the blazer he's wearing – navy blue with a white crest on the front pocket – look too big for him. He gets the short straw when it comes to clothes. Sam, the oldest, gets new, Jethro gets seconds, and Caleb gets new again because everything is too worn out, by the time he is ready for it.

Auntie Kate, what happens to you when you die?

Trust him to come up with this now. *That's quite a big subject for this time in the morning,* I breeze.

His eyes are shining as he waits for me to enlighten him.

Well, I imagine we go back to where we came from.

I should have realised he wouldn't let me get away with that.

He comes straight back at me. *Where is that?*

I grin in defeat. *That's the problem, Jethro. As soon as we're born we start to forget.*

14

He looks baffled more than disappointed. Quit while you're behind I self-counsel.

Have you seen the kite over there?

He shrugs. He always was the difficult one to distract. He takes after me. He's tenacious.

Maybe you should ask Mummy where we come from, I suggest, as I stride through the doorway on my way to the bathroom. *I was born before her, Jethro. I've had more time to forget.*

Funerals always make me want to laugh. *That's just hysteria,* my mother once diagnosed, when I confided in her about this. *It must have something to do with your father dying when you were only ten years old.* According to her, everything which happened in our family A.D. (After Dad), including her cancer, had something to do with him dying when Carrie and I were ten years old. I didn't even go to his funeral. The chapel of rest was the furthest I managed to get that terrible week. When the undertaker lifted the lid of my father's coffin so I could say goodbye to him, I was confronted by this waxy doll in a night shirt. He looked like a glove puppet. He looked like Punch. Drawing the undertaker aside, I remember asking him: *Don't you think he's wearing too much make up?* The man dipped his head three or four times in a fawning gesture, I imagine he thought respectful, before breaking it to me that since my father had laid dead on his side, for ten hours, his blood had pooled, creating a dark red stain under the skin. A lot of foundation was needed to cover over something like that. *Oh I see,* I said, struggling to take this in. Back at the corpse, I realised there were strands of what looked like cotton wool protruding from his eyes and mouth. *Maybe it's that he has been a little overstuffed then,* I tried. *In life, he had folds of flesh on either side of his mouth.* I put my hands to my face to demonstrate. *But, they seem to have been filled up with something.* I puffed out the lower part of my own cheeks to show him what I meant. He was staring at me with a curious expression. I was a species of child mourner he hadn't come across before, obviously. *It doesn't look like my father,* I finally admitted to him in case he was missing my point. Then, I withdrew from my pocket a bridge of four false teeth, wrapped in a paper hanky, which I pushed into his hand. *Would these help? The hospital gave them to Mum with his things. He lost the real ones in a motorbike accident.* The undertaker received my tiny parcel by dipping his head manically a dozen times, although not rapidly enough to conceal his astonishment. *Shall I leave you*

16

alone with the deceased? He was obviously having second thoughts about it. Perhaps, he was worried I would start rearranging my father's stuffing myself. Carrie was the sensible one. She stayed away. *I'd rather remember him the way he was,* she sobbed, as she watched me with my head down the toilet, retching up my guts afterwards. How right she was. It took me months to get the glove puppet out of my mind.

Leaning across Caleb to whisper to my sister, I ask: *Where's the wake being held?* But, my brother-in-law butts in before she can answer.

Do we have to go to the wake?

She turns to glare at him. *Of course, we do. Trevor's girl will have been up half the night doing the food.*

Goody. If it is in the banqueting suite at Trevor's pub, it will be a decent bash. I wave jauntily at some friends sitting a few rows behind me. They're staring straight at me but, ridiculously, they refuse to acknowledge me. Why do people always feel so constrained at funerals? There's a couple alongside them who are the spitting image of my next door neighbours in Deptford. It can't be them, can it? I wouldn't have thought we moved in the same circles. When I bought my flat, an ex-council place by the old wharves, it was the only one cheap enough for me to afford, but barely a year later, Bennett and Chelsee (Americans obviously) paid something obscene for theirs.

Jethro elbows me. *Have you seen her? What's she doing here, Auntie Kate?*

Who?

There at the back. It's the lady in the rocking chair.

I follow his line of sight. *The one who listens to your piano practice?*

He nods, earnestly, his black fringe flopping forwards. I must remember to remind Carrie it needs cutting.

The lady in the newspaper - the one with the glassy eyes, he whispers, dramatically.

It isn't possible to see her eyes from where we're sitting but it is hard to miss the fact she is dressed in a powder blue cocktail dress. Not the most suitable attire for a funeral, I would have thought.

What does she want, Auntie Kate?

That's what I intend to find out, Jethro, I declare, rising.

The coffin has been placed on two trestles, blocking the centre aisle, which makes it awkward to get past. The polished mahogany lid is crowned with a massive halo of sunflowers. They're my favourite flowers in fact but an unusual choice for a funeral wreath. I take the side aisle to the back of the crematorium instead. Jethro's glassy eyed lady is seated alone on the last pew.

Is anyone sitting here?

She examines me with an amused expression. *Does it look like it to you?*

Those seven words tell me everything I need to know about her. Each syllable is enunciated with cut-glass precision and coated with a watery (bottled not tap) disdain. This is what comes from being marinated in wealth and privilege in your mother's womb, I shouldn't wonder. This woman has a sense of superiority in her bone marrow. She is about my age, with long yellow tresses, a high Elizabethan forehead, and sapphire blue eyes. They're glassy, exactly, as Jethro described, although in me they conjure up the image of a porcelain doll. She's petite as a doll too. I feel like a dark tower as I sit down beside her.

Are you a friend of the departed?

Not, exactly, she answers. *Why are you?*

Her tone is flippant and I don't understand why. I can't think for a moment. I feel confused. I look around me. The hall where we're sitting is a simple white painted rectangle, with modern wooden pews. It is packed with police uniforms. We must be here to say goodbye to one of our own. But, I'm not sure...

My name is Belinda Montgomery and I need to speak with you, Detective Inspector.

That really surprises me. *Missing persons are nothing to do with me, Ms Montgomery. I only investigate murders.*

She is staring at me, strangely. *You really don't know, do you?*

Know what?

She flicks some imaginary dirt off the hem of her dress. *How have you been feeling recently Detective Inspector?*

Fine, why?

You haven't had anything happen to you? Anything...violent, for example? An accident, perhaps?

She moves her index finger round in a circle, as though trying to encourage me to develop the idea. Smaller circles with her finger touching her temple, accompanied by a low warbling whistle, would more accurately describe my reaction to her question. She is mad. I slide myself a little further away from her on the pew and look for my boss, Detective Chief Inspector Bixby, in the crowd. I saw him earlier with Fester and Nigs, who work with me. If I can attract their attention, we could get Belinda out of here, without causing too much of a disturbance. She must have gone missing because she is having some kind of breakdown. I see Bixby heading for the podium but, the moment I stand up to wave to him, Belinda pulls me down onto the pew again, and as I fall backwards beside her, I hear the screech of a car.

Hell's teeth! What was that? There is a deafening crunch and I feel nothing. *I don't understand.*

Belinda is looking at me as though she isn't sure what I'm going to do next.

Was it you who ran me over?

She shakes her head.

But this is a dream, right? I don't even bother to wait for her to reply because I know it isn't. *I have to get out of here. I have to...*

Don't you want to hear what they have to say?

Sliding to the end of the pew, I ease myself out into the aisle.

Do as you please, Detective Inspector, she hisses after me. *It is your bloody funeral.*

All I can think of is getting away. No, what I want to do is run away. But, that would feel too much like losing control and I have to keep a hold of myself - of whatever is left of me - otherwise...I head towards the double doors at the back of the crematorium which Val, one of the civilian workers from my office, is about to close. I can hear Belinda following behind me in her high heels, powder blue satin ones to match her dress. Bixby's deep voice with the pleasing singsong lilt of St Vincent resonates from the podium, around the hall.

Detective Inspector, Kate Madding, was such a handful. The remark is greeted by the laughter of recognition. Relief too. Relief at knowing they're still alive and I'm... *She was so full of life, she left me and everyone else around her breathless. She was one of the brightest and at times fiercest detectives I've ever had the honour of knowing. She did everything in a hurry. She spoke, ate, worked, got herself promoted, everything, faster than everyone else. It was as though she knew she wasn't going to have much time.*

I am through those doors before he can say any more.

Are you okay?

I glare at Belinda. *What do you think! Why didn't anyone say something? Why didn't I realise? I feel so stupid.*

You were probably too shocked to take it in. It was the same with me. Well, it is bound to be a shock, isn't it? She turns to look back at the crematorium to give me a little space to recover myself. *They're such awfully drab places, aren't they? No character at all. I definitely want to be done in a church when they find me.*

That's when I finally fall in.

You're dead, not missing.

She nods, grimly. *Which is exactly why I've come here to speak with you, D. I. Ghost.*

What should you do if you discover you're dead and didn't know it? I do what I've always done when something emotionally upsetting happens, I throw myself into work. I agree to meet with Belinda at my new office in the basement of my sister's house. It is full of junk but I manage to find a battered old civil service desk that Carrie picked up from a second hand store, back in the days when she did Phil's accounts, plus a couple of red plastic stacking chairs. Neither Belinda nor I actually need them. It is just as comfortable sort of hanging around. But, given the newness of our situation I decide they might help to foster an air of familiarity. The only passably useful item of furniture I add to my new haunt is a three tiered filing cabinet which Carrie painted blue for some reason. It has an empty set of buff hanging files in every drawer, hungry for distraction. I can't help wondering, as I survey this admittedly rather desultory scene, whether I should have set myself up in my flat instead, where there is at least a study tastefully furnished from IKEA. While I was living, this provided me with the perfect retreat from the commotion of the Murder Investigation Team's shared office; from the open sewer of smutty jokes running through it, specifically. But, in my afterlife I crave commotion. I am drawn to anything and anyone that lives; to my sister and her family most of all. I fill myself up with her and the boys as though life itself were catching.

Belinda is still wearing her blue satin cocktail dress when she arrives, or to be more accurate the memory of it lingers on in her like perfume. It is hard to describe how I perceive her. She gives the impression of herself as she was in life but the source of this impression is energy and not matter.

She coolly examines the microdot of order I've created in the middle of Carrie's unwanted debris and fixes me with her glassy stare.

I want to know what happened to me, Detective Inspector, she says, with the clipped dignity of a character in a Noel Coward play. *How I got to be...well, dead. And, my body is... Well, it is*

21

missing. I do realise it can't do me much good now but I would like to discover where it is.

Such a surreal brief: a dead woman who doesn't know how she died or where her body is. I always assumed when you died you'd know everything but it isn't like that at all. Both Belinda and I appear to be suffering from some kind of posthumous traumatic stress. Not the best starting point for an investigation. Fortunately, she isn't aware of my misgivings. I must be getting more skilled at keeping some of my thoughts to myself. This is a relief. Angst sharing isn't my thing.

I suggest we begin at the beginning.

Which is where, exactly?

Bixby my boss is fond of saying that a police investigation is forty percent fact and sixty percent luck. Luck Belinda and I are surely out of, which leaves us with what, exactly...I decide to start with the basics.

What's your full name?

Reassured by being asked a question to which she actually knows the answer Belinda immediately cheers up. *That's easy. My full name is Belinda Eugenia Isabel Montgomery but everyone calls me, Bim.*

Everyone but me she means. What kind of name is Bim for a grown woman?

I'd like you to tell me the last thing you remember, before you realised you were dead, Belinda.

Did that seem weird to her too? Apparently not, she launches into a long explanation.

I was on my way to the cocktail party my company had organised for some new clients - merchant bankers. You know what those are, right? Well, we'd hired a restaurant in Knightsbridge, near to our public relations agency. I set off in my BMW from home - I have a mews house in Greenwich, close to the river. It was about seven o'clock in the evening when I left. But, I never arrived.

I can't decide whether she is answering my question or trying to impress me because the words that leap out at me are: *cocktail party, merchant bankers, Knightsbridge, BMW, and mews house.*

22

Do you have any idea why you didn't arrive?

She smiles, tightly, at me. *Well, I'm thinking abduction and murder, Detective Inspector, the same as everyone else, but my mind is pretty much a complete blank from the time I left home. The next thing I remember I was wandering about in the street, in an extremely distressed state, but nobody could see or hear me. I didn't realise it, immediately, but I was dead.*

I read in the newspaper you went missing on June 7th.

The date has lodged in my mind because it was the same day on which I turned out to have died myself. Belinda's car was found abandoned in New Cross, the following day, only ten minutes drive away from her home. There was no sign of a struggle. Nor had the car broken down. Yet, it was obvious to the police that something untoward must have happened because her handbag - with her purse, driver's licence, and credit cards - was discovered under the passenger seat.

When does your memory kick in again?

Three nights and two days later.

This puts an end to that line of questioning. She could have been taken to the Outer Hebrides and back in that time. Her body might be anywhere. I change tack.

Does anyone stand to gain from your death?

The beneficiaries of my Will, I suppose, but they're all members of my family and frankly Detective Inspector none of them is strapped for cash. An account executive at work is likely to be promoted into my role but there's no way of knowing who yet. I won't be easy to replace, I can tell you that. My death is a disaster for the agency. They're bound to lose clients because of it.

Do you have a partner?

*Not as such...*She hesitates.

But?

It's a bit of a cliché.

What is?

I've been having an affair with my boss.

This is more like it. Most murder victims are killed by someone they know.

It's a him?
She nods.
Is he married?
No, what do you take me for? He's divorced.
So how long have you been seeing him?
Six months but we've kept it quiet. Nobody knows at the office. We didn't want anyone to feel uncomfortable about it. You know, working together, sleeping together. It could be embarrassing...
Would your boss have any reason to want you dead?
She pauses almost imperceptibly, before she bludgeons me with her rebuttal.

No, forget that, Detective Inspector! Definitely not! Not in a billion years! The man wouldn't harm a hair on my head!

I have my prime suspect. Call me a cynic but trusting the intuition of a murder victim doesn't seem like a good idea to me. Let's face it. They're not exactly likely to be the best judges of character, are they?

My desk at work is exactly as I left it. Nobody has taken so much as a paper clip. I feel proud to have been part of a team like that. I choose not to sit at it, however. I may be invisible but I don't feel it. Blind panic pulses through me every time someone living looks in my direction. My boss, Detective Chief Inspector Bixby, is on leave so I go to his office to use the computer there. I'm betting he won't have gotten around to blocking my access yet. Perhaps, they don't if you die which is a bit of an oversight as it turns out. As I wait for the system to crank into life, my attention is drawn by one of the framed photographs, hanging on the wall. It was taken last Christmas in our local pub. There we are - Bixby, Fester, Nigs, and I - rat-arsed and grinning from ear to ear. We had no idea then that, within six months, one of us was going to die. I don't know how - I'm not even touching it - but the photograph seems to leap off the wall at me. I'm so surprised, I let it smash onto the floor and before I can recover from the shock of this, the door flies open and Nigs comes in. He looks perplexed while he tries to locate the source of the noise which has brought him running. Spotting the shattered frame under Bixby's desk, he picks it up and bangs it against the inside of the paper bin to release the remaining shards of glass. He is about to place it on the table, when he does something extraordinary. He lifts it to his mouth and kisses it. He kisses me to be precise and stranger still I swear I can feel the caress of his lips on mine.

*How can you do that now, when you never...*No, that's not how I want to put this. I start again. *Why didn't you show me how you felt while I was alive, you idiot?* His brown eyes are moist. *I wanted you to so much it hurt,* I whisper to him.

No, I'm not being fair. It was always more complicated between him and me than that because I would have died before I showed it. It's what Belinda said, really. Working together, sleeping together. Is it ever a good idea? If Bixby had discovered there was something going on between us, there would have been hell to pay. Relationships between officers serving in the same team are frowned upon in the force. One of us would have had to put in for a transfer and I didn't want it to be me. I'd only just got that promotion. I wasn't going to make Bixby regret recommending me for it. There was still a buzz of attraction between Nigs and me. The bickering foreplay we kept up during our shifts together was the testament to it. *One day*, I promised myself, *one day*. How was I supposed to know I'd die before I got the chance? I was only twenty nine years old. There should have been time for everything.

He isn't handsome, Nigs, not in a traditional way. His face is one of those wonderful lived in ones but someone must have thought him gorgeous when he was a kid because that's what he exudes. He is dark and sexy, and he moves like syrup. Not that it does me much good now. I'm the ghost he is never going to lay.

When he leaves the room, I get this daft idea about following him home at the end of his shift. What's to stop me living with him in death as I never did in life? But before I can pass through the door after him, it opens again. He is back and this time Fester is with him. My two closest friends in all the world and we are together again. It feels so bitter-sweet. What am I saying? It feels great. I love these guys.

There, can you smell it?

Fester puts his nose into the air and sniffs, deeply. He shakes his head.

Try again, Nigs instructs. *It's there, I swear it is.*

I start sniffing too to see what he is on about.

I can't smell anything, mate.

Nigs looks disappointed. *It was there. It was! Kate's perfume, I'd recognise it anywhere.*

Fester pats him on the back. Nigs doesn't notice but there is concern in his eyes.

One of the girls down the hall probably wears the same brand, mate. Come on, why don't we get out of here. Let's grab a cup of coffee in the cafe around the corner.

He leads the way out of Bixby's office but Nigs lingers for a moment, still yearning for a trace of me.

I miss you Kate, he whispers, before he too walks away.

26

Shit, I should have grabbed him when I had the chance. One day, he'll find someone else and settle down with them. I'm never going to. Even better, I have an eternity in which to regret that. Isn't afterlife great!

What is up with you, Madding?

I spin around in surprise. The man I see before me is exactly the same as I remember - pasty complexion, grey curly hair, drooping moustache, and a massive paunch overhanging his belt like a multiple pregnancy.

Sergeant Ross, what are you doing here?

I've never been more pleased to see anyone. Robbie Ross was my boss when I was still in uniform. He died of a heart attack, seven years ago, right in front of me, while we were taking a break in the canteen. I've never smoked a cigarette or eaten a fry up since. Although, if I'd known I was going to die at twenty nine years old, I might have.

I should have guessed you weren't the type for eternal rest, Madding.

I don't remember being given much choice, actually.

Are you sure about that?

That flummoxes me. *What are you talking about, Sarge?*

You're the detective, you figure it out. He starts moving away from me again.

Where are you going? I want to talk to you.

Go home, Madding, you're needed there, he says firmly, before he disappears.

It is past midnight by the time I arrive back at my sister's house. It seems as quiet as the grave. I check on the kids and pick up Caleb's teddy from the floor by his bed where it has tumbled, snuggling it down between the sheets with his young owner. On the top bunk, Jethro stirs as I kiss his forehead but he doesn't awaken. I can't help wondering for how long my two youngest nephews will go on seeing me. Forever, I hope.

Downstairs, in the living room, Carrie has fallen asleep on the sofa waiting for Phil to come home. The television is murmuring in the corner. It is tuned to a news channel. Curled up in his armchair, Belinda is glued to it.

We seem to have acquired her as a house guest which wasn't exactly my intention when I agreed to help her find her body. For me, her constant presence contains all the awkwardness that flat sharing did when I was training, only Belinda doesn't steal my milk. It is one of the disadvantages about being dead, I'm discovering. There just isn't enough separation between work and home.

Good day, Belinda? She was supposed to go and check out the road where her car was found to see if she recognised it.

She nods, still fixated on the television screen.

Well, share it with me then.

Finally, she gives me her attention.

The police have found my body.

It isn't a pretty sight, although it is the knowledge of what it is that makes it so. Most people chancing upon it would probably walk straight past because the flesh has rotted away to a ruby-brown earthy substance, all but indistinguishable from the soil which partially covers it. There are still some slithers of leathery skin covering the bones, and a few tufts of mud-caked hair are visible. A couple of strips of fabric, stiffened with earth, are protruding too but not so much the casual eye would be drawn to them. A golfer discovered these remains by accident. Her ball had overshot the nearby green, landing in the bushy copse, which runs along the eastern perimeter of the course. She would have abandoned it but a hole in the fence, large enough for her to crawl through, enticed her to look around for it. She found it easily but in retrieving it from the mud, where it had come to rest, her hand came away with a matted lock of human hair.

The white suits of the forensic officers, who have been working on this grizzly find throughout the night, move carefully in and out of the trees. They won't attempt to remove the body until they've extracted every possible piece of evidence from the immediate vicinity, square metre by square metre, in a grid of their own devising.

The area is cordoned off and screened from public, and press, view but Belinda and I are positioned inside this barrier. She consumes the scene, voraciously. It is clear she hasn't yet realised so I tell her, bluntly: *This can't be your body, Belinda.*

Why not?

The decomposition is too advanced. This body must have lain here for months, possibly even years.

The anguish I see in her makes me feel cruel for confronting her with the truth.

Why can't I remember what happened to me? What's wrong with me?

Have you ever considered it might be better not to remember?

I need to know, Detective Inspector, she says, simply, as she turns her attention back to the grave.

I've no idea why the police used to ask women officers to do all the emotional stuff, back in the old days. It is just as well it was before my time because I've never been any good at it. There is something I don't quite get about feelings, my own as much as other people. Why does Belinda need to know? How will it help anything? She'd still be dead.

The forensics work, painstakingly, which for me means, excruciatingly, slowly. They dust and probe the site like archaeologists, hour after hour. While we are waiting for them to finish, I explore the surrounding terrain. I find myself wondering how this body could have been dumped in this spot. The dead weight of even a small corpse is difficult for one person to carry so lone murderers tend to dispose of their victims close to wherever they can park a car. The nearest road here – assuming a car couldn't have driven across the golf course without leaving some sign – is above the copse of trees. There's a steep incline so at least the killer would have had the help of gravity to roll the body down to the place where it is buried.

I go up to the road and retrace the route he might have taken. The trees are so close together, if he did roll it down, he would have had to stop every two seconds to move it in and out of the trees. It would almost have been easier to carry it, but the distance and uneven ground suggests to me that if he did, he must be incredibly strong. Strong people do exist, of course, and adrenalin pushes even the weakest ones beyond their usual limits, but I'm not convinced. Could he have used a wheelbarrow? I doubt it. The incline is too steep to control it – on one's own. That's what I keep coming back to. The position of this body would make more sense to me if two people had brought it down here together. Two men? A man and a woman?

What happens now?

I turn to answer Belinda only to find it isn't her who is addressing me. There's a small dark haired woman by my side. She is covered with mud - her long hair is plastered to her scalp with it - and she is wearing what looks like a soiled and tattered wedding dress. Her presence is not so much harrowing as harrowed. Whatever she has been through, I doubt I want to hear about it, but I'm too curious not to ask.

Is it you in that grave?

Her eyes are blue, and glassy. Another one. Is this how I appear to Caleb and Jethro? If so they've never mentioned it. I've only heard them describe Belinda as glassy-eyed.

Is it you, down there in that grave?

She nods. *I was murdered.*

What is the appropriate response to that? *Really? How interesting*! I can't decide so I do what I usually do when I feel uncomfortable, I gabble.

I'm Detective Inspector, Kate Madding. Or I was. Actually, I'm a sort of private detective now – not the London Eye so much as the London private eye. Yes, anyway, someone has asked me to help them find their body. She's down there, in blue. Do you see her? She was murdered, too. Well, she thinks she was, but she doesn't actually remember.

Would you help me?

I examine her muddy face. She is young this woman, barely out of her teens. Her expression is fluid and self-conscious.

Please, Detective. Would you?

She is looking at me tentatively as though she is frightened I might hurt her. Is this how she was in life or is it something to do with the way she died? If someone hated her enough to kill her, perhaps, she has a reason to feel suspicious about the rest of us.

But, you know where your body is.

Even by my standards it is an incredibly stupid thing to have said. She looks crestfallen, mistaking my words for the rebuff she half-expected.

Someone strangled me, she murmurs. *He called himself, Simon Says.*

Simon Says, like in the children's game?

Game?

Yes, my nephews play it. Well, Sam, the eldest, is probably getting a bit old for it now but the other two still do. You know how it goes, don't you?

She shakes her head.

The child who is Simon says something like, Simon says put your hands on your head, and the other children are supposed to do it. Then, he might say, Simon says jump up in the air, and they're supposed to do that too. It goes on like that really, until suddenly the one who is Simon just says: spin round - without the, Simon says, first. And any child who does it is out.

She stares blankly at me while she struggles to make sense of a single word I've said. Then, her face seems to clear a little as finally she gives up on my garbled explanation.

He dressed me in this gown and moved me into different positions like I was a doll. He got angry because I wasn't doing it right. It wasn't my fault. I couldn't move on my own. I must have been drugged. But, he strangled me, anyway.

There is an absence of emotion in her words despite the horrific experiences she is describing. I've witnessed this before in victims of traumatic crimes. It is as though they have to go to a faraway place within themselves in order to talk about it. It is a fragile solution because, sooner or later, the enormity of what has happened to them will break through their defences and traumatise them all over again. My instinct has always been to get as much information from them as I can, before they reach this point. I don't find it easy to listen, though. I've never liked the sick details of a murder. I can cope with any amount of blood and gore, I have a strong stomach, or I used to. It is the psychological stuff, the power games, the sadism, and torture that they suffer, I can't stand. That's what makes me want to vomit.

The silence between us is beginning to sound like a scream, so I ask her: *Do you remember what your killer looked like?*

The firmness of her response surprises me.

He was small, muscular, but wiry, like a weasel. He covered his head with a mask but I did see his face and hair. I'm not sure how. Perhaps, it was before he drugged me. I can't remember but I know he had ash blonde hair and...

She falls silent again.

What colour were his eyes? Do you remember?

They were bluish-grey. He had a pale complexion too and a moustache.

Would you recognise him again, if you saw him?
I believe I might.

It's a pretty good description, I murmur. And, if only I were alive it might be enough to track him down.

Does that mean you'll help me? I want him to go to jail for what he did to me.

I evade her gaze. He should be locked up, of course, he should. I'm just not very confident I can pull that off as D. I. Ghost.

Down at the grave, they're getting ready to move her remains. Dawn is breaking and the sky is luminous with the first rays of sunlight. A mobile canteen has arrived and a stream of the non essential white suits, hungry for their bacon butties after working through the night, is flowing noisily towards it. There is so much life in them, I can barely think.

What's your name?

Kerry Doughton. She points to the cordon around her grave. *The woman in blue has disappeared.*

Damn! She's right. Belinda has gone. I feel guilty. I shouldn't have left her alone for so long. She must still be upset. And, she never did tell me whether she recognised the street where her car was found. I ought to go and find her but I hesitate. Kerry remembers so much more than Belinda, I want to pursue her case too.

Kerry wins. I take her Bixby's office. It is on the fourth floor and the view from his window seduces me while we're waiting for the Missing Persons' Database to come up on his computer. I love the roofs of London. When I was a kid these were my land of opportunity. They let me peak at the possibility of a life beyond the confines of my family and neighbourhood. I'd sit in my classroom on the top floor of my Victorian red-bricked school and plot my escape across them, towards an indistinct but exotic future. I never guessed this would be an untimely death.

I might be wrong but I think the password has been accepted.

Yes, of course, I say, snapping to and punching in Kerry's name.

Within seconds there she is, except the woman pictured in the

33

photograph before me doesn't look anything like the muddy companion by my side. She is very blonde and very beautiful.

I print off her photograph while I am reading the information recorded there about her.

Kerry Doughton, a student, aged 20, went missing two years ago. She was on her way back to university, after arriving home, unexpectedly, to announce to her astonished parents that she wanted to leave. She missed her American boyfriend too much to want to stay in Nottingham on her own, she said.

He'd graduated from the same university the year before, and had returned to the States. Kerry's parents had never met him, and nor had anyone else. She kept herself to herself in the Hall of Residence where she was living and she didn't mix socially with the other students on her geography course, either. She was the quiet, studious sort. That's what her mother and father had always believed and they were horrified to hear she wanted to give up her degree and leave university, the year before her finals, for a man she'd only dated a matter of months before he'd gone back to his own country without a second glance.

They tried to talk her out of it. They were convinced they had by the time she set off again, a few days later, in one of the old cars they kept in the barn at the back of the house. She was supposed to be headed back to Nottingham to complete the last weeks of that term. Then, they'd have the summer vacation to bolster her resolve to return there in the autumn to complete the last year of her course.

They miscalculated. Kerry never arrived at her Hall of Residence. She disappeared without a trace.

The case wasn't more than the mystery of a few days, really. It was suspected she'd run off to America, possibly covering her tracks by driving to Europe first. The car was missing and cars don't just disappear unless someone drives them somewhere. She was listed as a missing person but her disappearance was never exhaustively investigated. Nor did the police put any resources into trying to find the boyfriend. Kerry's disappearance wasn't thought to be sufficiently suspicious to justify more than a minimum effort.

Her parents didn't make a fuss. They felt the police were right. By opposing their daughter's plan to leave university, they'd driven her away from them. Her passport was missing so she must have meant to disappear. All they could do was hope she'd relent as she grew older - maybe after becoming a parent herself – and let them know where she was living.

How awful for them to spend all this time believing she turned her back on them, when she'd been lying dead in that shallow grave.

Something else strikes me as I study her photograph. The muddy young woman beside me may not look like the one staring out from this screen but somebody else I know does. Belinda Montgomery.

Jethro is seated at the large round wooden table in the kitchen eating his breakfast. He swings his legs and hums between mouthfuls.

Is the other lady with the glassy eyes living with us now, Auntie Kate?

I want to start splitting hairs with him. Since neither Belinda, nor Kerry, is actually living, they can't be living with us. I stop myself from saying this, however. There is no benefit in arguing with a six year old. One way or another, they always win.

Glassy eyed lady, I mutter, distractedly, as though I have no idea what he is going on about.

The one in the wedding dress, he informs me, straightforwardly, as he fills his bowl with a second helping of cereal.

Now, I feel guilty. Kerry is a bit of a sight. He is probably frightened of her.

Her name is Kerry and she is a witness to a crime. That's why she is here. She is really a very nice person, even though she might look a little unusual.

A little muddy, he corrects me.

Yes, I concede, *a little muddy*.

I watch him, carefully. Despite my misgivings, he seems to be dealing okay with her bizarre appearance. Children are so adaptable.

Is Bim a witness to a crime too?

How on earth does he know her nickname?

Yes, that's right...She...

And, you're investigating?

Exactly!

I'm hoping this will put an end to the subject.

Are all your witnesses dead?

That stumps me for several seconds. He seems to have gone straight to the fault line running through everything I'm doing – my reason for not being. If they're dead and I'm dead, why are we bothering with any of this?

Y-yes, I admit to him, hesitantly.

Dead like you?

Will there be no end to this? *Yes, dead like me.*

His large brown eyes skewer through me. *Why can Caleb and I see dead people, and Sam and Mummy and Daddy can't?*

I-I don't know...Mummy can hear me sometimes, I think, in her dreams, I quibble

But, she can't see you like me and Caleb.

No.

Nor can Sam, or Daddy.

No. It probably has something to do with age, Jethro, I say, trying to head off his next question. *You remember I told you that death was like going back to where we came from?*

He nods, his fringe falling across his eyes. It definitely needs trimming. Why doesn't Carrie notice?

Well, young children are closer to that place than older children, and adults, of course, so they can see dead people better.

But, my friend Mikey is the same age as me, and when he was here the other day he couldn't see you.

He glances at the clock through a fine haze of hair. Mercifully, it is almost time for him to go to school.

Who's Mikey, I wonder, idly, before confessing: *I don't know why that was, Jethro.* I can tell from his face he is disappointed. *I'm sorry.*

That's okay, Auntie Kate.

His kindness makes me feel worse. *It could just be because we're flesh and blood,* I suggest. But, that can't be so because he can see Belinda and Kerry too. *Or perhaps some children are more sensitive to these things than others. You and Caleb might have a special gift.*

For seeing dead people?

It doesn't sound like much of a gift, the way he says it. *Yes!* I beam back at him to compensate for his lack of enthusiasm.

Does it mean that me and Caleb are going to die soon? Is that why we can see you?

I move around the table to give him a hug. *No, of course it doesn't mean you're about to die.* I'm not sure he feels my arms, but I hope he does feel how much I love him.

You promise?

I nod and stroke his face.

Cross your heart and hope to die?

I struggle to keep a straight face. *Yes, of course. Now finish your breakfast, it is almost time for your lift to school.* I notice a holdall in the corner of the room. *Have they changed the day for football practice, Jethro?*

No, I'm staying over with Mikey, tonight.

I wish he'd mentioned it before. I would have liked the chance to vet this Mikey first.

What does Mummy think about this?

It was her idea.

It was? That's peculiar. She hates them being away from her since I died.

She wants us all out of the house tonight – even Caleb.

Did she say that?

Yes, to her friend, Kay, yesterday, on the telephone.

How do you know that?

I was listening at the door.

Jethro! That's naughty! You shouldn't listen to other people's private conversations.

He smiles to himself as he waits for me to ask my inevitable question.

Okay, what else did she say?

She is going to tell Daddy she wants a divorce.

My heart leaps. Then, I think of Jethro. Does he understand what a divorce is? *And, what do you think about that?*

He shrugs.

Do your brothers know?

No

I hear the toot of a car horn outside, followed by pandemonium as he and Sam run about grabbing their school gear. They go to say goodbye to their mother and race outside to catch their lift. Two minutes later, the next door neighbour knocks. She is going to walk Caleb to nursery school with her own little son.

The house resonates with silence as soon as they've left. I sit at the breakfast table watching Carrie pour herself a cup of coffee. She has lost a lot of weight but at least the dark shadows under her eyes are slowly beginning to fade. She must be sleeping better. And, plotting too, apparently. I remember her telling Phil yesterday that he had to be home tonight because there was something they needed to discuss. I thought it was the kids. They will soon be breaking up from school for the summer holidays. Maybe that's what he thought too. I wonder whether he'll bother to do as she asked. The perfunctory *Okay, okay*, he gave her, might mean anything.

Have you asked someone to be here when you inform him you want a divorce? Like an army? Please tell me you are not going to be here on your own.

She looks about her. She has started sensing my presence but she cannot see me.

Kate, Kate, she coos. *Are you here? I'm going to do it. I'm going to tell him I want a divorce.*

You were supposed to move into my flat and then let the lawyer tell him about the divorce. That is what we agreed while I was alive so why change the plan now?

I don't care if he hits me. It will just make my case easier. That's what the lawyer said.

Hits you? Are you saying that bastard has been hitting you? And, when did this start? I knew she was scared of him, I absolutely knew it! *Why the hell didn't you do this while I was still around to help you? I can't believe your lawyer could be so stupid. I can't believe you're daft enough to listen to her. You must have a death wish. You're gambling that if Phil hits you, you'll survive. If you'd seen as many domestic murders as I have, you wouldn't take that risk.*

I have to do something about this but what? I retreat to my oldest nephew's bedroom to think about it. I need to make sure someone else is here when Carrie talks to Phil. But, how do I get them here? The only thing I can come up with is to write a letter to Nigs. I bash it out on Sam's computer.

Dear Detective Goldstein, I'm Kate Madding's sister, Carrie. She always spoke very highly of you when she was alive and it's for this reason I'm turning to you now. There is something I need to talk to you about, urgently. I realise it is short notice but I wonder if you could call at my house, this evening. Any time around eight o'clock would be fine. It isn't possible for me come to you because I have to take care of my three young sons. I hope you don't mind me asking you to do this, but since my sister died, I don't have anyone else who could help me. Yours sincerely, Carrie Hamilton, nee-Madding.

Getting Nigs to read my letter is going to be tricky. He hasn't yet heard of the paperless office. When I arrive at the police station to drop it off, I find his desk piled high with paper. It looks as though the waste paper bin has been upended on top of it. I have to wait until he goes to the coffee machine to clear a space.

Who's been playing about with my desk, he complains, the moment he returns. *Did you do this Fester because it isn't funny? I won't be able to find a thing now.*

Not me, mate.

Nigs picks up my letter. *Who put this here?*

One of the uniforms, probably, Fester replies, without looking up from his newspaper. When Bixby is away the boys like to play.

As soon as Nigs has read the letter, he shows it to Fester. *What do you think that's all about?*

I guess we're going to have to ask her that ourselves.

I can go on my own. You have that darts match to go to.

Fester rubs his bald head. He does this when he is thinking. *You masturbating again,* Bixby likes to shout across the office whenever he sees him.

No, I want to, for Kate. We owe it to her, don't we?

We could stop by after our shift.

Fine by me, mate, Fester agrees.

I knew they wouldn't let me down. I kiss them both on the cheek. Fester doesn't react but Nigs sniffs the air with a dopey

40

expression on his face.

Twilight falls early, bringing a drizzly end to what's been one of those peculiarly British summer days in which weather from all four seasons has come and gone. Dinner is eaten in silence. Carrie is wearing a figure-hugging, dark navy dress. It is a sensible choice for asking for a divorce, I decide - sober with a hint of sexy to foster regret. I only hope she has put as much forethought into what she is going to say to him.

She waits until Phil pushes his empty plate away before dropping her bombshell. Predictably, the moment she mentions the word divorce, he is on his feet screaming at her.

If you think you're going to take my kids away from me, you're even dimmer than I thought. He stabs the air with his finger. *You're an unfit mother, you are. You're mentally unstable. You've done nothing but cry since Kate died. That's what's caused this. You're having a breakdown. My mother will back me up and my sister.*

He is standing over her, preventing her from getting up from the table to escape him. Her lips are trembling and tears are streaming down her cheeks.

Through the window I can see Nigs and Fester pull up outside. I go out to meet them. It is not yet eight o'clock. Phil came home earlier than I anticipated. What am I going to do to get their attention? They are never going to hear him shouting out here - a vigorous breeze is agitating the canopies of the beech trees opposite the house, making the leaves rustle like pouring gravel.

I go back inside to see what's happening.

My brother-in-law has his hand around Carrie's throat. He lifts her from the chair like this and pins her against the wall. Her body slumps as though she is drowning on dry land. He is choking the life out of her.

Don't just stand there! Kick him in the balls! Poke his eyes out, Carrie, I yell to galvanise her but each shallow rasping breath she manages to take is a struggle for her so I turn on him, instead.

Leave her alone. Leave her alone, I wail.

It sounds lame even to me.

I will kill you, if you hurt her, I shout in his ear.

He slackens his hand a little and backs her along the wall out of the kitchen and across the passageway into the living room.

You think you're going to divorce me, do you? I'll see you dead first, you stupid bitch.

He slaps her face, gently, at first, like it is a game, but gradually the blows get harder.

She doesn't make a sound. Not even when he throws her to the floor. She is too scared. I can feel her terror in my own soul and I can't bear it.

There is a strange cracking noise behind me. It sounds like ice breaking under foot, but louder.

Phil hears it too. He looks around him to see where it is coming from but before he can figure it out, the room starts to vibrate. Everything around us seems to be moving in slow motion as though caught in a strobe light.

Suddenly, there's an almighty explosion and the air fills with a maelstrom of glass.

Carrie screams and Phil doubles over, covering his face with his arms and shielding her from the worst of it. An eerie silence descends, and I can see the shock in my brother-in-laws's eyes as he gazes at the windows in astonishment. Every single pane of glass in them has shattered.

Outside, Fester and Nig's footsteps are thudding up the front path. I go to let them in.

Mrs Hamilton, Mrs Hamilton?

Fester peers around the living room door. Nigs is right behind him. *The front door was open*, he explains, to my startled brother-in-law.

The hell it was. Was it you two who broke my windows? Get out of my house. I'm phoning the police.

We are the police, Nigs says, showing him his identity card and going over to my sister to help her up off the floor. *Are you all right, Mrs Hamilton?*

No, she is not, I answer for her, as he eases her onto the sofa.

You can't just waltz in here, uninvited, Phil tells him.

Like I said, the door was open. And, your wife looks upset.

42

Why wouldn't she be, someone just smashed our bloody windows.

Nigs looks from Carrie, to him. *Have you been drinking Mr Hamilton?*

What's that got to do with you? And, how do you know our name?

Fester crouches down in front of Carrie on the sofa. *Mrs Hamilton, can you tell us what happened?*

I recognise you two, now, Phil shouts over him to Nigs. *You were at my sister-in-law's funeral, weren't you?*

He and Fester ignore him as they coax my sister to speak.

Mrs Hamilton, are you alright?

I thought he was going to kill me, Carrie finally manages to gasp. *He grabbed me by my throat. I couldn't breathe.*

I've never felt so proud of her. I'm brimming over with sisterly love. I want to make everything in her life better for her. Then, I notice the way Nigs is staring at her and I change my mind.

There's a copy of a post mortem report on my desk when I return to my office. A note, from Bim, (I know, I know, but now Jethro and Kerry are both using her nickname, I feel strangely left out) is attached to the inside cover. *I came across this at the police station,* she writes. Poor Bim, I've been so preoccupied with Carrie and Kerry, she has been virtually working her own case. *It is your post mortem report. I thought you might be interested to read it. There are some case notes at the back which I've printed off for you too. Maybe it will help. xxx Bim.* What does she mean, help? Help what?

I scan the file, quickly, to see if I can tolerate learning more about the accident which killed me. My memory of it is fleeting, a few stills - the road, tyres, blood. Some deafening noises too: the revving of an engine, screeching, and a dull thud. That is pretty much all and I have a prejudice it might be better to leave it this way but, as usual, curiosity gets the better of me. I start to read and seconds later I'm completely gripped. To my astonishment, I discover I was run over twice. My thoughts about this crystallise slowly because the only explanation I can come up with is unbelievable. I was murdered! Someone must have hit me with their car and then backed over me, presumably to make sure I was dead.

It is with relief, therefore, I realise, as I read further on, that the forensic evidence doesn't bear this out. I was struck by two vehicles. The first was possibly a truck but I survived the impact of that. It was the second one which actually killed me. What are the odds of that - being struck twice by two different vehicles and neither of them stopping to report it?

I go upstairs to get an A to Z of London. I need to be able to locate what happened to me as the first step in trying to understand it. The post mortem report doesn't record where I was when I died but I remember Carrie mentioning the place to one of the neighbours. Hanswell Street, I think she said it was. Yes, here it is. I know this street, which surprises me only because my

44

memory has previously blanked that out. I never knew the name but the area, where it is situated, is familiar to me. It is a rat run between two main roads. There's an estate on one side, with a fairly unsavoury reputation and, on the other, a pub called The George. I go there sometimes or I used to. Was I there that night? I've no idea. It is still a blur.

A photograph falls out of the file. I have to turn it around this way and that to make any sense of it. God, I was a mess! And, this was taken after they cleaned me up. The report says I was thrown to the ground by the first impact which smashed my ribs, puncturing a lung. Then, the lower part of my spine was crushed as the back wheels went over me. The second vehicle was a car. It drove over my neck and that was it, lights out. According to the pathologist, who wrote this report, the two impacts occurred, one immediately after the other, as though the car was following behind the truck. Could it have been a police chase that went wrong? No, the police would have reported it. What about an illegal race? That would join up all the dots.

I turn to the case notes, Bim has printed off. An investigation was launched the day after my death but there was no CCTV evidence and the only person who saw the vehicles hit me was on the top floor of a block of flats some way away. He said the car that killed me looked like an old one - a Ford Fiesta he thought. I flick through the rest of the case notes. My car was found in the pub car park but none of the staff remembered me being there that night. There is also a mention of an analysis of some red paint found on my body. Is that here? No, I can't find it. I try and convince myself I should leave this here. I don't need to know everything. It is not exactly going to change the outcome. But, it's no good, I'm hooked.

I have to take myself off to the police station that dealt with my death to track down the missing analysis. I enter an empty office, looking for a computer terminal. Someone is already signed in to one, which makes it easier for me to access the information I want, but it also means I have to be quick about it, because they've probably only stepped out for a moment. I bring up the analysis of the paint found on my body and scan through it. It appears to confirm that the vehicle which killed me was an old Ford Fiesta, probably manufactured between 1995 and 2000.

Something flashes into my memory. The last thing I saw before everything went blank was a partial number plate. Three letters: TUL. Yes, that's right. Wait a minute, am I fooling myself? No, I'm right. It is becoming clearer to me. I lifted my head from the road and saw the number plate. I even started to memorise it but I ran out of time. The thing which bothers me most about this memory is that I'd previously assumed the screech I heard was the screech of brakes but that's not true. The screech was the noise the wheels made as the car turned into the street, at speed, and accelerated over me.

The door opens and a uniform enters. I try to close the window I've been looking at, before she reaches the desk and sees it, but in my panic I make a mistake and manage to crash the whole thing. Swearing under her breath when she sees the dead screen, she puts down the evening paper she is carrying so she can reboot the computer. Kerry's picture is on the front page.

I read the caption. *The body recovered a few days ago from a golf course in Bromley has been formally identified as belonging to missing student, Kerry Doughton.*

The murder team investigating her case must have checked out the Missing Persons file, I left on their desk. At least I was able to do that much for her.

The uniform leaves the office as soon as she has gotten the computer up and running so I log into the car registration database and enter the partial plate I can remember, cross referencing it with Ford Fiestas registered between 1995 and 2000. It doesn't get me as far forward as I hoped. There are too many cars listed here. It would take the living weeks to check them out. For me, it would be impossible. The only alternative is to squeeze the rest of that number from my memory. I picture the sequence of events that led up to my death over and over, focusing my mind on the final frame – the number plate. I recover what I think is the digit before TUL. Then, I go to work on these four and another digit slides into place, and another, until I believe I can recall the whole number. This I feed into the computer and hey presto, there it is, the car which killed me and, yes, it is a Ford Fiesta. I wait impatiently for the owner's details to come up onto the screen. Any moment now, I shall know the name and address of the person who took my life - accidentally, negligently, or on purpose.

When the information finally appears on the screen, I begin to doubt myself. It simply cannot be. I must have seen this number on the Missing Persons Database because the last registered owner is Leonard Doughton, from Chelmsford in Essex – the same Leonard Doughton who has just found out his daughter, Kerry, was murdered two years ago, when she and the red Ford Fiesta she was driving disappeared.

My flat is the place where I go when I'm feeling out of sorts. The ghosts of the past haunt me there as nowhere else. That's why I like it. Picking my way through a sierra of dust sheets, my life springs back into place, room by room, like grass after footfalls. I see Carrie on her hands and knees scrubbing the bathroom tiles when I first moved into this flat. Jethro leaving Pollock-like tracks on the wooden floors, on the day I let him ride around the open plan kitchen and living room on his tricycle. Most of all I see Nigs. And, this is truly odd, because on the few occasions he dropped me off, or picked me up from here, before or after work, I never once invited him inside.

Everything is as I left it. My ashes weren't even cool before Carrie put the flat on the market but she still can't bring herself to go through my personal effects. That's fine with me. I have anticipatory rage about what might happen when she does. I don't mind her giving a few bits to charity but if she slings anything out without consulting me, she'll pay. I never bothered to make a will so as my closest living relative she has inherited the lot. I wouldn't have wanted it any other way to be fair, except losing control over my home and possessions so abruptly does feel a little like being Sectioned under the Mental Health Act. Who says you can't take it with you? If I'd known Carrie was going to sell my flat from under me, I might have tried. The thing that really upsets me, though, is that I never expected to have to investigate my own death. My colleagues should have seen to that, themselves. I knew I wasn't expendable. You can't have a genetic double and not know that. But, I was erased from my life by a truck and a car and nobody but me seems to care a fig. Suddenly, I understand why Bim wants to find her body and why Kerry wants her killer put in jail. Now I want something for myself too - to know whether or not I was murdered.

All we have is a string of bizarre coincidences, I admit to my clients and Jethro, who is seated at the table in the garden with us, wearing the Sherlock Homes hat, I bought him last year for a fancy dress party.

But, they have to mean something, surely, Kerry suggests, brightly.

I am being cued in to join the murder victims' club but it is not in my nature. I'm not a joiner. I might have been killed, on the same night, and in the same vicinity in South London as Bim, and possibly by the same car that Kerry was driving when she disappeared, two years before that, but that doesn't mean our deaths are connected. Coincidences aren't evidence of anything. If I were able to present what I've come up with so far to Bixby, he'd laugh me out of his office. I don't want to say this to Kerry though. Her presence has been looking so much better over these past few days I'm reluctant to do anything that might upset her. She is less muddy now and there are blonde highlights beginning to show through in her hair. Strangely, Bim is looking worse. Bluish marks have appeared on her neck. I wonder whether she realises they are there? They must mean she was strangled like Kerry, I suppose. Was she drugged too? That might explain why they both have glassy eyes.

Didn't anyone ever tell you it's rude to stare!

I'm sorry, Bim, professional habit.

Kerry stirs. *I could be wrong...*

Bim interrupts her before she has the chance to go on. *And, why would that be?*

I just meant...

What? What? Spit it out.

I was just thinking it might be emotional.

Bim sighs, irritably. *Now, I have to ask a question to find out what you're talking about. Why is that? Say what you mean, why don't you?*

Kerry does as she has been told. *The bruising on your neck must be emotional.*

This produces a surprised silence.

Well, I suppose that would be quite perceptive...if it wasn't already abundantly obvious it couldn't be anything else – given I'm dead and my body is actually lying in an unmarked grave, God knows where! She turns to glower at me. *You're staring at me again!*

We'll find your body, Bim.

Yes, but when? She frowns at the green oblong table where we're sitting as though she can't quite believe in the existence of plastic garden furniture. *All this garden truly lacks is a pit-bull,* she mutters, bitterly.

I want to laugh but there is such a thing as familial loyalty. My sister's garden is a clover lawn which, during the summer months, suffers from alopecia. There aren't any other plants, shrubs, or flowers, because there aren't any borders in which to put them. A rummage of balls, bats, plastic bricks, toy cars, headless dolls, swords, and a batman mask, is all there is to draw the eye. No guns or other weapons of mass destruction because as the boys know their mother has a rule about these. They're not allowed to have them until they're over eighty five. Only Sam truly understands the significance of this. Jethro and Caleb still believe in a world in which the sequence 1, 2, 3, 4, 5, 6, 85 is not only possible, but highly likely, hopefully in time for Christmas. To help tire them out, and save on sedatives for Carrie, there is also a climbing frame, swing, and sandpit, as well as a play-shack capable of lowering the tone of any shanty town. I don't mind. I'm a native to the scrappy rectangles found at the back of South East London dwellings but Bim grew up in a manor house in Wiltshire with a back lawn the size of Orkney and Kerry on an arable farm in rural Essex.

I might be wr...

Bim stops her with a savage look. *Let's dispense with the preamble shall we? What is it you want to say? Come on, out with it?*

I try to mitigate her irascibility by smiling encouragingly at Kerry.

I was just think...
Didn't I say no preamble?
I'm sorry, I just meant...
Meant what?
...they can be very child-friendly.

Kerry furtively monitors Bim's reaction. Unlike the two of us she has no experience of surviving sisters. She is doubly unlucky in that both Bim and I are older than her. She is never going to hold her own. This is the only thing Bim likes about her, of course.

What is she going on about?

I shrug out of sheer self-preservation.

...pit-bulls. They can be really sweet tempered.
Don't tell me you used to own a pit-bull.
They can be lovely.
A geography student and a pit-bull owner, aren't we lucky? Bim glowers at me, again. *Do you think it's possible that you could have upset someone so much they paid to have you run over, Kate?*

I am beginning to suspect that Bim isn't happy with me for agreeing to help Kerry, while I am still supposed to be searching for her body.

Spare a thought for the offspring present, I grumble, glancing nervously at Jethro, who is crayoning in a colouring book of dinosaurs.

Fortunately for me, he doesn't seem to hear. Caleb, playing in the sandpit at the bottom of the garden, is probably out of range of our conversation. Besides, he only understands us when we communicate very slowly and deliberately.

I don't know what you're worrying about, Kate. Your nephews see dead people!

That's not the point. Carrie would be apoplectic if she knew we were discussing any of this in front of them.

Then, we'd better not tell her, had we.

My sister puts her head out of the back door right at that moment making us jump guiltily.

Caleb and Jethro go and have a pee before we go out, she

shouts.

When there is no response from either of them, she comes out to take a closer look. Caleb is still in the sand pit building something avant garde. His mother smiles, indulgently, at him. He was a blonde haired angel with a halo of curls when he was born but gradually the Madding genes have asserted their supremacy, turning him into the olive skinned, dark haired, sand-speckled, cherub he is today. Sam my eldest nephew is the only one who looks as though he might hang on to his father's blonde hair but even he has our dark eyes and skin.

What an interesting house, my sister tells her youngest son.

We turn to examine it - a little sceptically it has to be said.

Now come and wash the sand off your hands, we're going out, she adds.

It's a plane, Jethro corrects her.

The rest of us study it anew. It doesn't look like a plane to me but then it didn't look much like a house either. Carrie is wise enough not to pass further comment on it.

Did you hear me, Jethro? We're going out. I have to do some shopping.

He continues colouring in his dinosaur book and I await the explosion. But, Carrie without Phil has become a more relaxed mother. She buys herself some time rather than colliding with him head on.

Where's Sam?

In his room, we all chorus.

He is always in his room even though the summer holidays have just begun. He has taken Phil's departure the worst. Not that he was ever the kind of father who took much of an interest in him while he was living here. It is the loss of the hope he could one day become such a father which has hit Sam so hard, perhaps. A couple of meetings have been arranged with him since he left; on neutral territory, with - in view of the violent offence of which he is accused - a chaperone. But, Phil has failed to show up both times. Something always seems to come up at work, just like it did before he and Carrie split up. Caleb and Jethro show no obvious signs of suffering from his lack of attention but Sam does and, really, it is obvious even to me that three growing boys need a male figure in their lives to relate to. Carrie knows this too. She hears the information about Sam's whereabouts as an accusation and finally loses her patience

Jethro how many more times? Put that crayon down, have a pee, wash your hands, and change your sandals, in that order please, because WE ARE GOING OUT.

I don't want to go, Jethro tells her, sulkily.

Jethro, do what your mother says, I chide, gently.

No.

Carrie is standing there weighing up her next move. He is a bit big even at six to be forcibly removed from the table.

Jethro, please, I encourage.

But I want to stay here with you. I want to be part of the murder investigation team.

Carrie frowns. *What are you talking about?*

Jethro, leave it there, please, I warn him, quickly.

He looks up at his mother. *I want to stay here with Auntie Kate and her...*

Don't you dare mention Bim and Kerry, Jethro, don't you dare. Your mother isn't going to understand.

He blinks at me sourly from under his Sherlock Holmes hat.

Carrie puts her arm around him. She talks quietly because she doesn't want Caleb to hear. *Auntie Kate is dead, Jethro. You know that. We went to her funeral. I understand you miss her. We all do. I miss her, terribly, myself. But, she is in Heaven now.*

We all laugh at that, even Caleb whose ears started to wag the moment she dropped her voice.

It's not funny, she says, uncertainly.

Auntie Kate is sitting there, Jethro informs her, pointing at me.

Jethro, we agreed this was to be our secret.

No, you decided that.

I don't know what to say to that, because he is right. I disliked myself at the time for saying it but I wanted to spare us all – well, me and Carrie principally – all of this.

Okay, if this is what you want, be my guest.

Carrie asks, tersely: *I decided what?*

I don't want to go out shopping. I want to stay here with Auntie Kate who is sitting there. He points at me again.

Carrie straightens up and turns round in a circle. Reeling, is the word which comes to me as I watch her.

Jethro this is very important. Are you telling me you can see Auntie Kate?

YES, he shouts in exasperation. *Can't we Caleb?*

Carrie's hands go to her mouth in horror. *Caleb too?*

She spins around to find him.

He has left the sand pit to get closer to the fun. He nods his head, earnestly.

And, does she talk to you?

Of course she talks to us, Jethro says, as though she is being particularly dense.

Jethro, there's no need to talk to your mother like that.

He shrugs.

Carrie doesn't know what to do, or say, next.

Jethro is studying me. *Prove to Mummy you're here, Auntie Kate.*

Carrie follows his gaze to what to her is an empty chair.

This is your show not mine.

I get up from the table, ready to walk away, and his eyes fill with tears. I have never seen such a look of wretched disappointment on his face and I feel as though I am failing him, irrevocably. I sit down again and lean across the table to pick up a crayon.

Carrie almost dies of fright.

Pass me your book, Jethro. He slides it to me. *He is telling you the truth and I will look after him if you want to go out shopping,* I write.

My sister runs inside the house.

Make her believe you, Jethro whines to me.

How can I if she runs away from me?

Tell her something only you two would know, Bim suggests.

Carrie comes back out of the house and picks up the book to read what I've written again. She almost can't believe she is entertaining the idea that I'm sitting here. The only reason she is

54

is because she has felt my presence herself. She has had the same thought as Bim.

What were the names we invented for ourselves when we were small?

Flopsie and Maisie.

After Jethro has repeated what I've said, I watch Carrie calculate whether she might have told him these names before. She thinks not but...*Where did we hide granddad's false teeth?*

Tell her, we didn't hide them we flushed them down the loo.

Jethro laughs. *Did you Mummy? Did you flush them down the loo? Did you get into trouble?*

She nods. There are tears in her eyes. She rips out the page on which I have written.

Jethro makes a face.

It's only one dinosaur out of a whole book, Jethro and it's mine now. She writes on it: *I don't want to communicate through the boys. They've been through enough, already.*

Fine, I reply, using another of Jethro's crayons.

I have a million questions.

I probably don't have one single answer.

We can't do this now. It would be better when the boys are in bed. And, I do have to go out. Can I leave them with you, or not? Will you look after them? I want an honest answer, Kate. Are you really capable of taking proper care of them?

Of course, I am - the same as always.

Only dead!

I ignore her remark. There's no point us falling out this early on.

Those helmet heads have only arrested Reece for my murder, Bim announces, as she arrives in my basement office.

Who's Reece?

My man. My boss. Remember? I told you about him. I was there at his house when they came for him.

And, they actually arrested him? On what grounds?

I don't know. They didn't spell it out. They just asked him to accompany them to the police station.

Bim didn't work in public relations for nothing. She likes to spin the facts.

It's probably just routine, I reassure her.

But, what if they pressurize him into making a confession? He is very vulnerable without me. We have to do something, Kate.

She means I have to do something.

Yes, but...

But, what?

You have no memory of what happened, Bim. Who is to say he wasn't somehow involved with your death?

She doesn't so much give me a withering look, as wither herself from my office. I'm not sure whether I'm more irritated with her, or myself, as I watch her disappear. I knew I should have immersed myself in her case. If I was any kind of serious detective I would have paid Reece a visit, followed him even, by now. I would have acted on that first stab of suspicion I had about her involvement with him, during our initial interview. If only I hadn't been so busy working with Kerry on a photo-fit picture of her killer. And I've been spending a lot of time with my sister too. That's right! This is all Carrie's fault. The familiarity of my conclusion satisfies me on every level. It assuages the guilt I feel for failing Bim and distracts me from her case all over again.

I have owned up to Carrie not only about the existence of Bim and Kerry but also about my role in investigating their murders. She took it better than I expected. My new state seems to have afforded me some kind of celebrity status in her eyes. I feel uncomfortable about this and relieved at one and the same time. We've developed a technique for communicating she, and I, which used to be called automatic writing. She holds a pen, loosely, and rests it on a blank page, while I steer it for her. She appears to be genuinely pleased to have me around.

The thing I hate most about being dead is the passivity of it, I confided to her, that very morning. *It seems to me I am only kidding myself about still being a detective. What I really am is a wait-ive and watch-ive. Apart from being able to do a few conjuring tricks, I am pretty useless. I can't question the living, only the dead, and that doesn't seem to have yielded any great advantage so far.*

I never expected my words to her to be so graphically borne out, only a few hours later.

Bim reappears, rousing me from my thoughts. *I have been with Reece a great deal of the time since I died,* she informs me, archly, *and I'm a witness to the FACT this man is totally devastated by my disappearance. There's no way he could have killed me. Absolutely none.*

She is so resolute about it I don't have the energy to argue with her.

Let's see if there's anything on the News about it, I suggest, instead.

I switch on the portable television Carrie has donated to my basement office. It is tuned to Bim's favourite current affairs channel. Having worked in public relations she uses twenty four hour news broadcasts like dialysis.

We sit through a sixty minute cycle of stories without there being anything about her, or Reece. Then, Kerry shows up to watch a Soap she has started to follow. But, if we turn over, Bim is going to expect me to do something much more taxing than watch television to prove I'm helping her. We are still bickering about it as a banner headline - *Missing PR: Breaking News* - flashes across the bottom of the screen.

This is it, this is it, Bim exclaims, excitedly.

There is a police search under way in some woods in South East London which is believed to be connected with the

57

disappearance of Public Relations Executive, Belinda Montgomery, the presenter, an attractive brunette, whose hair is so lacquered it doesn't move with her head, reports. *The woods, known locally as Oxley Woods, are close to the home of her boyfriend, Reece Baxter, who was driven away in a police vehicle earlier today. Detectives hunting the missing woman have confirmed that he is helping them with their enquiries.*

I round on Bim. *Why would they be searching the woods near his home, if he didn't have anything to do with your disappearance?*

Because they're cretins!

As a former cretin, I take umbrage at that. It's so typical of the general public. You want us to do something about it when you get yourselves murdered but the moment we do, you vilify us. The police wouldn't waste time and money mounting a search of the woods near Reece's house unless there was a reason to suspect him.

She disappears in a huff, again, and while we wait for her to calm down, Kerry flicks over the channel to the Soap she wants to watch.

Okay, if you really want to know, he was accused of aggravated rape when he was a student, Bim volunteers when she reappears, ten minutes later.

Yep, that would do it, I say, dryly, as Kerry turns the television back to the news channel, before anyone can tell her to.

It was done out of malice. The charges were dropped because the woman retracted her statement. She told the police she couldn't bear the thought of being raped again by the judicial system. She made the whole thing up, more likely. She was some kind of balm pot, apparently.

And, how do you know that?

Reece told me.

Oh, well, it must be true, then!

Don't be so unpleasant! He didn't have to tell me about it. I would never have found out otherwise.

Somehow that doesn't console me.

She has made a habit of this kind of thing, Kate.

Of course she has! Her gullibility is astounding.

No, it's true. She made a similar accusation against a professor at the same university, before Reece even graduated.

Says who? Reece?

She ignores the remark and ploughs on with her defence of him. *There was a story in one of the newspapers, recently, about her doing something similar to a work colleague too. That's why he told me about it. He showed me the cutting. He was debating whether he should contact the police. He didn't want her to ruin this man's life the way she'd tried to ruin his.*

Bim, this is a tricky subject, you must see that. It's so easy to accuse a woman of making this kind of thing up. Most rapists do. And, it does happen that some women get picked on time and time again. That DOES happen, you know! Now, I want you to think very carefully about the question I'm now going to ask you before you give me an answer. Okay? Have you ever considered the possibility she was telling the truth?

Of course, I have. I'm not so much of a fool not to. And, I can see how he could get himself misinterpreted.

Misinterpreted? We're talking about aggravated rape, Bim!

I know that! Why don't you let me finish? I was just trying to tell you he has that tendency men sometimes have to over-sexualise things. But, MY experience of him is that he is absolutely clear no means no. I've felt embarrassed once or twice by his sexual innuendos but I have never ever felt sexually threatened by him. He likes women too much to physically hurt one.

I don't want to be argumentative but frankly I doubt her judgement. What kind of woman has a relationship with a man who has been suspected of aggravated rape? *Well, let's hope your body doesn't turn up in Oxley Woods or his goose is cooked.*

It won't. Reece had nothing to do with whatever happened to me. He was already at the restaurant where the party was being held when I set off from home that night.

I pounce again. *How do you know that?*

He rang me before I left the house.

And, what? Told you he was at the restaurant?

59

Don't say it like that. The other people there must be able to confirm his whereabouts.

Kerry, who is flicking back and forth between the news channel and her soap, pauses to ask: *If Bim's right and Reece really can prove where he was, why would the police be bothering to interview him?*

Bim gives her a ferocious glare.

He is her boyfriend, Kerry. They have to talk to him. He is going to be a useful source of information about her. But, if they're digging up Oxley Woods because they suspect him, either there's a hole in his alibi or they think he paid someone else to murder her.

Why are you doing this? You're supposed to be my friends, Bim whines, miserably.

More Breaking News in the missing PR woman case, flashes across bottom of the television screen, putting an end to our argument.

Police searching in a South East London wood for the missing Public Relations Executive, Belinda Montgomery, have cordoned off an area from public view, the presenter reports. *They haven't confirmed whether or not they've found human remains yet, but we are expecting a statement from a police spokesperson shortly.*

The finding of human remains in Oxley Woods is confirmed on the front pages of the early editions of the next day's newspapers, which actually hit the streets in London, at around 11pm that night. We know by then, from visiting the site ourselves, what the media do not. It can't be Bim. The body that has been found is even more decomposed than Kerry's. On the inside pages of the same newspapers, every salacious detail that can be wrung from the life of *public relations playboy, Reece Baxter, aged 41,* has been printed. The fact he's been released without charge doesn't seem to count. Bim is wretched on his behalf. She has us all staked out at his house *on suicide watch.* (Well, that's her intention. Mine, if I'm honest, is to see whether I can find any hard evidence against him.) It is a particularly cheerless place: all style and no personality - minimalist modern, with a hint of

Japanese for entertaining the easily impressed. Very expensive too, I shouldn't wonder, but completely soulless. I'd top myself too if I had to spend any amount of time here. Despite his lamentable taste in décor, the man himself is a dish. I can see why Bim fell for him. With his brown wavy hair, pallid complexion, Mediterranean blue eyes, a high patrician forehead, and fine boned nose, he pushes the barrier of handsome into something closer to beautiful. He dresses well too, even in distress, which makes him vain, perhaps, but I'm prepared to admit, after only a short time there, Bim's instinct is correct. Reece is no murderer. He is too devastated by the unfurling events - by Bim's disappearance most of all, and now by the possibility it is her in that grave; that she really is lost to him forever. And, even if he is faking this, from the moment she went missing none of his behaviour points to him being the killer. He even hired a private detective and on his advice offered a reward for any information leading to her recovery. That doesn't seem like the action of a murderer to me. Unless he is an extremely clever one...No, the longer I observe him, the more I believe in his innocence. Bim is right to worry about his mental state too. He is dangerously depressed. For hour after hour, he sits on a stool in his kitchen with several bottles of tablets on the gleaming work surface in front of him, while we take turns to talk him out of joining us.

You will only confirm in the mind of the public that you really are Bim's killer, if you do this, I try.

And, all investigation into her disappearance will cease, Kerry follows up, to the accompaniment of Bim whimpering, dramatically, in the background: *Don't do it Reece. Don't do it, darling. Live for me. Live for us.*

I am prepared to send the bottles flying from the table, before he ever has a chance to reach for them, if only to shut her up. But, mercifully, as dawn breaks, he voluntarily places them back in the medicine cabinet himself from where they inexplicably fall into the toilet, and are flushed away. He is a PR man, whose reputation will be in ruins ahead of his business, if he isn't quick to act. He has realised this from the moment the police first took him in for questioning but thanks to us (who would have thought three dead people would turn out to be such brilliant life coaches) he is finally ready to fight for himself using what he understands most – how to manipulate public opinion. He calls in several favours from the journalists he knows and persuades his ex-wife to talk to them about his gentle character and his love for Bim, whom he was apparently planning to ask to marry him. (This produces more whimpering from his intended.) The owner of the restaurant where the cocktail party was being held, agrees to make public the fact that, not only was he there on the evening Bim disappeared, but he was also there most of that afternoon too; from before the time when she left the office to go home and get changed, which means his alibi is as solid as they come. The police have nothing. Trumping all of this, the private detective he hired reveals a piece of evidence, hitherto undiscovered by the police, (what an almighty cock up). Bim's car was recorded on a security camera, at seven minutes before eight, on the evening she went missing, being driven by a man in the same vicinity, but not the actual street, where it was later found abandoned. The picture quality is so grainy it is difficult to make out the driver clearly but it isn't Reece. They are possibly about the same height but Reece has dark hair and the man in the car is fair.

I've promised to babysit my nephews while Carrie goes for a job interview at a local supermarket. It's a part-time position as a cashier so she'll be able to fit it around the boys' school hours, when Caleb starts full time nursery in the autumn. She is not doing it for the money. She received a large payout from my life insurance as well as inheriting my flat. But, now she's a separated woman, she needs to get out of the house and make new friends. She is in a state when I go upstairs to check on how her preparations are going. She's already dressed, in a blue polka dot skirt and a summer weight short-sleeved blue jacket, but she is feeling upset because Sam hasn't returned home from the game of football he is supposed to be playing with his friend Ryan, in the park.

I knew I shouldn't have agreed to them going out on their own. They're only nine years old. Anything could have happened to them.

Calm down! He'll be fine. He is probably on his way home right now. You just go to your interview and I bet he'll arrive back two seconds after you leave.

But, what if something has happened to him?

Nothing has happened to him. He is just doing what nine year old boys do. They play football and forget the time.

This conversation is carried out without having to write anything down. Carrie's psychic skills are coming on a treat. She still can't see me but she can hear me in her head.

Her eyes are glistening with tears. *What if he has been run over?*

Part of me is angry with her for making my death the cause of her continued suffering. It is me who's dead, not her. But, I can also recognise it must have, genuinely, shaken her universe. The one thing we know with any certainty when we're born is that one day we're going to die but we live our lives as though that day, probably, isn't today, or tomorrow. Thanks to me, Carrie can no longer make that assumption. The worst has already happened and it is going to take time for her to ignore the fact it could quite easily do so again.

Carrie, if anything bad had happened to him, I'd know. Go to your interview, and you'll see, he'll be here by the time you get back.

Are you sure?

Carrie!

Okay, okay, you win, I'll go.

She rushes about, collecting her essential interview anxiety relieving items - paper, pens, antiseptic wipes, plasters, and lip salve - until there's no more space in her handbag.

Boys do what your Auntie Kate tells you, she calls to Jethro and Caleb who are watching television in the living room.

They don't answer.

Wish me luck, she says to me, as she hurries out the door.

You don't need it. The job's yours, I call after her.

I sit on the arm of the sofa next to the boys as soon as she leaves. They're lying in a heap, Caleb's head resting on one of Jethro's calves, Jethro's foot on Caleb's stomach.

Jethro looks up at me. *Has she gone?*

Who's she, the cat's mother?

Has Mummy gone, he rephrases, begrudgingly.

Yep.

Oh. He goes back to watching his programme.

Where's your brother?

He kicks Caleb, making him yelp. *There,* he says.

Your other brother.

This causes him to look at me, briefly. Carrie has finally trimmed his fringe and I catch a flicker of something I can't quite pin point in his eyes.

He is playing football in the park with Ryan.

Pull the other one.

He looks back to the animal programme he is watching to avoid my penetrating gaze. *He told Mummy he was playing football in the park.*

And, what did he tell you?

Nothing.

64

Jethro?

I gave him my word I wouldn't tell anyone?

I'm not anyone. I'm a ghost so you're safe.

He considers the loophole I've offered him. *He has gone down the mall with Ryan.*

To do what?

I don't know. Nick some computer games, probably.

I feel shocked which is nothing to how Carrie will react if she finds out about this.

You say that as though it is a normal family pastime. Is it?

He shakes his head. *Not with me, it's not.*

And, never will be?

He doesn't answer.

Promise me Jethro because if you ever pull a stunt like that I'm going to know.

I promise, okay? Don't have a go at me, Auntie Kate. I haven't done anything. Sam's the deli- quent.

Mmm. We'll talk about this, later, when you're not glued to that screen.

I take myself off to the kitchen to have a ponder about all of this. I've no idea why some rooms are better for thinking through emotional quandaries than others. It is not like I was much of a cook in life but I feel closest to my mother here. Before she died from cancer, six years ago, I'd hang around her when something was troubling me. I didn't need to talk. Her presence alone was enough to help me sort things through. What I'm trying to decide now is whether I should go and get Sam before he robs a shop - possibly the same shop where Carrie is hoping to work as a cashier - or abandon him to his fate and stay here with my nephews of six and three who are far too young to be left on their own. Fortunately, Kerry shows up in time to rescue me from my deliberative loop. She has been to check on the CCTV camera footage of the man filmed driving Bim's car the night she went missing to make absolutely sure it couldn't be her killer. But, the picture quality is so bad his own mother wouldn't be able to recognise him.

I want you two to stay here while I go out to look for Sam, I brief my two youngest nephews. *You're to do as Kerry tells you. And, you're not to answer the door to anyone except your mother, okay?*

Okay, they repeat, flatly.

Look at me when you say it so I can see you've understood, I command.

Okay, they repeat more loudly, turning to face me.

First I go and search Sam's room. I'm looking for evidence and I soon find some. He seems to have accumulated more games than I remember him having, a few weeks ago. I'm furious with myself about this. Why didn't I notice these earlier? Apart from Sam, I'm probably the most regular visitor to this room. I'm the only one he can't keep out in truth. He can't see or hear me but he does talk to me, usually just before he goes to sleep. It is touching. He asks me for little favours like I was God. Most of them are beyond my control. Some of them show me how sad and confused he is. I never expected this, though. To demonstrate I'm here for him, I've taken to putting a few pieces of his jigsaw in place whenever I'm in his room. He loves the things. He always has one on the go. This might not seem like much of a relationship to anyone else but I think he likes me doing it. And, it is the best I can do under the circumstances of being dead. Apparently, he needs more.

I locate him in the mall without difficulty. I can always home in on Carrie and the boys. I've arrived too late, however. He didn't come home at the agreed hour because the store detective from a mega media store has apprehended him and Ryan for shoplifting. It is the first time I've met Sam's best friend because at their age they seem to change them with their clothes. This one was promoted after my demise which is a pity because I might have tried to steer my nephew away from him, if I'd seen him coming. He is a parchment-skinned, mousey-haired type, who even at nine I can tell will suffer from acne the second he reaches double figures. He even has a hint of that shifty embarrassment which sometimes arrives in boys at adolescence, because they know the rest of us know about puberty too and are very probably monitoring them for signs of it just so we can laugh behind their

66

backs. I feel sorry for the poor kid. One look at him tells me he is too off-putting to have been loved enough, but shoplifting sure as hell isn't going to be the way for him to scrape his self-esteem off the floor. He and Sam are trying to talk their way out of it but the manager is on the point of calling the police.

He is a well-scrubbed sort in his thirties and he has heard it all before. He doesn't care about the age or personal circumstances of these *tea leaves*, as his cockney dad would have called them, or *thieves* as he prefers to think of them himself, rather than the more modern *shoplifter* which, in his opinion, rather misses the whole point of this being a crime. Stealing is stealing and anyone caught doing it in his store is going to feel the arm of the law, limp-wristed though this appears to have become nowadays. Carrie and Ryan's parents will have to be summoned before the boys can be searched. I don't want that to happen. I don't want any of this to have happened. And, if I hadn't died maybe it wouldn't have. I feel responsible so I decide to do something about it.

I set off the fire alarm. The manager and the store detective haven't seen the movie. They, immediately, run out of the office to take a look at the shop floor while the boys dart down the back stairs like harden criminals and out through a rear door, which has been mysteriously opened, into the car park. They're full of bravado about having gotten away with their petty larceny, until they check their bags, and find the games they'd slid inside them are missing. They can't believe their eyes but I can see from Sam's face, he has an uncomfortable notion
who might be behind this magic.

As soon as he gets home, he hurriedly climbs the stairs to his room, pursued by a shout from Jethro of: *Auntie Kate has gone out looking for you.*

His answer is to slam his door, loudly, behind him. His mouth drops open once he is inside.

I've made a pile of his ill gotten gains and on his notice board there is a message for him constructed out of letters clipped from that day's newspaper headlines. GET RID OF THESE TOMORROW! AND IF YOU EVER DO IT AGAIN I WILL

PUT YOU IN JAIL MYSELF.

You won't tell Mummy, will you, he begs.

I write on his computer: *Was that the last time?*

Yes, I promise.

Well, of course, he'd promise me anything right now so do I trust him? I think the answer to that is I'm going to have to keep a very close eye on him indeed.

Then, I won't, I write. *But, if you break your word to me, there'll be trouble.*

He looks up and down and around the room as though uncertain where a ghost could be expected to hang out. *Thanks, Auntie Kate. You won't regret it.*

I leave his room, worrying about the wisdom of our agreement. Sam's thieving is obviously some kind of cry for help and his mother has a right to know about it. But, she will never take the job, I'm already aware she has been offered, if she finds out about this.

Congratulations, I call to her, as she enters the house.

She laughs. *How did you know I'd got it?*

Before I can answer, she starts talking into the mobile phone she is holding to her ear. *No, sorry, I was talking to... to...someone else. Thanks for phoning, again. It was really thoughtful of you. Bye.* She flushes. *That was Nigs. He wanted to know how I got on.*

I'm about to ask her how he knew about the interview, (and since when has he taken to phoning her on her mobile), when she adds: *He mentioned they've just found another body in Oxley Woods.*

68

The police have cordoned off an area of disturbed ground which they've identified as being a possible grave. They've yet to excavate it though and until they do any talk of finding human remains is premature. They are combing the surface, before beginning to remove the earth, and as I watch them, I have the same thought I did about Kerry's grave. The part of the woods where the bones were found, a few days earlier, is close to the perimeter, but this spot is deeper inside and, if it does turn out to be another grave, it seems too far from the road for one person to have risked the physical exertion involved in carrying a dead weight all that way.

Kerry joins me. *Don't tell me they've found another one.*

It looks like they think so.

How many bodies are there in these woods?

Scary, isn't it. I used to bring the boys here to play when I was alive.

Have they identified the other one they found yet?

She and I haven't had a chance to catch up properly thanks to the drama with Sam. Earlier that morning, before getting roped into babysitting for Carrie, I'd gone to the check on what the forensic pathologist had managed to discover about the bones.

I shake my head. *It's a woman and they think she has been dead for about three years. There was one interesting thing. She has a petite frame like you and Bim. If she also had blonde hair....*

Kerry interrupts before I can finish my sentence. *Do you really think the Weasel could have killed Bim too?*

This is the name we've started to give the man who murdered her, born from her description of him. It robs him of his humanity just as he robbed her of hers, but it is also our way of trying to make the idea of him less frightening. If you can call the bogeyman, Ferret Features, he stops being one. Well, that's the theory.

I shrug. I don't want to alarm her. It is only a half-baked idea anyway. In reality, serial killers are very few and far between.

69

Well, anything is possible at this stage, I guess.

We continue to watch the white suits work in silence. It is the path of least resistance with Kerry who is not one for small talk. That's fine by me, but Bim keeps complaining that she is suffering from something called Only Child Syndrome, which she read about in Vogue, or so she claims. She is a little hazy about the details. The only bit she has managed to retain is something about sometimes having to coax people who are only children to talk, not because they are shy, but because they demand that level of interest before the deign to open their mouths. I'm not sure that this is a fair description of Kerry. It seems to me she is simply rather quiet and shy. And, given everything she has been through that's not really much of a surprise. I suspect she'll emerge from her shell in time. She is certainly looking better, week by week. She is completely blonde-haired now, although still with a mud-stained face and the tattered wedding dress.

A low murmuring begins to circulate around the site. We move towards the grave to take a closer look. Thirty centimetres of earth have been removed and bagged for further analysis, but now they appear to have stopped work and are taking photographs.

Why are they getting so excited, Kate? The grave is still full of earth.

I've no idea. Then, I notice it. There's a tiny blue satin eye winking up at me through the dirt. *It is her. They have finally found Bim.*

I go in search of her, hoping I can reach her before she hears about her body on the news. I'd rather it came from me. I check all her usual haunts but to no avail, she is nowhere to be found. When I get back to the woods, she is there, watching her body being exhumed from the shallow grave where it was dumped. Suddenly, I am uncertain what to say to her. Should I congratulate her on finally discovering where she is buried? After all, this is what she had wanted from the beginning. Or should I commiserate with her because lying there limp and dishevelled in her blue satin cocktail dress she makes such a pitiful sight? Either way, she is dead, I suppose. I can only hope finding her earthly remains brings her some peace.

I can't believe it, she exclaims, suddenly.

I turn to comfort her but she appears more outraged than distressed.

Where are my shoes, Kate?

Baffled, I examine her presence.

Not, those ones, silly. She points at her corpse. *My blue satin high heels are missing!*

She is right. Her body is wearing a pair of black court shoes.

They're not mine. They're hideous!

Oh, I don't know, I think they go all right with the dress, I quickly reassure her.

Don't be stupid. How can they? They're synthetic! I wouldn't be seen dead wearing synthetic shoes.

This plunges us all into an awkward silence. Bim seems to be more upset about the shoes than she is about the state of the body wearing them which seems odd to me since the stains on that cocktail dress are definitely coming from the inside.

I was wearing Reebok trainers when I went missing, Kerry says, after awhile, as though belatedly catching up with the conversation.

Relieved to hear her say anything, I ask: *And, what did you have on when your body was found?*

She lifts the hem of her wedding dress to reveal the impression of a pair of matching white slippers.

What is it, Kate? Are you all right?

I don't reply, immediately. I'm too busy having an epiphany moment. *Oh m-my God,* I eventually stammer. *Why didn't I think of this before?*

Think of what?

How many times has a breakthrough in a case come from something so trivial it seemed irrelevant at first?

Come on. Tell us then, Bim orders.

You might not want to be seen dead in that pair of black court shoes, Bim, but I'm betting I know the corpse that would.

71

Petite blonde, Gertrud Weiss, was found dead in the boot of her boyfriend's car almost exactly one year ago. The couple had arrived in Britain from Austria, a few months previously, to take up positions as German language assistants, at two South London private schools. If everything worked out during the final term, they would be hired again for the coming academic year. It had seemed like an open and shut case at the time. They were overheard having a humongous fight the night Gertrud disappeared, wearing the skirt, blouse, and black court shoes she'd worn to work that day. And, the only physical evidence on her body – naked except for a pair of Reebok trainers when it was found – pointed to the boyfriend, Karl Grüner. Okay, it was circumstantial but three months ago, he was convicted of her slaying and he is now serving a life sentence as a Category A prisoner, at Her Majesty's pleasure. I was the lead detective during the investigation. I found Gertrud's body in the boot of that car and I arrested Karl for her murder. There was no doubt in my mind I'd got the right bad guy. I was happy to go into court to testify against him. His character didn't help him much. When I interviewed him, he came across as cold and detached - exactly the type who'd kill someone without showing remorse. He denied it but I expected that. Wouldn't most psychopathic killers do the same? Damn! I truly believed my instincts about him were sound! How could I get the geezer so wrong? An innocent man has been incarcerated for a murder he didn't commit and I'm the one responsible for putting him there.

How the hell am I going to get him out of prison now I'm dead?

This is the question I put to Bim and Kerry, after I have shared the while sorry tale with them, when we return to my office.

We need to be absolutely sure the Weasel killed this woman before we worry about that, Bim soothes.

It has to be him! He leaves the same signature each time. Gertrud's body was wearing Kerry's trainers. And, the black court shoes Gertrud was wearing when she disappeared were in that grave with you, Bim.

What about my wedding slippers then? Who is the owner of those?

I haven't a clue, Kerry. Those woods could be full of corpses wearing each other's shoes for all I know.

Was Gertrud drugged and strangled too?

Yep.

We should try and find her, don't you think, Bim says. *Maybe she knows something which will help us.*

But, she could be anywhere by now.

We could always go to her parents' place in Austria. If she's still around, she is bound to pop in to see them, from time to time. Why don't we make a holiday out of it? We could do with one after everything we've been through. Do you know the address, Kate?

It's probably on file, somewhere.

Bim's smile broadens. *Maybe I could squeeze in some skiing.*

I sigh to myself. *I haven't had a proper holiday for years. I always fancied going on one of those round the world cruises. I just never had the money, or the time while I was alive. I bet those boats are full of ghosts trying to see the world.*

We won't be able to go to Austria until after my funeral though.

But, they haven't even released your body for burial yet, Bim. And, nor are they likely to for some considerable time I keep to myself.

Reece is arranging a memorial service for me. It's going to be wonderful.

Kerry and I exchange a look. I wonder whether she too is desperately searching for an excuse not to go. The media are bound to be there. It will be a circus.

You will change into something more appropriate, won't you?

I see she is referring to me which surprises me. I'm not the one in a cocktail dress.

What's wrong with what I have on? It never occurred to me that how we appear in our afterlife could be changed. I assumed we'd have to spend eternity wearing the same thing.

Bim pulls me over to the old mirror at the back of my basement

73

office. There's no image there when I look for myself in it.

Shit, I'm a vampire!

You have to concentrate. You have to think yourself into being.

But, I'm dead.

Don't be argumentative. Think, you. Go on.

A hazy image appears and fades, and appears and fades, again. It is me, all right. I'm wearing the clothes I was run over in, a navy trouser suit and a yellow silk blouse. They'd look fine if they weren't heavily stained with blood.

I'm appalled. I had no idea. *Is this how Jethro and Caleb see me?* Bim and Kerry are strangely quiet on the subject. *Why didn't you tell me?*

They probably don't even realise what it is, Kerry reassures me.

You're kidding, aren't you?

It just looks like a rusty stain, particularly now the crusty bits have fallen off.

I feel mortified. *How do I change into different clothes?*

That's easy. You create a picture of yourself in whatever clothes you want to wear.

If it's so easy, why are you still wearing your blue satin dress?

Because I like it! It was brand new too. I'd never worn it before the night I was killed. I shall be changing into something different for my memorial service though.

I try and picture myself in another outfit but the navy suit is still clinging to my image in the mirror. What clothes do I like? What clothes did I used to have in my wardrobe? I can't remember.

Bim grimaces at Kerry. *Why do I think our D. I. Ghost isn't much of a clothes horse? Come on the pair of you, we can go up West and hunt for ideas.*

In the West End of London, it is Christmas already – it is the end of the summer everywhere else but for London's swankiest shops Christmas always comes a little early. The afternoon sunlight is dulled by the garish cheer. The sheer abundance of it beckons. Bim, my self-appointed personal dresser, finds me another navy trouser suit but this one from Harrods. It is more expensive - had I actually bought it - than anything I have ever worn, more expensive than my entire wardrobe put together, probably. She matches this with a collarless white Indian cotton shirt. When I picture myself in the mirror I find I look good and even better, stain free. For Kerry, she chooses a medium weight plaid tunic with a dark blue jacket. She looks a little like a French school girl but it suits her.

Bim wants to surprise us with her outfit.

It's unlucky to see what the deceased will be wearing before the morning of her memorial, she announces, half jokingly – I think.

I nod but say nothing. How much more bad luck could she have than being murdered?

She shows up to her memorial service in a black lace flamenco dress with a veil. She does a twirl so we can admire it. Kerry gives me a helpless look. I'm going to have to lie our way out of this on my own.

Wow! I think it really works, I do... You look very... funereal, but in... a Spanish flamenco, kind of a way.

It is enough. Bim beams back at me.

I love it so much I might make this my eternity dress, instead of the blue satin.

She seems so absurdly happy for someone attending their own memorial service, I decide the news about our trip to Austria being off can wait. I've remembered Gertrud's parents are dead. She has no living relatives. The school where she was working had to pay for her funeral and her body was buried in a South London cemetery. I was there but I'd managed to blot this out somehow. Lord knows where she'll be now.

The interior of the church is dazzling; the candle-shaped electric lights, clustered along the walls, making the gold behind the altar, and the stained glass windows, glitter. The pews, stalls, and lectern are ornately carved and reek of polish and old wood. There are vases of white roses everywhere and at the top of the side aisle stands an easel with a portrait of Bim, painted especially for the occasion.

The Service itself is excruciatingly sentimental. There's barely a dry eye in the place by the end of it. Reece gives the eulogy as

Bim dances flamenco – well, gives her interpretation of a flamenco dance - around him. She is having a wonderful time. Her wake afterwards is to be held at a posh hotel, down the road. I don't see the point of going. I can't eat, I can't drink, I don't know anyone, and they wouldn't be able to see me, even if I did. I make my excuses to Kerry, at the end of the Service, because Bim is off with the fairies, tangoing her way up and down the central aisle.

Outside the church, I linger to watch everyone else leave. I have asked Bim to take note of anyone she doesn't recognise, but she is so wrapped up in herself, I doubt she'll remember. I myself don't see anyone more suspicious than two detectives, who are standing around in the car park, doing the same as me. There are a million petite blondes in designer label clothes but nobody who looks like the Weasel. As the crowd breaks up and heads in small groups toward the hotel, a woman walks towards me so briskly I expect her to pass right through, before I have the chance to move aside. Instead, she comes to a halt abruptly in front of me. She is a tall brunette, pear shaped, but she carries her weight well, or dresses it well, I should say. She is wearing a dark suit, beautifully stitched - handmade, I shouldn't wonder. She is in her forties, with a lean face that is handsome more than attractive, because her jaw line and lips are a little too firm for a woman. Her eyes are clear and intelligent and I sense in her a lack of artifice which appeals to me. I imagine you'd always know where you were with her.

D. I. Madding?

I'm shocked. I would have sworn she was alive.

D. I. Madding, she repeats, more loudly.

She is alive. I can see her breathing.

You can see me?

She looks about her to make sure nobody can overhear her.

Yes, I can see you.

Who are you?

My name is Margaret Dryer and I don't know why but I've always been able to see spirits, ever since I was a small child. I have a message for you. It was given to me in a dream. She

76

laughs. *I know what you must be thinking. I normally dream messages for the living, not the dead.*

I am not sure whether I find this reassuring, or not.

Bim didn't mention she knew any mediums, I say, suspiciously.

Bim? Oh, the deceased, yes, I mean, no, I didn't know her but her memorial was mentioned in the newspaper and I was told in my dream you'd be here.

I might be the dead one out of the two of us but she is beginning to freak me out.

The message was in German. Do you speak German?

I stare at her in astonishment. *Not one word.*

Well, that's okay because I looked up the words for you in a dictionary. She takes out a piece of paper from her handbag. *I've written them down for you. I am not sure if this will make any sense to you but the message appears to be: GET HIM OUT OF PRISON NOW OR ELSE!*

The cemetery where Gertrud Weiss's body is buried is a vast jumble of graves, many of them dating back more than a hundred years. Bixby once told me that the quickest way to get to grips with the culture of a foreign country was to visit a graveyard, eat a meal, and watch a television programme. I never travelled enough to put his theory to the test but from the slithers of social history inscribed on the tombs here, I suspect he was probably right. Our ancestors have borne so many trials to get each one of us here, our births are a miracle of endurance, centuries long. Entire families lie in this graveyard obliterated in a matter of months by the flu. Or sometimes solely the children perished, broods of ten brothers and sisters succumbing to the same childhood diseases our children today are sent to parties to catch. And, weaving through all these tombs is the slow march of sons, fathers, and husbands, shipped home from their colonial duties, in wooden boxes, from countries no longer known by the names engraved here. Like them, I have become a full-stop in my family's history. My children too will never be born.

As I wander through the lichen-covered stone slabs and wind-blasted angels, I don't see many spirits hanging out here, despite the legions of bodies buried around me. Graveyards aren't the spooky places they are made out to be by the living. It is not us who disturb their tranquillity but their own fear of dying, I suspect. If they only took ten seconds to think about it, it would be obvious. Why would we want to stick around our rotting corpses, when we no longer have any need of them?

I have come here at Gertrud Weiss's request. She told Margaret Dryer who gave me her message that she would be waiting for me by her grave. I'm not sure she is going to like what I have to say to her. Getting her boyfriend, Karl, out of prison is going to be a lot trickier than getting him in there was. My final resort has been to leave a file on the desks of the detectives investigating Bim's murder, highlighting the links they have to make: the shoes that disappear from one victim and reappear on another; the fact that Gertrud was not only a petite blonde like the others, but both she and Bim – her autopsy report has confirmed this – were raped post mortem. There are also posthumous puncture wounds through the palms of all three women's hands, as though they had been nailed to something. I've laid it out before them, as clearly as I can: THERE IS A SERIAL KILLER ON THE LOOSE AND GERTRUD WEISS IS ONE OF THE VICTIMS. As soon as the message clicks, they will have to take steps to release Karl from prison.

Gertrud is sitting on the bench by her grave, looking about her, impatiently, as I approach.

There you are, at last! You certainly took your time. I have things to do, you know. I want to get to the British Library before it closes.

Her English accent is perfect but there's something not quite right about the inflections in her speech that gives her foreignness away. She seems younger than she did when I saw her last. Well, she was lying on a mortuary slab at the time. There's no hint of the skirt and top she was wearing when she was abducted either. She appears to me in a pink and white tracksuit, with white slip-ons, and a pink bandanna. Bizarrely, she seems the epitome of health.

A confetti of blossom drifts through us, from the trees around the edge of the graveyard, as I sit down beside her on the bench. Two council workers are sweeping the petals into heaps so they can be cleared away.

It is the work of Sisyphus, she comments, when she sees me watching them.

I'm not a complete ignoramus. I have heard of the Myth of Sisyphus. I just haven't got a clue what it is. I've no intention of admitting this to her, however. She is only in her mid-twenties and she is studying for a doctorate. Or she was. That was her reason for wanting to spend a year in London as a German assistant. Karl too. Brain boxes, the pair of them. Not that I have any reason to feel cowed, I reassure myself. I'm not the one wearing a pink bandanna.

You did a good thing, this morning, she tells me. *But, if they don't pick up on it, I will expect you to do more. Karl is important to me. What happened to him wasn't fair. You weren't fair.*

I feel myself begin to bristle.

You judged him as a British man, she continues. *You never took account of his foreignness, not in a positive way, only as something sinister.*

She is the one who isn't being fair. I bent over backwards to offer him an interpreter, but he refused one. I didn't come here to argue with her, though.

I want to talk to you about your murder. Do you remember what happened?

There's something I have to say to you first.

I leave space for her to go on but she doesn't speak.

Which is?

I have been very angry with you, she says, without a trace of the emotion to which she is laying claim. *Destructively so. I have stood beside you and hurled every abuse, I can think of. I've wished you dead a million times.*

That's okay. It wasn't you who killed me. Now getting ba...

But, I may have weakened you, made you more careless, or less able to protect yourself.

You really believe that's possible?

We're all capable of that much. We are not supposed to do it but we can influence the living, affect their mood, and even their actions without trying too hard.

I don't know how to react to this information. It seems far-fetched to me.

Forget it, I have, I tell her, lightly.

She smiles, and I notice the peachy skin, the pale blue eyes, and the crown of white blonde curls she had in life. It is the kind of face only truly beautiful in youth. In time, those same features would have slipped into homeliness. Not that this will ever matter to her now.

What is it you wanted to ask me?

What can you tell me about your murder, Gertrud?

Very little, and I prefer to be called Gerte.

Do you have any idea what the person who killed you looked

80

like?

I have a fuzzy image of a man. He was small with thinning, blonde hair and penetrating blue-grey eyes. He must have been about thirty or thirty five.

I show her our computer-generated image of the Weasel, the one I helped Kerry to develop.

That's him, she confirms, without hesitation. *Who is he?*

I was rather hoping you would be able to tell me that. Do you remember how he managed to abduct you?

I was in a bit of a state when I left the flat where Karl and I were living. We had a row, that night. He wasn't happy here, he wanted to go back home, but we'd only been in London a few months. I thought we should give it more time and I was desperate to continue my research at the British Library. So I walked out in a huff. I took the car with the intention of driving around until I'd calmed down. Our car, it was registered in Karl's name, but it belonged to both of us which means, just for the record, Detective Inspector, my body wasn't found in his car, it was found in mine!

This is pretty much what he told me at the time of her murder and I didn't believe him. Bixby always said that getting it wrong went with the job. *Did you see the word, infallibility, written anywhere in your job description, Madding,* he'd bellow at me. *Our job is to collect the evidence. It's for the CPS to decide whether there is a case to answer and the courts to tease out whether that case stacks up.* They didn't do that with Karl, though, and despite Bixby's consoling words, I feel bad for initiating the chain of events that led to this injustice.

Gerte waves her hand in front of me to get my attention. *Can we move this along please?*

The car was found outside your block of flats. Can you remember where you were attacked?

I've no idea. I didn't really know London. I do remember calling in at a garage, a repair place, at some point. There was a strange knocking sound in the engine and, as I was passing, I saw someone still working there. I stopped and asked for his advice. The guy fixed it. Didn't charge me, either. He said it was nothing.

Are you sure he wasn't the one who killed you?

No, he was nothing like him. This guy was tall, good looking too; a really nice man.

And, you remember leaving the garage?

Yes, without a doubt.

Do you know where this garage was?

I haven't a clue.

Why do you think the murderer left your car outside your home? It seems an odd thing to do.

He must have wanted me to be found quickly, for some reason, but I don't ...

Remember, I say, finishing her sentence.

There's something I do remember. Not from that night but from the night you were killed.

But, you were already dead by then.

Yes, but I still saw you that night. I like to ride the buses, you see. London's such an exciting place. I've explored it quite a bit since I died. I'm not sure, exactly, where it was but it was south of the river, somewhere near Greenwich, I think. That was where the bus was headed anyway. You were talking to someone. I saw you from across the main road. You were up a side turning. I didn't see who it was you were talking to, but they were driving a BMW, a newish one. Well, it was very shiny, it looked new to me.

And, you're certain it was me?

Beyond a shadow of a doubt. I followed your investigation into my murder with considerable interest. I would have recognised you anywhere. You were standing next to the driver's window.

Of the BMW?

Yes.

But, you didn't see the driver?

No, only the number plate. I remembered it because the next day it was all over the newspapers. It was the same car that PR woman was driving when she disappeared.

It is not that I doubt her but I need to be absolutely certain about what she is telling me. So I take her to the road in New Cross where Bim's car was found abandoned. She insists this was the

82

place where she saw me talking to the driver. I have to accept what she is saying, and if I'm reluctant to do so it is no reflection on her. I'm just at a loss to know what to make of it. The only two possible scenarios, I can think of, which explain it are that, either, I was talking to Bim, immediately, before she was abducted, or to her abductor, as he was dumping her car.

What time was this?

It must have been about eight at night.

That decides it for me. If Bim left her house in Greenwich, at seven that evening, she wouldn't have been sitting in her car in New Cross, at eight. Not unless her car had broken down. But, it was newish, as Gerte said, and when it was discovered by the police, there was no sign of a mechanical fault. Besides, even if she did break down, it must have been before seven thirty for her to only have gotten as far as New Cross. She would have had over an hour to phone for help, or warn her colleagues she was going to be late. Yet, there were no calls made from her mobile, after she left her house that night. No, the most likely person to be driving Bim's car at eight o'clock, that night, is the same tall blonde haired man who was recorded driving it, several minutes, earlier, on the security camera footage Reece's private detective unearthed. If Kerry is right and the Weasel is small in stature, it couldn't have been him. So who was it?

I devote several hours to checking the only real lead we have, the computer generated image of the Weasel that we produced, based on Kerry's description, against the police mug shots of men with a history of attacking women to see whether I can identify him. There are hundreds of faces that could be him. I seem to see him everywhere. But, there is no one photograph which screams, unequivocally: *Look no further, I'm the one!* If I were a living detective, I would probably follow up on some of these men but, ironically, with eternity stretching out before me, I can't be bothered. I think of delegating the task to Kerry but she wants to spend the weekend at her parents' place. She feels the need to do what she can to comfort them in anticipation of the publication, in the mainstream media, of a rumour leaked by the police that will link her murder with Bim's. The term serial killer has yet to be used but it is surely only a question of time. Soon every aspect of the women's lives will fall under public scrutiny and anyone who claims to have known them will be offered money to reveal all. Kerry's former American boyfriend, who managed to hold his peace during the two years in which the police believed she'd run away to be with him, is already preparing to step into the limelight of fame by association. He is to be flown to London from his Chicago home and lodged in a five star hotel with a minder at the expense of a Sunday newspaper. *I never realised she was missing, otherwise I would have come forward sooner,* he will lie. Well, it sounds better than: *I wouldn't have come forward at all, if this Sunday newspaper hadn't found me and paid me to do so.* Bim is taking time off too to go to Italy with a dead friend, called Fabian, whom she met a few days ago at her old office. He was killed in a skiing accident in the Italian Alps, the Christmas before last, which curiously hasn't seemed to dampen his enthusiasm for the place. *I am so thrilled to have come across someone from my own milieu,* she informs me. Neither Kerry nor I could be expected to understand anyone as deep as her, obviously. I am tempted to ask what poor Reece might think about her jaunting off with another man but I feel too miffed about being tossed aside as a class reject to make it sound like a joke.

I eschew the company of Carrie and the boys when I get back to the house, despite feeling hideously alone. Instead, I make myself even more miserable by staying glued to the old desktop computer that Sam has donated to my office out of gratitude for my silence over his shoplifting. Every dead person I know - well Bim and Kerry (I don't count Gerte because riding around London on buses and going to the British Library isn't my idea of fun) - is having a more exciting afterlife than me. I've remained trapped in the past whilst they're beginning to move on, I grizzle to myself as I work. But, trying to catch a serial killer has to be worthwhile, even if it doesn't have the same cache' as weekending in the Italian Alps, I reason back against myself. Is that why I'm doing it though? Or am I simply too scared to discover what I'd be left with without work? I have wasted my life! Carrie has birthed three kids in the same time it has taken me to rise to the dizzy heights of being D.I. Ghost.

Predictably, I distract myself from these depressing thoughts with yet more work. I believe I have identified another possible lead and I force myself to pursue it despite my wretchedness. If Kerry was wearing wedding slippers when her body was discovered, the odds are these were taken from her predecessor – possibly, Jane Doe, the unidentified bones, the police dug up in Oxley Woods, a few days before they found Bim. What if the wedding dress was this woman's too? There can't be many brides who have vanished into thin air. She has lain in those woods for about three years according to the forensic pathologist so if I check newspapers from around that time, maybe I will come up with something.

I scan the headlines in one of the national newspaper's archives, going back four years, to be on the safe side. A missing bride is bound to have attracted media attention but, dishearteningly, I find nothing. Surprise, surprise, I've hit another dead end!

My disenchantment chases me upstairs to my sister's living room, as night falls, where I find Jethro and Sam fencing each other with plastic wands. Their shrieks of laughter do little to dissipate my self-pitying mood. They are so full of life, it hurts. Carrie is in the kitchen cooking tea - fish fingers - which typically she manages to burn. Neither of us inherited our mother's cooking gene. When she calls the boys to the table to eat them, I sit in Phil's chair, watching them pick off the black bits, while I bask in their sheer exuberance at being alive, like the pallid heat from a winter sun. They ignore me. I might be a ghost but familiarity still breeds contempt. A few listless hours later - spent watching the box - I read Caleb a bedtime story, and play a game of chess with Jethro, before lights out. Then, I go to check on Sam. We've started a new jigsaw, a 500 piece one, and we're collecting the straight edges to form the outer rim. It is a picture of the universe. It was Sam's choice. I would have preferred something brighter with people in. But, this one is more difficult than anything we have attempted before, which is why he wanted it.

Sorting through a pile of pieces, he asks: *What do you think about Mummy having a dinner date with that friend of yours?*

He is able to hear me in his head now, like Carrie.

Which friend?

That detective, Nigs.

I can barely contain my rage. I've only been dead for five minutes and she has pinched my bloke. And, as for him! He hasn't exactly gone on holding a torch for me very long, has he? To add to my misery, I remember it was me who brought them together. I never should have written that letter to Nigs. I should have let Phil murder my sister, instead!

Auntie Kate? Are you still here?

I sense Sam is about as happy with this development as I am and I consider joining forces with him to stop it. Or turning him into a gun I can load against my sister. But, he has already been through so much my conscience gets the better of me. He is finally beginning to settle down. How could his mother do this to him?

Dinner date?

I might as well find out all the gory details and Sam is clearly dying to tell me everything he knows.

86

They're going out to dinner, tomorrow night. To a restaurant! We aren't invited.

Mummy hasn't asked me to babysit. More than that, she hasn't mentioned one bloody word to me about it. If she thinks she can exclude me by going out to eat, she has another think coming.

We're getting packed off for the night to friends.

Ryan?

Yeah.

Great! Personally, I blame Ryan for leading my innocent nephew astray. Maybe now is the time to put Carrie in the picture about the shoplifting. That might stop her from going out on this date, with Nigs.

My flat has been let to a Sikh couple called Jaswinder and Jitendra, whose grandparents emigrated to Britain from the Punjab. They're friends of my next door neighbours Bennett and Chelsee and have signed a six month lease while their own house in Richmond is being renovated. The place was just sitting there empty waiting for the sales market to pick up so Carrie and I thought, why. not? Jitendra is an accountant and his wife, Jaswinder, an interior designer. They have a little son called Surinder. They speak a kind of Punjlish among themselves, using the words from each language best suited to encapsulate whatever it is they're trying to express. I understand them. This is one of the pleasant surprises to being dead, languages foreign to me in life are intelligible now. I find that thrilling. London is so rich in different cultures there really is no need to travel the world. I've just never had the opportunity to enjoy this diversity before because I've invariably entered people's lives on the heels of a tragedy. But, now, for the first time, I can find out more about what they're like, without them knowing I'm around. It is so strange. When I lived, it was the dead who preoccupied me. I had to die before I developed a curiosity about the living.

I find an excuse to have dinner with my new lodgers, at least once a week. My kitchen used to be the place where I sometimes dished up a takeaway but now it is in the hands of an accomplished cook. The food Jaswinder prepares tempts every sense I no longer have. The taste is in the smell. How does she do that?

As they eat the meal she has cooked, they all take turns to talk about their day and when they've finished I tell them about whatever is troubling me.

It was much more than a physical attraction between Nigs and me. We liked each other. I mean really liked each other. It's that feeling you get of being seen through by someone. But, seen through in a nice way. Seen through and still liked. No loved. Loved for being yourself. I'm beginning to think it was the biggest mistake of my life, not to have acted on my feelings for this man. The closest I got was at a colleague's birthday party. I stepped out into the garden to get away from the smoke and noise and there was Nigs, sitting alone on the terrace wall, gazing up at the moon. We'd both had a bit to drink and I remember thinking this was good because the only way I could overcome my objections to having a relationship with him was to get them drunk. I asked him what he was doing out there on his own and the next thing I knew I was in his arms. We were just about to kiss when someone bellowed for me from the back door. I can't even recall who it was. Nor, why they were looking for me. We both jumped away from each other. The next morning Nigs said: About last night. And I said: Forget it. It never happened. And, from then onwards it was as though it never had. You probably think, Jas, this almost-kiss doesn't entitle me to be as livid as I am with my sister for going out with Nigs, particularly given I'm now dead. But, there was so much more between us than actual deeds. It may have been all in the air but it was there. That should count for something, with Carrie. We had an agreement, when we were young, that if one of us liked a boy, the other one left her to it. We treated boys the same way we did the parents, we divided them up. Then, there were never any fights. If she doesn't cancel her date with Nigs, I promise you, there's going to be one hell of one now.

My house guests listen politely to my outpouring, without passing comment or judgement upon me, which if I'm honest is precisely why I like talking to them so much.

I wait until Carrie has fallen asleep to lay on the bed, beside her, and whisper into her ear her own worst fears. *If Phil finds out you're dating the detective who arrested him, your case against him might fail, you know. He might think you were having an affair before you split up. There's no guarantee he won't find out. He could be suspicious there's something between the two of you, already. He will probably kill you, this time, you realise. And, even if he doesn't, it will have all been for nothing anyway, because knowing your luck with men, Nigs will turn out to be as*

89

bad as him. No, what am I saying, he will turn out to be even worse.

She tosses and turns to get away from the terrible dreams I am causing her to have but I take no pity on her. I'm determined to ensure that this dinner date doesn't go ahead. She will ring Nigs first thing in the morning to cancel it. Then, I will then find a way to make certain it is never rearranged.

There's a noise, downstairs. One of the boys must have woken up. Maybe, they need a drink. Or, perhaps Caleb has wet the bed and gone to the living room to sleep on the sofa, rather than awaken Carrie.

I go to take a look.

A figure is sitting in the dark at the kitchen table. For a split second, I think it's Phil because it does seem familiar, but another moment on, I fall in.

Sergeant Ross, what are you doing here? He looks fed up. *Is everything, all right?*

Ah, Madding, I was wondering when you'd show up. I think we need to have a little chat, don't you?

I gather from having worked for him in the past, I'm in trouble.

What do you want to chat about?

You think rules are for everyone else except you, do you?

I am not sure what he's talking about so I try to deflect his question by changing the subject.

I'm in the middle of a murder investigation, Sergeant.

No, you're in the middle of becoming too involved in what is over and done with.

What do you mean?

I've just said what I mean. What is it you didn't understand about it?

I have a nasty feeling this is about Carrie. *I'm a ghost, we're supposed to hang around the living,* I reply, sullenly.

Well, as it happens you're wrong. You're not a ghost. Ghosts are little more than sound and picture bites of experience that get trapped in time and space. Someone hits play and they play. What you are, is a spirit; an earth bound spirit, apparently. That's where you might be going wrong.

90

I'm where I want to be.

Oh, is that right? Well, if you're so content why are you trying to interfere in your sister's love life?

I'm not! All right, I might be - a little. But, only for her own good. He likes me, not her.

He liked you, he corrects me. *And, you did nothing about that. Now, he likes her and she will. That's the difference between you. You always convinced yourself you were the stronger one, didn't you? Has it ever occurred to you, you were mistaken? She was the one who was able to do without you. She was the one who could move on alone.*

Yes, to the creep she married. That was her first move. You call that strength?

She can live without you is my point - if you let her. Can you exist without her?

What does it matter now?

It matters because, if you too want to move on, you're going to have to find that out.

Then, we've just lapped the circuit, Sarge, because I don't want to move on.

You are the most stubborn...What is it you do want, Madding?

I want a result in this case.

He nods. Then, let life happen. That's my advice, for what it's worth. You don't have to be so afraid any more.

Part of me wants to ask him what the hell he is going on about. I'm dead. How can I let life happen? But, the stuff about being afraid provokes some kind of resonance in me. I don't want to admit it, though.

I do know I'm more angry with myself, than Carrie, I offer, instead.

And?

I shrug. *I guess I'm beginning to wonder whether I wasted my life. Did you ever feel that, Sarge?*

Yes, but I see it differently now. Life isn't the big deal, you know. It's just one rung on the ladder.

To where?

He laughs. *Just work your case, Madding. Let life happen. And, you might discover the answer to that, yourself.*

I didn't say anything before because I wasn't sure how you'd feel about it. I used to wonder whether you had a thing for him yourself. You sort of lit up whenever you mentioned his name.

Carrie is confessing to the dinner date with Nigs, and pissing me off with her analysis of my interest in him, at the same time.

I've decided to cancel now anyway. I don't know what I'm getting myself into. He might turn out to be worse than Phil. And, even if he isn't, what if Phil found out? It might tip him over the edge into a full blown homicidal-mania.

I almost can't bring myself to do this. *Cancel? Of course, you shouldn't, cancel. It's good you're beginning to get on with your life. And, there's no need to worry about Nigs. You couldn't find a better bloke.*

You really think so?

I do.

What about Phil? He'll kill me if he finds out I'm seeing the detective who arrested him.

He won't find out, and if he does, Nigs will do everything he can to make certain he can't hurt you again.

You really believe this is okay? You don't mind me going out with him?

Me? What should I mind? No, I'm all for it.

I'm letting life happen, I tell myself. But, I'm also aware that instead of undoing last night's work, I'm creating a new scenario in which I've not only given this relationship my blessing, I've positively encouraged it. It is the last time I shall interfere, I promise myself. But, I know myself better.

Carrie goes to the hairdressers to prepare for her big night out so it is back to the computer for me. I've decided to do another trawl of national newspaper headlines, looking at everything that mentions *bride* or *wedding dress,* during the same time period as before. It is a mammoth task. It takes most of the day but this time I get lucky. I find an interesting news story from three years before, under the headline: JILTED BRIDE IN SUSPECTED SUICIDE.

Jackie Brand, a twenty six year old fitness trainer, from St Albans, was engaged to be married to Brian Jones, a driving instructor, from Sheffield. But, on the morning of her wedding, she disappeared after her husband-to-be called things off. She was already dressed in her wedding gown and veil when he rang to dump her. Nice fellow. After, hanging up the phone, she told her bemused relatives she had to pop out, without revealing what had happened. Maybe, she felt too embarrassed. Her mother thought she was having a last minute fit of nerves as she watched her drive away. But, everything was arranged and she knew Jackie loved Brian to bits so she didn't doubt she would be going through with the ceremony. She probably just wanted to lap the block a few times to calm her anxiety. When she wasn't back in time to leave for the church, her brother was dispatched to discover whether she was already there, and to have a word with the minister, if she wasn't. It was only then they discovered the groom and best man were missing too. A rumour went around the congregation that Brian had never really wanted a big wedding and he and Jackie had decided to elope.

Mr and Mrs Brand decided that the reception should go ahead as planned. There was no point in wasting all that food and booze. It wasn't until they returned home they discovered a telephone message from Brian. He was at his flat in Sheffield, he said. He wanted Jackie to call him there. They rang him, immediately, and for the first time they learned why neither he, nor Jackie, had been at the church. That was when they started to grow concerned for their daughter's safety, and they informed the police. Forty eight hours later, Jackie Brand's white Renault 5 was discovered, where it had been abandoned, close to the Humber Bridge. No trace of her was ever found, although suicide was strongly suspected. That's what the police thought and even her parents believed it was the most likely explanation.

The last known person to see her alive was a patrol man from one of the breakdown networks, who was named in a local newspaper as Gordon Richards. Jackie phoned the central number that Saturday, at 12.30pm, from the M1, near the Leicester turn off, where her car had broken down. Richards managed to get it going again at the roadside, three quarters of an hour later. He remembered her particularly because of the wedding dress she was wearing, of course. She told him she was going to Sheffield but her runaway groom maintained she never arrived.

There is no photograph with this story. I wonder if she had any taken before Brian called the whole thing off? I have a dim recollection of Carrie posing for several in her wedding dress - flowers clasped to her belly to hide the bump - before leaving for the church, when she was wed to Phil. Most of them had me, the reluctant bridesmaid, standing beside her. She made me wear this metallic bluey-grey thing with a lace trim. Why, I would have liked to know? I mean every colour under the sun goes with white so what was her reason for wanting to make me look like Navy frigate? Our mother said it was so I didn't deflect attention from the bride, being her identical twin and all. But, dressed in that monstrosity, I doubt anyone was able to take their eyes off me. Maybe Jackie did something similar – had photographs taken at home before the ceremony, I mean. (I'm sure Carrie was unique in her desire to humiliate her only bridesmaid.) It is too much to hope for probably. Besides there is not one shred of evidence that she was actually murdered, and even if she were, her killer would have to had to have known she'd been jilted to come up with the plan of making her disappearance look like a suicide. All of which makes the boyfriend seem like the best fit. The police would have looked at him pretty closely though, I imagine, and he did have a witness to vouch he wasn't involved. The best man was with him from the time he left the hotel in St Albans, where they were staying, until the moment the police hammered on the door of his flat in Sheffield. It all rests on the dress then. That's my only lead. I need to find out what it was like. If it is the one Kerry was buried in, Jackie joins our club, and the Weasel is her killer. And, if I can prove, at least, to my own satisfaction he was, another possibility comes into play. Casting suspicion on the boyfriends could be as much part of his signature as swapping the shoes. Brian, Karl, and Reece were all implicated to varying degrees. Karl was actually convicted, and Bim was buried in the woods opposite from where Reece lived. Kerry was thought to have run away, but if her disappearance had ever been treated as suspicious, her boyfriend too could have found himself at the heart of a possible murder enquiry. It suggests to me that the Weasel has prior knowledge. He either has to be researching his victims, in advance, or he is acquainted with all these women.

Sometimes it is possible to tell from looking around a house that a family member who once lived there died under brutal circumstances. It's nothing to do with black crepe, or ribbons, nor any of the usual trappings of mourning. It's just the feeling you get of time standing still. Often, it is the meticulous cleanliness too, as though the place has been scrubbed from top to bottom to rid it of the stench of death. Jackie Brand's home in St Albans is like this. The living room is misnamed. It gleams like an empty mortuary slab and is as empty and lonely as a graveyard. Upstairs, her bedroom has been embalmed, just as she left it, behind the locked door. There are even strands of hair in her hairbrush and a faint whiff of scent lingers on her pillow. The only thing that has changed, in this house, since her disappearance, three years ago, is that all traces of her relationship with Brian and their impending wedding have been expunged. Time stopped when she died, but in the memories of her family she has been fixed at an earlier point, before the seeds of the tragedy which carried her away were formed. The photographs of her on these pristine walls stretch from her babyhood up until the year she finished her college course. That must have been when they thought the path that led her away from them opened up before her. There are hundreds of pictures of her as a baby and small child, and tens of her during her teenage years. There are even a few from her early twenties, because she was still theirs then. Yet, there is not a single one of her from the moment she met Brian Jones. These survive only in the family album, but even there they have been carefully chosen to exclude his image, their engagement, and wedding day. In all the photographs of Jackie on display she is laughing. This is a feature of a suicide, I learned during my years on the force; the photographs are always happy ones. They belie the silent scream of unanswerable questions that, over the years since her disappearance, will have slowly become a litany of unacknowledged accusations. *How could you do this to us? How* *could you kill yourself without a word? Why did you do that without once giving us the chance to talk you out of it?*

I am not sure what I wish for them. That Jackie really killed herself. Or that in all the time they have blamed her and themselves for her death, she was the victim of a serial killer. Better than either of these, of course, would be that she is still alive somewhere and married to someone who cares for her a lot more than Brian Jones ever did.

Feeling frustrated and sad I decide to visit the regional office of the breakdown organisation where Gordon Richards works to see what I can turn up about him. I've no idea how I can find a way of asking him whether, by some miracle, he still remembers the dress Jackie Brand was wearing when she went missing but it has to be worth a try. I find myself sharing a computer with an obliging young woman with a Midlands accent. I only have to whisper in her ear two or three times what I want and she brings up the staff database onto the screen for me. Gordon Richards is no longer listed as a member of staff. He left about eighteen months before to go travelling abroad. A personnel note recorded on his computer file says they would be prepared to take him back when he returns. He was a good worker, obviously. His is an odd age to go backpacking though. According to this, he's in his thirties. Another note on his file records that the human resources department supplied the financial reference for the mortgage he used to purchase a house in Leicester, six years prior to his departure. I make a mental note of the address. Provided he hasn't sold it since, I might as well go and take a look while I'm here.

It is a redbrick Victorian terraced house, three up, and three down, in a quiet road, I find, when I get there. The name written on the card underneath the doorbell shows he still owns it. Down a short flight of stairs to the right of the main entrance, the old coal cellar has been converted into a small bedsit with its own front door. I do a quick tour of this, first. It has been let to a male university student, a psychology undergraduate, who has yet to

98

grasp the fundamentals of taking care of himself. There is a touching list of cooking instructions stuck to the greasy cooker hood in the kitchen, which includes the following: *Frozen peas – boil for three minutes.* Upstairs, in the main house, the walls are all covered with embossed wallpaper and painted beige (the same as the bedsit, only cleaner). Gordon likes to keep a tidy place. You could eat your dinner off the vinyl flooring in his kitchen, which can only mean someone is around to clean it. The décor is disturbingly bland. After only a few rooms I'm beginning to long for colour. Anyone who likes this amount of beige has to be a bit odd. The fridge contains little, except a few bottles of beer, and a pack of butter. Perhaps, he is still away, after all. But, when I open the freezer, I see it is just that he is a convenience meal junkie. It is stuffed with frozen pizzas, pies, and TV dinners for one. Upstairs, predictably, his bedroom carpet is beige, as is the duvet cover, and the curtains. I open his closet door with trepidation but, for his clothes, he favours dark blue slacks and jeans, with lighter blue shirts and navy jumpers. He doesn't own a suit but he still has his uniform, pressed and covered in plastic. There are enough clothes here to indicate he is definitely back from his travels. Why hasn't he returned to his old job then? Could the rent from the bedsit downstairs be enough to keep him going? I'm about to leave when I spot a photograph of a man, I assume to be him, holding a flight of darts, at what looks like a pub darts match. He is fair-haired and clean shaven. I search the drawers of a bureau in the living room for another less visible photograph I can steal. I find one in an envelope of prints, dated four years ago. He is standing outside a caravan with his arm around an elderly woman. Could this be his mother? All of the other photographs in the envelope are scenic shots of a rugged coastline. It might be somewhere abroad. I'm not sure. But, wherever it is, it looks cold and windy to me. I doubt that would bother Gordon. Judging from these pictures, he is more into flora and fauna than sunning himself on a beach. I can't find any photographs of his recent travels. I rifle through the other drawers but there's nothing. Is that strange? Probably not. When you're snooping around someone's house everything seems sinister.

By the time I get back to Carrie's house, she has left for her dinner date. I go to my basement office with the intention of conducting a case review. It is the only thing I can think of which might distract me for the required amount of time. I can't settle, however. The house feels like a mausoleum without my sister and the boys. Perhaps, I should go and check on how my nephews are getting on at their respective billets like the responsible aunt I aspire to be. But, naturally, all I really want to do is spy on Carrie and Nigs at the restaurant. Technically, I'm not supposed to know where they're dining. My sister didn't volunteer the information and, in deference to Sergeant Ross, I didn't ask. It would be easy enough to locate them though. I could home in on Carrie on the dark side of the moon, if I had to. I wrestle with myself, for several minutes. Well, all right, for at least three. But, it is a foregone conclusion. I'm just not woman enough to stay away.

It would be better to go early, before things warm up between them, I reason. The final moments, when they might arrange another date, should definitely be avoided – if only out of politeness. In the end, I wait until I'm summoned by them. This isn't exactly what they do but they are both thinking of me at the same time, which has a similar effect.

The restaurant is a French bistro near Dulwich. At street level, there is only a reception area and cloakroom. The dining room itself is reached by climbing down a narrow metal spiral staircase to the basement below. It is a converted wine cellar with low ceilings and plenty of intimate alcoves. The brick walls have been painted white throughout and hung with a collection of Cartier-Bresson photographs to create a sensual, yet sophisticated, ambience. The tables are covered with blue and white checked table cloths and each one is decorated with a vase of lavender, and an empty bottle of Bordeaux, stuffed with a candle. The air is suffused with the aroma of fresh bread and garlic.

I'm shocked to discover the extent of Carrie's make over when I lay eyes on her. Ever since we were children, we've had the same shoulder-length bob of hair. This is what suits us. But, now, she's had hers butchered. Whatever possessed her to do that to herself?

It looks sort of spiky, which is a kind way of saying it sticks up all over the place. Even the colour is different. Her natural colour is jet black, like mine, but she's gone and had some red lowlights put in. The final colour bears no relation to anything that could be found in nature. Only a toxic chemical could produce a shade like that. She just doesn't look like her anymore. Or, perhaps, it is more that, for the first time since we were born, it is me she doesn't look like. I bet she's regretting it. It's obviously a disaster. Why didn't she tell me what she was planning? I would have stopped her.

She and Nigs are talking about the murder case. Very romantic! He is in the middle of explaining to her that the police believe they might be dealing with a serial killer and he and Fester have been assigned to the enlarged murder investigation team.

It means I am going to be working 24/7.

I thought from watching Kate that was a normal week for you guys.

Nigs laughs. *She was a bit extreme.* Lifting his nose in the air he sniffs.

Instinctively, I back away from him before Carrie can notice.

He is looking gorgeous, tonight. Tall, dark, and delectable, with blue-black hair and a five o-clock shadow. There is no doubting the testosterone in this man. He is wearing a blue collarless shirt and jeans. He is smart but casual. Perfect. Carrie is a little overdressed, or - depending upon whether you can get past her plunging neckline - under-dressed, by comparison. She should have worn trousers. I would have. Instead, she has put on a wine-coloured silky thing, I've never seen before. It is probably the only thing she could find to match the lowlights. At least, it is an A line. She'll be able to eat whatever she wants without it showing.

I shan't be able to see much of you for the duration, which is probably just as well, because I have to give evidence against your husband at his hearing in a few weeks. If the court was to find out I had any kind of personal relationship with you, it might complicate matters.

She looks disappointed.

When the court case is over.....It will be...well... different.

He smiles shyly at her and she gives a nod. This must have been where I went wrong with him. I was too good at verbal communication.

There is something else I wanted to tell you.

She is all ears.

It is about Kate.

Is that another look of disappointment on her face!

You know it's strange but I often seem to smell her perfume.

Carrie smiles, tensely.

I did just, then.

She glowers at me over his shoulder. She can't actually see me, I reassure myself, but she obviously suspects I'm here.

*It would be just like Kate to...*She is going to say, *spy on us*, or *ruin my date*, something like that, but she stops herself. *It would be just like her to find a way of coming back, if she could,* she says, instead.

She was special wasn't she?

I knew it! He may be out with her but he is still carrying a torch for me. And, now she has changed her hair she doesn't even look like me! No wonder he wants to back off. Of course! That's why she did it. That is why she had it hacked off. She wanted him to like her for herself and not because she looks like me. Poor baby!

Wasn't she just, my sister finally manages, through gritted teeth.

The detectives working her case have turned up a security tape of Kate in her car on the night she was run over. There was a tall blonde haired man with her.

What was that? I don't want to confirm Carrie's suspicion I'm here by talking to her but I do want her to question him about what he has just said.

Who was it?

We don't know yet. There is another recording taken just over twenty minutes beforehand of a man driving the car of one of the murder victims, Belinda Montgomery, who disappeared on the same night. It isn't very good quality but the forensics have managed to enhance it. It is possible the man driving the murder victim's car and the man riding as a passenger in Kate's car are one and the same.

A worried expression creases Carrie's forehead. *What does it mean?*

It could mean a lot of things: that she knew him; that she was driving her car under duress; that she was murdered too. Or.... that.... she was involved with these murders in some other way.

What other way?

Good girl, that was my question too.

Well, it's only one possibility and nobody believes it but they still have to eliminate it from the enquiry.

I don't understand.

I do, and I am livid.

There is a theory this killer may have an accomplice.

I hope you're not saying they think that Kate...

She sounds really indignant, bless her. I take back every mean thing I thought I had about her dress.

Like I said, nobody believes it. But, in view of the two recordings they have to rule her out, that's all. They might want to ask you some questions about her too. It is nothing to worry about. They just have to do their job.

Her loyalty towards me has moved him. The more she talks about me, the more his interest in her quickens. I can read it in his face. Isn't my afterlife becoming ironic! I'm going to bring these two together, over my dead body, whether I wish to or not.

The police think I murdered you, I announce, punitively, to demonstrate to Bim and Kerry how I've been made to suffer while they've been away for the weekend.

Kerry is sympathetic. *That's terrible. How do you know?*

One of my old colleagues told my sister.

Bim is curiously quiet.

Don't tell me you think it could be true?

No, of course, I don't. But, you have to admit that you don't have much of an idea how you're involved in all this.

Assuming I am, you mean.

Well, that is one of the things we're trying to find out, isn't it?

And, how does she imagine abandoning our investigation to enjoy herself in the Italian Alps is going to help us to do that, I ask myself, bitterly, before filling her and Kerry in on what I've been up to during my weekend of hard graft.

There are no photographs of the wedding dress at Jackie Brand's house but the motorway patrol man, Gordon Richards, was the last known person to see her alive so I was thinking we could try and find a way of asking him what it was like.

Bim looks at me as though she thinks I'm mad. *A man isn't going to remember a wedding dress he saw last week, let alone three years ago! There has to be another way.*

Well, you think of one then.

That's him, she exclaims. *That's the Weasel. How on earth did you find him?*

She is looking at the photograph of Gordon Richards I stole from his house.

No, that's the patrol man.

It's the Weasel, I tell you!

It is? He looks different from our computer generated image.

No, he doesn't. It's definitely him. I recognise him.

I should be thrilled but *reliable witness* isn't exactly a description I associate with Bim. *But, you said you didn't remember what he looked like,* I point out to her, suspiciously.

104

I don't, but I'm still absolutely sure that's him.

I almost can't bring myself to pursue this.

And, why is that?

I don't know. I just have this really powerful feeling about it.

Well, that'll stand up in a court of law. What about you Kerry. Is this the man, you remember?

She pours over the photograph. *I might be wrong...*

There are worse things. Tell us.

He doesn't have a moustache.

So?

Without the moustache, I can't tell whether it's him or not.

I feel like screaming. With witnesses like these, is it any wonder we are getting nowhere fast.

Perhaps, Jackie Brand would be able to identify Gordon Richards as her killer, Kerry suggests.

And, do you know where we can find her, because I don't?

Forget Jackie Brand, we should find out everything we can about Gordon Richards, first, Bim proposes, instead.

Well, I suppose it wouldn't do any harm, I acknowledge, grudgingly. *There may be something I missed. But, he left his job to go back-packing, Bim. If he was abroad when either you or Kerry were killed, he is not the Weasel, whether you think you recognise him or not.*

Bim and I conduct a meticulous, room by room, search of Gordon Richard's house, while Kerry moons about by herself trying to intuit whether there is any evidence there, from what I can gather. We all meet up in one of the spare bedrooms a few hours later to share what we've found, which is precisely nothing.

One of us is going to have to stay on and see if he shows up. If he does, she should follow him about a bit, until we can figure out what to do next.

Bim and I both turn to our junior partner, Kerry, and wait for her to take the cue and volunteer, but she seems to be lost in her own thoughts.

Hello, earth calling Kerry, Bim teases.

She doesn't respond.

105

What is it, Kerry?

I've been expecting this to happen, Bim whispers to me when she still doesn't answer. *She has been replaced.*

What are you talking about? Replaced by what?

A triffid, of course.

Yes, very funny. She looks upset to me.

You think? How can you tell? She is not like you and me, Kate. She was studying for a geography degree. I mean, what kind of person studies geography when it isn't compulsory? She's a triffid, you mark my words, and it'll be our turn next if we go on hanging out with her.

Kerry, please, what's the matter, I try again, ignoring Bim.

I'm probably wrong...

But?

I think I may have been here before.

Oh, I know, I know, don't tell me, Bim gushes. *You were Cleopatra in a former life!*

I look daggers at her. *Do you mean in this house, Kerry?*

Sorry, I might be mistaken.

Mistaken how, exactly?

It's just that I remember being in a cellar. It had the same layout as the bedsit below us, only there was a trap door where the stairs are.

Is that it?

Yes.

The basement bedsit here has the same layout as the cellar where you were held?

Yes.

Bim smirks and mouths: *Triffid!*

Well, I suppose it could have been converted, during the last two years. It's a pity your memory isn't a little more specific. Sixty per cent of the older houses in this country used to have cellars, you see, Kerry.

If it wasn't this house, it was one very much like it.

Her point, exactly, Bim mutters.

Kerry appears to hesitate. *There's something else.* She places the centre spread from a newspaper, on the beige nylon bedspread

106

of the single bed, where we are sitting. It's yellow with age. *I found this in the hall cupboard.* She points to a story, headlined: WOMAN FIGHTS OFF ATTACKER.

Bim and I scan it.

A Leicester woman fought off a suspected abductor when her car broke down in a lane, in the outskirts of the city. A man stopped to offer her assistance, claiming to be a mechanic, but instead of fixing her car, he tried to grab her from behind and drag her into his van. The woman, Gail Martos, aged 30, fought back, and he was eventually scared off by a passing car, driving away from the scene at speed. The police have issued a description of him. He is probably in his late twenties, or early thirties, white, of small to medium height and frame, with mousy blonde hair. He was driving a blue Renault. The woman escaped unharmed.

I feel like an idiot. Kerry's mooching about the place has obviously worked better than I gave her credit for. I saw this newspaper in the cupboard but I didn't think of examining it.

Bim asks me: *Could this man be our Weasel?*

It is possible. What happened to this woman might explain how you were abducted from your cars too.

Why did Gordon keep it?

Souvenir? But before we get too carried away, let's remind ourselves that we don't know he has anything to do with this. It could be a coincidence.

A coincidence he was the last person to see Jackie Brand and a coincidence he has a newspaper article about an attempted abduction in his hallway cupboard?

Is there a date in this article?

The attack happened four years ago on June 5th, Kerry informs me.

I groan.

What's the matter?

I can't believe I didn't realise this before. You two and Gerte were all murdered in June. And, guess which month Jackie Brand disappeared in?

When you think about it, being a motorway mechanic is a

107

brilliant job for a serial killer, Bim says. *It places someone in the perfect position to win over a woman's confidence by pretending to help her. And, what is she going to chat about while she waits for her car to be fixed? She's going to tell him about her life, her family, and her boyfriend.*

There is only one Gail Martos listed in the Leicester telephone book. She lives on a modern estate of starter homes in the suburbs of the city. She is another petite blonde. It is the only thing about her that stands out, in truth. Dressed in baggy clothes with a headscarf covering her hair, she puts effort into not being noticed. She is like a blurred photograph you can't quite make out. I could study her for an hour, turn away, and not remember a single detail about her. She has all but faded from this world, yet she is very watchful of everything within it. Her eyes dart about her, suspiciously, as we watch her open her front door and disappear inside.

It is obviously a woman's house. The walls are painted pastel colours - peaches and pinks, mainly - and at the windows, there are chintzy curtains. The living room has been colonised by a pack of cuddly toys, which perch on every arm and cushion of the three piece suite. No human being, other than Gail herself, could ever feel comfortable in this room, not when a sudden movement could send several of the furry creatures flying to the floor.

We wait twenty four hours for her to receive the letter which, after much deliberation, we have decided to send her. When it finally arrives, the postie has to knock because it's too bulky to squeeze through the letter box.

Gail examines the envelope but she doesn't open it. She puts it in a bag and takes it to work with her.

This is how the three of us come to spend the day with her in the back room of the flower shop, where she is employed to make funeral wreaths, and wedding bouquets.

Bim keeps sneezing. *It's the pollen. It's aggravating my hay fever.*

You're dead for heaven's sake! How can you have hay fever?

The only answer I get is another sneeze.

Gail works with only a tiny radio tuned to a pop station for company. It is a warm day outside but this room is chilly - for the flowers, we assume - and she wears fingerless mittens to keep her hands nimble. She is dressed in jeans, a short sleeved white blouse, and a baggy navy blue jumper which reaches down to her knees.

Between sneezes and sniffs, Bim is humming Eleanor Rigby, the radio station's Hit of the Day, as we watch Gail wire a bouquet together. We've heard the Beatles version three times and Bim's rendition twenty - at least.

Well, I'm sorry, she declares when Kerry and I moan, as she starts the song all over again. *I think it's really apt. I do. Look at her. The poor creature is so lonely, it is pathetic.*

Maybe she has a rich internal life which compensates for the lack of people in her life, I point out, equitably.

Does that look like a woman with a rich internal life to you?

We all turn back to Gail.

It is hard to tell. She doesn't seem unhappy to me. She is just...self contained.

Nutty, Bim interjects.

In her own world, Kerry trumps us both.

She does like her little routines, I suppose.

It's called Obsessive Compulsive Disorder.

Don't exaggerate, Bim.

I'm not. She checked the front door was locked five times before we could leave this morning.

Kerry asks: *Do you think our envelope has upset her?*

I nod. *I don't suppose she gets much mail.*

Maybe, she'd feel better if she actually opened it, Bim scoffs.

I doubt it, given what's inside.

She's lucky. She managed to fight him off. Heaven knows how!

We all examine Gail again.

Do you envy her?

I'm angry that she is alive and I'm not.

I might be wrong but I think we should try to come to terms with being dead. It's not so bad, is it?

It is to me, Triffid!

Well, when this is over, and we've caught this killer, I'm going to do something meaningful with my afterlife.

Bim rolls her eyes.

I'd like to ask Kerry what she'll do. No, I'd like to ask what I should do. She is right, though. None of us is in any position to criticise Gail. We cling to the living and our investigation and she to her cuddly toys and little routines. What's the difference, really? None of these things are doing us much good. We are comforted by them, but what changes?

For lunch, she has a sandwich bought from a snack bar a few doors up the road. We have an exciting ten minutes, waiting in the queue with her, trying to guess what she will order. Bim suggests banana and walnut on rye. I try bacon, lettuce, and tomato, on white. But, Kerry is the one of us who truly understands this woman. She wins with tuna and mayonnaise on wholemeal.

The afternoon passes slowly. We play I-spy for a while and at four o'clock the owner of the shop, a plump woman in her fifties, called Madge, who speaks with a slightly affected southern accent, drops by for a cup of tea, and a chat. She lists the customers she has had, that day, by what they've bought.

The dozen red roses – his wife's birthday – was followed by a poesy of sweet peas. Then, came the lilies and, after that, more roses, but yellow ones, this time. Oh yes, and an order was placed for a couple of wreaths too, she says, capturing a strand of nicotine blonde hair and twisting it back up unto her bun. *The funeral is next week; one of the teachers at the local school. She died of* ...She mouths the word, cancer, and presses her lips together in a grim yet satisfied smile, her eyes glistening with the self-bestowed importance of imparting her sad news. *She was riddled with it her mother-in-law said. It started...*Her voice drops to a whisper...*down under.* Cupping her hand, she raises her eyebrows to reiterate the unspeakable nature of the body part to which she is referring.

Kerry looks at us perplexed.

She means Australia, Bim enlightens her, with a snigger.

An hour later, we're travelling home with Gail, on the bus, convinced that when she gets there, finally, she is going to open our envelope. Yet, unbelievably, she stalls again until after she has cooked herself her dinner - a pork chop and salad followed by rice pudding - which she eats seated at her kitchen table. Pushing her half-finished dish of rice pudding away, she reaches for her bag and extracts our envelope.

The moment has come. We can barely believe it, nor conceal our excitement. She pulls out the letter which we printed off onto official police letter-headed paper and reads:

Dear Miss Martos, we are writing to you regarding your attempted abduction in Leicester, four years ago. Please find enclosed here two envelopes, marked A, and B. You should open A, first. In this, you will find a computer generated image of a man. We need to know from you whether or not you think this could be your attacker. In B, you will find a photograph of a man and we need to know from you whether or not this man could be your attacker. To help you, you will find on the sheet, attached to this letter, a multiple choice of responses, covering a continuum of possibilities from, "Yes, I am sure this is him" to "No, I am certain this is not him". Please complete this questionnaire and return it to us in the prepaid envelope provided.

The main risk in our approach is that she realises it is a hoax and tears the whole thing up but to our delight she follows our instructions. She opens envelope A, slitting the flap with a knife, before sneaking a look inside. As she pulls out the contents, her reaction is immediate. She cries aloud, stands up from her chair, and drops the computer image.

There is no question about that, ladies. She recognises him, Bim trills.

I not going to quibble with her but at best her reaction means that Kerry's description of her killer strikes some kind of chord with her too. I am expecting a more muted response to the photograph in envelop B, because a computer generated image can't fail to make someone look like a psychopath, whereas a guy with his arm around an old lady has to be a bit of a sweetie. But, the moment she pulls this photograph from its envelope, her hands start to shake, the vibration rapidly travelling up her arms to her torso, where it soon rushes in all directions, until the whole of her body is trembling. It reaches her lips last, making her teeth chatter, as a strange mewing sound emanates from deep within her.

We look at each other in alarm, uncertain what to do as she flees past us on the way to the bathroom, where she is violently sick. She is still clutching the photograph in her hand and noticing it, she throws it away from her.

We hover around her feeling useless and guilty for being the cause of her distress. It was a game to us. I'm not sure I ever believed she would be able to recognise either of our pathetic exhibits. That Gordon could really turn out to be The Weasel seemed too much of a long shot. But, Gail's reaction is both sobering and shaming. We've upset her, deeply. And, we might actually be on to something too.

When there is nothing more in her stomach to bring up, she hauls herself up from the floor and staggers to the living room, where she heads for the sofa. Here, she immediately curls up into the foetal position, and clutching an ear-less teddy to her, she closes her eyes.

She didn't finish her rice pudding, Bim says, forlornly.

As Gail drifts off into exhausted sleep, Kerry sings her a lullaby to prevent the Weasel from stealing into her dreams and disturbing her again.

I watch her breathing in and out with a mixture of fascination and shock. My thoughts are fragmented by a caravan of unanswerable questions. Can we rely on the outcome of our experiment? Did she really recognise Gordon Richards as her attacker? Or could her reaction merely be hysteria, brought on by the stress we've put her under? If Gordon Richards was the one who tried to abduct her, why would he stay living and working in Leicester, for the best part of two years, before he went off travelling? She could have run across him, and recognised him as her assailant, at any time.

We should feel triumphant, shouldn't we?

Neither Kerry nor I answer Bim who has asked the question.

Then, why do I feel so terrible?

She is expressing the sentiment of us all. One by one, we curl up too, Kerry and I in the armchairs and Bim on the hearthrug, each of us cradling a cuddly toy.

AUTUMN

It is Halloween and I'm doing my best to bring a white sheet with two black eyes and a circle for a mouth to life but, according to my nephews, I'm not moving it correctly.

How come I'm the one who is dead and yet you know more about ghosts than me?

You have to make it look like there's a person under the sheet, Auntie Kate, otherwise we can't take you trick-or-treating, Sam explains, patiently, for the hard-of-thinking.

Shouldn't that be the other way around? I'm the one who is supposed to be taking care of you.

Carrie has gone to a Halloween party with Nigs and I'm the only babysitter she could find. I have strict instructions to A: stay out of sight – which I can't help but manage. And, B: keep the boys inside the house. It is part B of my responsibility which is proving to be the most difficult. All dressed up with nowhere to go, my nephews are too nine, six, and three years old to understand their mother's insistence that trick-or-treating isn't a British custom. Besides, her stand against Americanizing our culture is obviously self-serving. The truth is she wanted to go out and there was nobody living who could take the boys from house to house. This is why against her orders I have agreed to let them trick-or-treat the houses in the next street, where we don't know anyone, provided I accompany them. The plan has floundered on my inability to make the sheet look as though someone living is walking under it, however.

It's okay Auntie Kate, it's not your fault, Sam my wizard of an oldest nephew says, kindly. But, I can tell from the faces of Dracula and the Mummy that disappointment hangs heavy in the air.

My subsidiary task is to oversee sweet distribution when the neighbours' kids who haven't heard that trick-or-treating isn't a British custom come calling. Without an adult here, it would be one sweet for them to avoid a trick and the rest of the packet for my nephews. I'm not doing too well with this either. I forgot my sheet when Harry and Davey, the brats from two doors down, came around, and when I offered them a toffee apple, they ran away screaming.

If you scare all the kids away we could eat the rest of the sweets ourselves. Then, we might not feel so bad about you being unable to take us trick-or-treating, Jethro tries.

I particularly like the use of 'might not' in that sentence.

A baffled expression settles on his sweet face. *Does that mean we have a deal?*

I feel so sorry for them I can't bring myself to refuse.

They stand giggling in the hallway waiting for our first victims to knock.

Two witches greet me when I open the door. They have their father with them - at least I assume that's who it is under the weir wolf make-up

That's really clever, boys, he says, when the tin of sweets levitates off the hall table towards his offspring. *How do you do it? Is it on some kind of thread? It's very good. You can't see it, at all. Just take a couple of sweets, girls. Leave some for everyone else. 'Night, boys. Great trick!*

Harry and Davey are pathetic, Jethro mutters, glumly, as they walk away.

Caleb punctures me with a quizzical expression which I suspect has something to do with wondering what dead aunts are good for. While Sam is looking wistfully at the receding back of a father prepared to take his children trick-or-treating.

Carrie should never have gone out to that party. She always was man bloody mad. It just wasn't apparent because she got with Phil when she was so young. She is obviously one of those women who need a man by their side in order to define themselves. Now, she is latching onto Nigs, when really she needs to be here with the boys and her recently deceased and extremely traumatised older sister.

Do it how you did with Arry and Davey, Caleb whines.

Harry, I correct. *Okay, when the next ones call, you lot have to*

116

hide behind the door. If they can't see anyone at all, they'll know it's a real ghost.

I lift the tin into the air, ready, as we hear footsteps approach. *Open it, Sam, before they knock, but do it slowly like in a haunted house.*

As the door creaks wide, my life and death flash before me. Carrie is standing before me, her hand outstretched, holding the key.

She sees the tin in mid-air and goes ballistic.

Are you completely mad, she shouts, barging past me. *When Maggie rang me to tell me what happened to Harry and Davey, I knew you were pulling some kind of bloody silly stunt. She was threatening to report my 'babysitter' to the police, if I didn't come home and investigate what was going on. Bed, now, all of you! No arguments. We'll talk about this in the morning. Don't look like that, off you go, and don't forget to wash the makeup off. Not you, Kate! Put that tin down. You, I want to talk to now.*

She waits until the boys are in the bathroom, before she explodes again. *I had to leave Nigs at the party. Did you do this on purpose just to ruin my date?*

I only wish I'd thought of it.

No. You should...We just... I'm sorry Carrie but you're going to have to change out of that shower curtain if you want me to take this seriously. Who are you supposed to be anyway?

I'm the murdered woman in Psycho, she states with misplaced dignity. *Why? Isn't it obvious?*

Not to me, it isn't.

Well, the fake knife fell off. It was supposed to be sticking out of my breast, like this. See? Wait a minute. I understand what you're doing. Stop trying to change the subject. Where was I? Yes...What would have happened if the neighbours had called the police first and me, second? If they found out there was nobody here with the kids – nobody living, I mean – they could have taken them away from me. She starts to cry. *How could you be so thoughtless! I'm all they've got, Kate. There are no grandparents for them to turn to, no living aunt, and now the poor little things have lost their father too. I'm all alone here. Do you have any idea what that*

117

feels like? I'm scared, Kate! That's what it feels like. I have three small boys to rear on my own and that scares me rigid.

She is crying so hard by now there is snot running down her lip. I wish I didn't notice this but I just can't stop being her shit of a big sister.

How many people do I have to lose, Kate? How many?

Her voice has the same cadence as the hook in a song - those few notes that get you every time you hear them, filling you with pain and yearning. I want to tell her I'll make everything up to her because I feel so terrible but what's the point? She'll never believe me. She knows me far too well.

Gerte has taken to dropping by my office on her bus tours of London so I can update her on how the investigation is going. She has an analytical way of thinking, reminiscent of my boss, Bixby, which frequently turns these meetings into impromptu case reviews. It is hard to keep hold of the fact that she is one of the murder victims herself because she seems so happy. Dressed in her pink and white tracksuit and pink towelling bandanna, her presence shows no sign of the strangle marks, or glassy eyes, that Kerry and Bim still have.

As she appears before me, she is holding a polystyrene cup of coffee which she has snaffled from the café on the corner. She can't drink it, of course, but she likes to marinade in its aroma.

I tell her about my plan to go to Sheffield to take a closer look at Jackie Brand's boyfriend, Brian Jones. I don't believe he has anything to do with our inquiry but I have a theory Jackie might be there. I've searched everywhere else for her so it can't do any harm to try.

You have no actual proof she was murdered.

She disappeared from her car, though, Gerte. *Just like the others. Just like you. And, Gordon Richards is a pretty good suspect for doing away with her.*

It only fits as a hypothesis. You don't have one shred of irrefutable evidence against him and we already know where that leads - to innocent people going to jail for crimes they didn't commit.

Karl is bound to be released soon.

So you keep telling me, but that doesn't change the circumstantial nature of your case.

It is not easy being D.I. Ghost, you know. The police procedures, I used in life, don't work now I'm...I 'm about to say now I'm in spirit, but the phrase feels so alien, I falter. *Now I'm...whatever,* I mumble, instead.

Well, if it did turn out you were right about this man you'd be way ahead of the police. You just have to prove it, beyond a shadow of a doubt, is all I'm saying.

And, what happens then? I can hardly arrest him, can I?

You'll think of something. You'll have to because the alternative would be too grotesque to contemplate. After putting all this energy into trying to identify him, just imagine what it would feel like to have to sit back and watch while he goes on slaughtering women.

Brian Jones is still at the same address where he was living when Jackie went missing three years ago. It is a light and airy maisonette with two bedrooms, occupying the upper floor and attic of a large Georgian house, in one of the city's leafier suburbs. It should be a pleasant place to live. Yet, the scene Bim, Kerry, and I, encounter upon our arrival is one of devastation.

I wouldn't have thought they had a lot of tidal waves in Sheffield, Bim muses, as we explore.

The central heating pipes are fractured. The doors and windows don't fit their frames. There are stains on the carpets and up the wallpaper. The stairs creak and the ceilings on the lower floor are so badly cracked one of them has actually caved in.

Bim screws up her nose. *What is that smell?*

The reek of boiled cabbage is pervading every room, despite the sickly-sweetness of the air freshener that someone has used to mask it.

The electrics are a little eccentric, I say. *The lights in the bedroom refused to work when I switched them on, only to spring to life of their own accord, a few minutes later.*

Perhaps, some of this damage could have been done while they were putting out the fire in the kitchen, Kerry suggests.

I had forgotten the fire. We all look through the charred door at the scorched walls, work surfaces, and cupboards.

She is right, you know, Kate.

I smile at Bim, sardonically, while I wait for her barb.

Well, it had to happen sometime. She probably studied water damage in geography.

I wish you wouldn't talk about her as though she isn't here, I whisper.

Most of the time she isn't!

Why would she want to be?

It's like the Marie Celeste, Kerry says, dreamily. *Do you think anyone is still living here?*

The sound of a key going into the lock, in the front door,

121

answers her question. It's Brian Jones. He doesn't look anything like how I imagined a jilter would, which makes no sense at all since I have never given the matter a second's thought before. Possibly, I expected him to be wickedly good looking, an obvious Lothario and not the stolid, uninspiring specimen standing in front of me.

Dark haired and clean shaven with metal rimmed glasses, he has an enthusiast's face, by which I mean there is something both eager and purposeful about it. I could picture him chasing up back numbers of The Beano on eBay. Am I being unfair? Why should I worry about it? Where he is concerned, I'm a sister. How dare he do what he did to one of us?

He isn't on his own. There are two women with him and only one of them is alive. This is when we finally begin to comprehend what's actually going on in this maisonette. Brian's arm is in a sling. He fractured it falling downstairs, late yesterday, and has spent most of the night in the Accident and Emergency Unit of the local hospital. Were he a child, the doctors working there would have reported him to his local Social Services Department, some time ago. Since Jackie died, he has presented them with a long list of suspicious injuries. Last year - the one in which his living, as opposed to live-in, girlfriend moved in with him - was the most calamitous by far. Barely, a week went by without one of them having to seek medical attention. Neither of the young couple believes in the paranormal otherwise the word *poltergeist* might have come crashing into their vocabulary by now. Between them, they've experienced such a run of bad luck in this maisonette, they've decided to move. A new start, in a new home, is all they need to herald in a more tranquil epoch in their lives. Fat chance! Jackie is sure to be moving with them.

We should feel appalled. I am sure Gerte were she here with us would be. Kerry almost is, at least, to the extent she decides to pop back to Leicester to check on whether Gordon Richards has shown up, rather than spend any time in Jackie's presence. Bim and I, however, are entranced by her skill in manipulating the material world. What we can do is child's play compared with what we see going on here.

I think your body may have been found, I inform my heroine, when we persuade her to take rest from blowing dust and dirt onto the accident prone couple's wet washing, in the communal gardens downstairs.

So?

I'm not sure what to do with that so I press on. *You may have been buried in a wood in South East London and if we're right, probably, it means you were murdered.*

Now, tell me something I don't know, Einstein.

Why is she being so irascible? I didn't murder her. *I was thinking you might like to wreak revenge on the person who did it.*

What do you think I am doing?

Are you trying to tell me Brian Jones killed you?

I'm not trying to tell you anything.

I study her, perplexed. Her manner may be ugly but I can tell from her presence that in life she was extremely beautiful. She reminds me of a Modigliani portrait: oval face, pale skin, and a full-lipped sensual mouth.

Bim is evidently thinking the same. *Good bones,* she jokes, quietly, to me, as Jackie begins to twang the washing line, so forcefully, a few of the clothes pull free from their pegs and drop onto the floor.

Her eyes aren't glassy though. And, although she is petite, her hair is brunette, not blonde.

What are you two wittering on about?

We were wondering whether you were blonde when you were murdered, Bim bravely answers.

What the hell has it got to do with you?

Before we can reply – and neither of us are eager to – Kerry appears beside us.

He is still not there, she tells us.

That's mine. Take it off, Jackie demands, as soon as she realises what she's wearing.

Kerry is flustered...*I...He...It's not my...*

Take it off, I said. *Take it off now, or I'll make you regret it.*

You're having a go at the wrong person. Kerry hasn't done

anything to you. We haven't done anything to you, I protest but she ignores me.

Did you hear what I said? TAKE IT OFF NOW OR YOU'RE FOR IT!

Bim starts muttering behind me: *I don't know why she's still wearing it anyway.*

Shut up, Bim. It's not helpful, I whisper, fiercely, to her.

But, I showed her how to change it, didn't I? We both know she can because she did it for my memorial service. You haven't gone back to wearing the clothes you were run over in, have you? So why is she wearing that old thing again?

Why shouldn't she? You're still wearing your blue cocktail dress.

Jackie's vibration is beginning to throb, violently, but Bim doesn't take the hint. *Anyway all this shrew has to do is picture herself in the stupid dress and it's hers. It would suit her a lot better than all that leather gear she has on. She looks like a biker.*

She manages to make *biker* sound like a close cousin of the sewer rat. Fortunately, for all of us, our unfriendly poltergeist is focused on the wedding dress Kerry is wearing to the exclusion of all else.

Look at the state of it! It's completely ruined. It cost me a fortune that dress. I'll never get that dirt out.

You're mad, Bim tells her. *What do you need a wedding dress for? Haven't you heard? You're dead, you silly witch!*

Kerry and I instinctively back away from them.

What happens, next, astonishes me. They burst into laughter and, instantly, the atmosphere of hostility that clings to Jackie evaporates.

Sorry, ladies, being angry does become a bit of a habit.

That's the trouble with eternity, Bim gushes to her new friend. *It's so same-y.*

Kerry and I stay where we are, a safe distance from the pair of them.

What was it you asked me? Oh yes, my hair. I was blonde when I was murdered but not a natural blonde. She begins to swell with rage, again. *I dyed my hair blonde because that prick said he preferred it that way,* she shrieks, pulling his smalls from the line and flinging them beyond the garden, into the fish pond, next door. As she turns back to us, her expression softens again. *The day after I was murdered, I reverted to my true colour. Now, ladies, why don't we go indoors and talk. I've finished out here, for today.*

She leads the way to the beleaguered couple's bedroom.

This is the epicentre of my activity, she announces, proudly, dancing about. *I think of it as my bunker.*

It is practically in darkness because the cords of the two window blinds have broken, leaving them permanently down. I can just make out that the wardrobe door is open. The central clothes rail has collapsed and a quartet of Brian's suits are wrestling in a heap of earth and cat excrement, on the floor. We sit down, gingerly, on the bed.

Now, ladies, what else do you want to know?

Did Brian Jones kill you?

I ask her this, straight out, because I want this interview over and done with, before she finds another excuse to get cross with us again.

She pulls at a thread on the bedspread, until a small hole forms.

The way I see it, yes, but technically, no.

What do you remember about the day you were abducted?

Virtually everything, I should think. It was supposed to be the most important day of my life. And, it was, but not for the right reason.

I sense a storm brewing against Brian, again, so I hurry on. *Let's take it from the top. What happened after you left your house that day?*

I was on my way to Sheffield to kill that bastard. She points through the wall. *What kind of animal waits until your wedding day to call things off? How could he be so cruel?*

We nod, vigorously.

Did you reach Sheffield?

No, I was on the M1, close to Leicester, when the car suddenly died on me. I phoned my recovery service and they sent a patrol man out. He told me I'd run out of petrol. I felt such a fool. He

125

claimed I wasn't covered for that so he made something up for his control room, which I thought was really good of him, because he didn't have to. Then, he offered to drive me to the next service station to get some petrol. I didn't suspect a thing. I was genuinely grateful to him. I got into his van without a second's concern. I felt safer being with him than staying on my own beside the car. He was wearing a uniform and driving one of the recovery service vans. What was there to fear?

I show her the photograph of Gordon Richards.

That's him. But, he had a moustache, when I met him.

I glance at Kerry. Richards with a moustache matches the description she has given of her killer.

What happened next?

He drove off the motorway. He said the nearest garage was close to the exit but we ended up in the middle of nowhere. He stopped the van to have a slash. I was beginning to have misgivings about him by then. But, what could I do? I talked myself out of it. I did get out of his van but there was nowhere to go. When he came back, he started screaming at me. I couldn't make out what he was saying. He was calling me a whore, I think. He was off his trolley. I was so shocked it sort of paralysed me. He hit me quite a few times. I fell to the ground and he kicked me. I was begging him not to hurt me. I must have fainted. When I came to, I was in a cellar.

This is the evidence we've been missing. We've found our killer.

Do you know how he got you inside?

He covered me up with a blanket, that's all. Isn't that incredible? He lived in a row of terraced houses, this guy. It was a quiet road but it was all built up. There were tons of neighbours and he brought me into that house, under their noses, while it was still light. Yet, nobody noticed a thing.

What did he do about your car?

He was proud of that. He boasted about it. He hitched back to the M1 with the keys and some petrol. He dumped it in a service station car park, initially. But, later, after I was dead, he moved it to the place where it was found.

126

Didn't his control room wonder where he was?

It was the end of his shift and I was his last job. He called in and told them he'd hand the paperwork in the next day. They said that was okay.

Did he drug you?

No, he'd beaten me up pretty badly and I kept passing out. He didn't like that. It made him angry. He made me sit in a chair and he was moving me like a doll. Simon says do this, or do that, he kept saying. But, even with him working my limbs, I couldn't do anything, really. That was spoiling his fun. I was bleeding too. He didn't like that, either. Too messy for him, I guess. He got fed up in the end and strangled me.

What was it about do you think? What was the point to the game?

I've no idea. Does it matter?

Now, the interview is going smoothly and she has apparently calmed down, Bim chooses this moment to ask*: So why didn't you do something about him after he killed you?*

I can't believe, she just said that. I wait for the explosion.

Like what? I was dead, Jackie replies, with surprising, equanimity.

But, you still could have done something, surely, Bim persists.

*Bim, you...*I start to say.

She cuts me off. *If she'd done something, Kate, I might still be alive.*

Bim, that's not fair, I tell her.

Jackie laughs, nastily. *What was I going to do? What are you going to do to stop him? He could be killing someone else, right now.*

None of us reply.

That's the problem with your stupid investigation, she goads. *Do you think, if you leave a 'Gordon Richards did it' note, for the police, they are going to arrest him?*

The least you could have done is haunt him and not your ex-bloke, Bim retorts.

Why would I want to do that? It wasn't personal with Gordon Richards. I didn't exist for him. What he did had to do with him, not me. But, with Brian, it is different. He did that to me! And, now he is paying for it. All right?

But, Gordon Richards murdered you, Bim exclaims, exasperatedly. *If that isn't personal, what is?*

Jackie doesn't answer. Not, directly. She sends an ornament flying through Bim to the wall, behind, where it smashes into smithereens.

I have to grovel - a lot - to persuade Jackie to visit Gordon Richards' house in Leicester. She only agrees on the condition Bim stays away. My purpose in bringing her there is to make sure she recognises the house as the site of her murder. It falls into the category of crossing a t, and dotting an i but it needs to be done. Being dead is all the sloppiness we need in this investigation.

He has converted the cellar since I was last here, she explains.

I avoid Kerry's gaze. She was right about recognising it.

That's where I was kept and killed, Jackie continues. *It was only after I died, I got to explore the rest of his beige palace.*

I draw her away from Kerry, under the pretext of showing her something.

Did he do anything to your body once you were dead?

Well, it didn't bury itself.

That's not what I meant...

He put it in a chest freezer for three days and then drove it to London in his blue van and buried it in some woods.

But, he didn't defile it in any way?

She doesn't respond for several stunned seconds. Then, she asks, hesitantly: *Defile, in what way?*

I hesitate. I don't want to tell her everything that was done to Bim and Gerte. *Did you have any puncture marks in your palms?*

Puncture marks? Is that a joke?

According to the post mortem reports, the others did, I say, quietly, checking to make sure Kerry has wandered off on her own. *Two of them, for sure. Kerry's body was too decomposed to tell, definitively, but there were broken bones in her hands.*

Why would he do that?

I shrug. *I guess sickos get sicker if they're not stopped.*

Is that a dig at me?

No, no, of course not.

And, you're sure the same guy murdered us all?

I think it's possible but I'm not sure of anything yet.

I do remember him cutting off a chunk of my hair. He cut it off at the roots. And, before you ask, I haven't a clue why.

While we have a look around the basement studio flat, Gordon's tenant, a sandy haired psychology student, is hunched over a book. Eyeing his domestic clutter – the empty takeaway cartons, unwashed clothes, a bike chain, several thick psychology tomes, and a tabloid newspaper – it is hard to imagine that this is where Kerry and Jackie were murdered.

Kerry sits down next to him and lays her head on his shoulder.

Jackie nods towards her. *Is she okay?*

I give her a helpless look. *Hey, Kerry, are you okay?*

She glances up at us. *I can remember what happened to me on the day I was murdered now. It just came back to me. Well, I think it may have been there before but I couldn't bear knowing about it.*

Slowly, she recounts the sequence of events that led to her death. It is another chilling tale. On her way back to university, she came off the motorway at Leicester to get something to eat. She stopped at a small parade of shops where she bought a kebab, which she ate in her car, before driving off, again. A couple of minutes later, she noticed a van behind her. The driver kept flashing his lights. She couldn't work out why until she heard a loud clunk under the car and she saw in her mirror that part of the exhaust pipe had fallen off. She pulled over and so did the car behind. Gordon Richards got out. He was nice to her at first - helpful. He said he'd fix it for her but then suddenly he grabbed her and held his hand over her mouth. He must have had something in his palm. Whatever it was, within a few seconds, she passed out.

Was he on duty?

He couldn't have been. He was wearing casual clothes - jeans and a navy jumper - and he was driving a blue van which had no company markings. I think it must be the same one Gail and Jackie remember.

Were there no other vehicles on the road? No one who could have seen him?

It was open countryside. One or two cars did pass by, but not at the crucial moment.

He's bold, isn't he? He likes taking risks.

I bet he gets off on it, Jackie sneers. *It probably makes the pervert feel potent.*

I wonder whether he knew the exhaust was going to fall off. All he had to do was tamper with it while you were getting your kebab and then follow you.

Bastard, Jackie exclaims.

There is something else I've remembered, something strange, Kerry says. *After I was dead, my body was taken somewhere else, outside of Leicester. It could have been in London. I might be getting this all wrong but I think it was some kind of outbuilding.*

It is the bugbear of every murder enquiry: how to organise information to make sure that any leads aren't buried under a mound of irrelevant detail. I no longer have the benefit of a police computer programme to do this and so I resort to a more basic approach. I open a file and call it: *The Weasel.* Then, I list his known, or alleged, victims, sequentially, highlighting the key aspects of each attack and killing, starting with Gail - the only one of us who got away with her life - to see what emerges.

1. Gail Martos, petite blonde, florist, 30 years, single. Failed abduction after her car broke down four years ago (June 5th). Attack takes place on a country road, outside Leicester. Attacker is driving a blue van. He describes himself as a mechanic, and offers assistance. He grabs her from behind, and tries to drag her into his blue Renault van. She has identified him as being Gordon Richards. The description issued to the media at time of her attack also matches Gordon Richards.

2. Jackie Brand, petite blonde (dyed), fitness trainer, 27 years, engaged to be married. Abducted one year after Gail Martos was attacked (June 6th) after breaking down due to running out of petrol. Gordon Richards is the breakdown mechanic sent out to help her. He drives her to a country road, accessed from the Leicester turn off of the M1. There, he attacks her and takes her to the cellar of his home where he *moves her about like a doll* and when he gets fed up with this he strangles her. Her car was left on the M1, then moved to a service station, and later dumped near the Humber Bridge. Her body was kept in a deep freezer, for up to 3 days, and then driven to London in the back of his blue van. It was buried in Oxley Woods.

3. Kerry Doughton, petite blonde, geography student, 20 years old with an American boyfriend. Abducted a year after Jackie Brand went missing, (June 1st), from a country road, on the

outskirts of Leicester, while on her way back to Nottingham University. Gordon Richards follows her in his blue van from a parade of shops where she has stopped to buy a snack. He flashes his lights to make her pull over and when she does he offers her his help, before drugging her and taking her to the cellar of his home in Leicester. He dresses her in Jackie Brand's wedding dress and shoes, plays the *Simon Says* game and then strangles her. She is driven somewhere else. It is possible her body was refrigerated for up to a year because the decomposition was less advanced than the date of her murder would imply. She was found buried on the edge of a golf course in London. Some of the bones in her hands appeared to have been broken.

4. Gertrud Weiss, petite blonde, language assistant, 24 years, Austrian, lived with boyfriend, Karl Grüner. Abducted a year after Kerry Doughton (June 3rd) in unknown circumstances. She remembers driving around London after a domestic row. She also visited a garage somewhere in South London, where a mechanic checked over her car for her, before she drove off. She has identified Gordon Richards as her killer - despite not being able to remember what happened to her. He was no longer working for the recovery service, at the time of her murder, and was supposedly travelling abroad. She was drugged and strangled. Her car was missing for a week before being discovered outside the flat she shared with her boyfriend. The car had no mechanical fault. She was found in the boot, naked except for a pair of Reebok trainers (possibly Kerry's). According to the pathologist, who examined her body, she was raped post mortem. She also had post mortem puncture wounds through both her hands, consistent with being nailed to something. The only physical evidence on her body belonged to her boyfriend, however, and he was convicted of her murder.

5. Belinda Montgomery, petite blonde, PR executive, 30 years old, with a secret lover, Reece Baxter. Abducted a year after Gertrud Weiss (June 7th) in unknown circumstances but she was driving from Greenwich to Knightsbridge on her way to an office

party, at the time. Her car was found abandoned in New Cross, the following day, with no mechanical fault. I was seen talking to the driver of her car, in the same road, at about 8.00 pm, on the night of her abduction. And, a tall blonde male was filmed driving the car, several minutes earlier. The same or a similar man was also recorded in the passenger seat of my car at about 8:15pm. According to her post mortem report, Bim was drugged and strangled. She was raped post mortem too and had the same post mortem puncture wounds through her hands as Gerte. Her body was buried, wearing Gertrud Weiss's shoes, in Oxley woods.

6. Kate Madding, tall, dark, Detective Inspector, 29 years old, and single. Killed on the road that runs past the George pub on the same night as Belinda Montgomery was abducted (June 7th). It was a hit and run involving two vehicles – a truck and the same car Kerry Doughton was driving, when she disappeared two years before. She was seen talking to the driver of Bim's BMW, and filmed with a tall blonde man in her car, shortly, before she died; possibly the same man who was seen driving Bim's car, earlier the same night.

QUESTIONS: Did I know something about Bim's disappearance that got me killed? Who was driving the vehicles which ran me over? Did they know each other? Was it an accident or murder?

I want you out of here! Do you hear me? You're not supposed to be here. You're dead! So go away and be dead, somewhere else!

Carrie is stomping through the house, screaming at me. First, she tries my office. Then, she goes to the living room. Next, she takes a look in the kitchen. And, finally, she goes back to my office again. She is livid because Phil's lawyer has found out about her dinner date with Nigs, which has put her case for assault against him in jeopardy. I'm pretending I'm not here until she calms down. It is not my fault. It has absolutely nothing to do with me.

You're here. I know you're here. You're always here! I can't keep you out! Kate? Kate? She picks up the computer. *I am going to smash this onto the floor, I swear, if you don't answer me. One, two, three...If I get to five, it's Mechano.*

I think she is serious and it is so unfair because I've only just finished inputting all that stuff about my investigation. I have no choice but to break cover.

You have no right to hold me to ransom like this. I'm working on a very important case, you know.

I don't care, go and work on it somewhere else, she snarls at me, unpleasantly.

Why are you taking this out on me? I haven't done anything. All you have to do is claim you agreed to meet Nigs because he wanted to ask you some questions about me and my death. That should do it. It's pretty much the truth, anyway.

I knew it! You were there, weren't you? How dare you spy on me! Get out, right now. Do you hear me?

We seem to have gone full circle.

I don't see why you are being so nasty to me, Carrie.

I'm not. This is my house, not yours. I have a perfect right to sling you out of it.

But, I'm dead, you can't keep me out!

I realise this is a mistake, the moment I say it. A red blotch has appeared on her neck, the tell-tale sign she is about to go into meltdown.

And, don't I know it! It was bad enough having to put up with you interfering in my marriage when you were alive. But, this! This is unbearable! I WANT YOU OUT!

Arguing with Carrie is like playing tennis. All I have to do to win the match is keep her running about the court, chasing the balls I bat back to her, until she is exhausted.

Interfere in your marriage? Why, because, I let you cry on my shoulder?

You were always coming between Phil and me, you know you were. You were jealous, that much was obvious.

All I have to do to lose an argument with Carrie is get sucked into the fray, emotionally. That is what the word *jealous* has just done. It sucked me in. Suddenly, winning the match isn't important, just as long as I can pulverise the witch.

Listen to me, you traitor. The only reason I came between you and Phil was to save your neck. And, this is the thanks I get. Who do you think got Nigs and Fester there, that night? You know the night your wonderful husband tried to kill you because you told him you wanted a divorce.

But, that was when you were already dead. What about the things you did to interfere, when you were alive? You fancied him, didn't you? Go on, admit it. A wife can sense these things.

A wife can sense these things? Oh please. You've been paralysed above the clitoris since the day you met him.

Were you having an affair with Phil?

Was I what?

You heard. Were you having an affair with him?

I am not going to dignify that with an answer.

That proves it. You were.

You're mad. If you want me out of this house, I'll go, but you're going to have to rent me an office somewhere else, first.

I'm what?

You heard, I parody. *You inherited a lot of money from me. The least you could do is use some of the life insurance payout to rent me an office - my own space where I won't be subjected to your silly whims.*

135

*I am not renting an office for a ghost. You're dead! Dead
people don't have offices.*

*I'm not a ghost I'm an earth bound spirit. And, what would you
know about it, anyway?*

Dead people really have offices? I can tell from her voice,
curiosity has punctured her outrage. *If I do rent you an office...I
can't believe I'm even entertaining this idea. But, if I do, would
you move out of here for good?*

If that's what you want.

You would only come here when you were invited?

By you, or one of the boys, I qualify. *Yes.*

By me, she corrects.

You are not keeping me away from my nephews, I warn her.
And, if you try, I shall tell them.

*You would too wouldn't you? You were always telling tales to
Mum and Dad.*

I can see this is about to degenerate into a list of every
narcissistic slight she has ever suffered at my hands and I want to
spare us both the tedium of that.

Rent me an office and I'm history.

*I want to know whether you were having an affair with Phil,
first.*

*I already told you, I am not going to dignify that with an
answer.*

*Is that because you were, or you weren't, having an affair with
my husband?*

This is so insulting, Carrie. How can you even think it of me?

*Nigs said there was a man, a passenger in your car, who was
filmed on a security camera, the night you were run over - a tall,
fair haired man. That sounds like Phil to me.*

*Oh, for Heaven's sake, woman. How many tall, fair haired men
do you think there are living in this part of London alone?*

You phoned him that night.

I did? I feel shocked by this. *How do you know that?*

I checked his mobile the night you were killed.

*You must have been really devastated by my death to make time
for that.*

136

It was a habit. I didn't think. Whenever I came across his phone, I used to check his incoming calls. You spent your last moments phoning my husband and I'd like to know why that was.

I've no idea.

She narrows her eyes at me.

Honestly, I haven't. I can't think of a single reason. I despise him. You know that. Whatever the reason I rang him that night, I can guarantee there was absolutely nothing going on between us.

If you don't remember, how do you know?

For the same reason in your heart of hearts, you know, you idiot. It is impossible. Even if I did fancy him – which I didn't – I would never have acted on it. Never! You're my sister.

I can sense from her grudging acknowledgement, the storm has blown itself out, but now I'm feeling resentful. I never realised she had such a low opinion of me. She is judging me by her own standards, obviously! It is she who is after my bloke, not the other way around. That is the real reason she wants me out of this house. So she can carry on here with Nigs, behind my back.

Apparently, sisterhood doesn't mean as much to you as it does to me. I have no intention of staying where I'm not wanted. Goodbye.

I hang around long enough to listen to her begging me to come back.

Don't go off like that Kate. Not in a huff. I didn't mean it. I didn't. Come on, talk to me. You can stay here as long as you like. Do you hear me? Kate, Katie?

Her revelation has unnerved me. In spite of loathing Phil, in the first years of their marriage, before his unpleasantness ripened, he was apt to produce the faintest stirring in my ovaries. My treacherous eggs weren't bothered by how boorish he was. Why, I've no idea. They were moist with lack of clarity on this point. But, I think it may have had something to do with him being outrageously *physical*. The man is so much in his own body it is positively unseemly and he is far too comfortable about this for it to be quite decent. Anyway, whatever the anatomy of it, without regular injections of reason, his Eau de Neanderthal was all the

137

charisma he would have needed to get his sperm on my eggs. I lied to Carrie. I *can* see the attraction of Phil, I always have, but I really wouldn't put it any more strongly than that. I can see the attraction but I've never actively desired the man; although I might have wondered what it would be like, once or twice. He did try to kiss me, a couple of times, though he claimed he'd made a mistake, afterwards. This happens when you are an identical twin. Carrie and I are used to being confused. Sometimes, we've played on it. But, the people closest to us were never usually fooled. They recognised some difference in us that others couldn't detect. Shouldn't Phil have had same knack for distinguishing us? I've long suspected he did. That he hid behind the pretence he couldn't, in order to try it on with me. I never responded. I pushed him away. So why was I phoning him on the night I died? Could Phil be the Weasel's accomplice or is that too much of a leap? If it was him that Gerte saw me talking to at the wheel of Bim's car, if I'd run into him unexpectedly and could identify him, wouldn't he have had a pretty good motive for wanting me out of the way?

I hold Carrie to her agreement to rent me an office. All the time I'm doing it I believe I shall back out, at the last moment. I just want her to feel wretched for turning on me the way she did. Then, when the last moment finally arrives, I discover I'm going to go through with it. I really would prefer my own space away from her and the boys. Absurdly, it is because I have a life; well, an afterlife, technically speaking. I never had much time for friends outside the job, while I was living, but since my death my social circle has expanded. We're interesting folk us earth bound spirits. We all have a different take on afterlife and we share a determination not to go into the Light. If you go into the Light you don't come back. That much is common knowledge. You go to another dimension; a higher plane, possibly. But, it is a ladder, with no snake. It is permanent. And, the whole point of being an earth bound spirit is that we don't want to go anywhere else. I'm slightly miffed I haven't been offered the choice, though. Why haven't I seen it? Aren't I sufficiently evolved? It is disturbing. This is one of things I talk about with the other spirits, I meet: *Have you seen the Light.* I know so much about it - little though that is – I'm tempted to lie. And, I am beginning to wonder whether this is what everyone else is doing too. Could the Light be nothing more than a dead person's urban myth?

Carrie has set aside half the money she was awarded from my life insurance policy to cover my business expenses. I have to admit this is generous of her. It should be enough to keep my detective agency going for some time, which - given I don't have a single paying client, and I am never likely to - is essential. The office we decide upon is on the top floor of a Victorian pile, tall and narrow, with four floors, in Greenwich. On the street level, there is a Spanish restaurant; on the first floor, a solicitor; on the second level, an accountant; and, right at the top of the stairs, there's me. It's the attic, so it's small, but with views to die for. (Well, the odd snatch of the Thames between the roof tops, opposite.) There is a tiny reception area, a back office, a toilet, kitchenette, and a large cupboard.

I can't believe I'm actually renting an office for a ghost; is my sister's mantra, throughout the process of signing the lease.

I'm not a ghost! How many more times? I'm an earth bound spirit, I protest, but it's useless.

Well, whatever you are, we can agree you're dead, can we? That's the real point I'm making here.

It is so unfair. We have nothing against the living. Why are they so prejudiced against us?

I put a small sofa in the reception area and, in the back office, a large round meeting table and some chairs.

This prompts from Carrie: *Explain it to me, again, why a ghost needs a sofa, and a table, and chairs?*

A computer, telephone, and fax are also purchased and installed, but only after I have to endure several variations on the theme of: *And, what exactly are you planning to do with your telephone apart from look at it?*

The cupboard, I decide, should be used for storing files and miscellaneous items of which, mercifully, there are none as yet, limiting the scope of my sister's barbs. She puts the remainder of the money into two accounts. They're in her name but I will be able to manage them, using the internet, which will at least obviate the need to secure her cooperation for every fiscal move I make. The first account contains enough money to cover the rent and basic costs for a year. The second contains what's left over. We hum and ha about whether to put a plaque by the front entrance, eventually coming to the conclusion that we have no choice because even though my business technically doesn't exist, there is bound to be post, if only from the landlord. The Madding Agency is the name we hit upon. It is vague enough to discourage the casual visitor but sufficiently specific to be a postal address. The letterheads I have printed bear a different name: The Madding Detective Agency.

We import and export art materials; Carrie tells my neighbours in the building, through clenched teeth because before I died she liked to believe she never lied. *But, we trade across the dateline so we keep rather odd hours. You're unlikely to come across any of us, during the normal business day. In fact, it will probably seem to you as though nobody is ever here.*

She gives the landlord an alternative version. *I'm renting the office to write a book away from the intrusion of my family. The plaque by the door was placed there by some friends as a joke. There is no Madding Agency, as such. There is only me, Carrie Madding, the would-be writer, beavering away on my masterpiece into the wee small hours.*

When I finally get rid of her, I sit in my office trying to figure out how I can make my phantom business pay. The life insurance money won't last forever. I will need to make enough to cover the rent, and other costs, after the first year has passed. Clients, I will have no shortage of. Word has gotten around about me, already. But, how on earth am I going to turn a waiting room full of spirits into an income stream?

One of the spirits I find in my waiting room, seeking my professional help, is a capable sort, called Denise.

I died on the operating table in a private hospital while I was having a nose job done, she informs me. *The anaesthetist was high on cocaine. He lied his way out of trouble, naturally, but I don't think he should be allowed to get away with it, do you? I was only nineteen. I want you to get him struck off.*

I have to tell her – and all the others – that until the Weasel is caught, I won't have much time to do anything else.

I'll manage the waiting list while you're pursuing this other case, if you like, she offers. *You don't have to pay me, either. I'll barter my work, for yours.*

I hire her on the spot.

In life, she was a tall, stringy type, with short cropped afro hair, skin reminiscent of a plump black plum and a mouth that moves up and down at the corners like a wire under pressure. In death, her presence also has a bloody and misshapen nose.

I flick through the files she opens for each of my possible clients. There is enough work here to keep me going, easily, for a year. There are those who've been wronged like her and want justice, but many of the spirits in these files are still touchingly involved with the lives of their loved ones. It is on their behalf and not their own they wish to engage my services. Working for the living is attractive, because they would at least be able to make a donation towards my office expenses. But, how would they know it was me who'd helped them? It is going to be tricky, I can see.

I visit Carrie's house when I am not working but only at agreed times. At the boys' bedtimes, on Sunday afternoons, and whenever anyone invites me there by thinking about me. It is a better arrangement than before because when I'm there, I'm there for them, and not preoccupied with my murder investigation. In the evenings, after the boys have gone to bed, my sister sometimes uses me as a sounding board about her plans for the future. Her job in the supermarket has made her a few friends and given her back her confidence, but it is not what she wants to do for the rest of her life. Returning to education is the obvious option, but she isn't keen.

I'm thinking about going into business offering secretarial services to companies who don't want to employ a secretary full time, she announces one evening.

It sounds a great idea. So great I'm a little suspicious. *Is it yours?*

Yes...well, no, it was actually Denise Boulay who suggested it to me.

Who is she?

Your Financial Controller.

I don't have a financial...what, you mean my office manager, Denise? How the hell do you know her?

She sent me an email and now we're using Instant Messenger to communicate. She was a small business adviser for one of the banks before she died.

Was she? I had no idea. Are you sure? I thought she was only nineteen. She has never mentioned anything about being a business advisor to me.

Her suggestion is that you rent me some space in your office. I front the business but we use some of the spirits, on your waiting list, to do the work. She thinks it would be the best way of

142

financing the detective agency.

Is she insane? Who is going to employ a secretary they can't see?

No, you don't understand. That's the point of it. The work is all done remotely by computer. It's a virtual service. They don't have to sit in the office so it doesn't matter whether they're visible or not. And, it's not just secretarial services we'll be able to offer. Basically, any spirit with book keeping, web design, or computer skills will be able to barter their services, in return for the detective agency taking on their case. The money they earn will go to cover the detective agency's expenses.

And, you will be based in my office?

Our office. I'll be paying half the costs. Or the Madding Agency will. The Madding Detective Agency will pay the other half. It will probably take about three months to set up if you agree, Denise reckons. What do you think?

A virtual secretarial services agency, staffed by spirits, apart from you?

Yes.

In my office?

Our office.

I think I'd like to talk it over with my lodgers first.

Are they the lodgers who can't see or hear you?

They're the ones.

Were you always this eccentric?

Carrie, I'm not the one who wants to go into business with a bunch of stiffs! I just want to mull it over, okay?

I disappear to the bar of the restaurant on the ground floor of my office building, before she can say anything I'll want to make her regret. Eccentric? Me? And, what about Denise? Who is this woman I've employed? If I catch her studying a map of Poland, she is definitely for the push.

I sit on a stool next to an old man who tells me he is looking for his wife. *Maybe she has walked into the Light,* I suggest to him. But, it turns out he isn't even sure she's dead. I think of offering him my professional services but then it occurs to me that just because a man spends his eternity looking for his wife, doesn't

143

mean he actually wants to find her. Most of the spirits I run into here are doing *the tour*. Well, that's what I call it because they seem to be permanently wandering about the world. I like them. They have the pleasing social ease of frequent travellers and I love hearing about their journeys. The old man who is looking for his wife is hooked on disaster. He travels to typhoons, earthquakes, air crashes, and fires, in search of her. He has just returned from a volcanic eruption and is in the middle of describing it to me, when Denise rushes in with one of her own.

The Weasel has turned up in Leicester!

With his blue van?

No, I think they said it was white.

A Renault?

A Ford.

I thought it was too much to hope for that he'd still have the other one.

She smiles at me, facetiously. *Why, don't you like Fords?*

You know it's not the make of the van I'm bothered about, Denise. It's not being able to get hold of the forensic evidence that might have been inside the blue one. If it were strong enough, the police could have arrested the Weasel straight away, before he has the chance to kill again.

Bim and Kerry want to know whether you are going to join them at the house.

I can't, not yet. Something has been nagging me about the tall, blonde man who was recorded riding in the passenger seat of my car the night Bim and I were killed, and I think it's time I checked it out.

I don't even know where Phil is living now. I have to pick up his trail at work. I spend a tedious few hours at the garage, waiting for him to go home. I loathe all things mechanical and cars are no exception. There is nothing I understand about them and even less which interests me. It is ironic really that I was killed by one: a peculiarly vengeful fate.

He finally closes the doors at seven at night but before he leaves, he invites the three mechanics still there to have a drink with him. They go to The George which I find unsettling. I am not sure which of them suggests it. It gets lost in the lads' banter they keep up. But, it creates a tangible, if tenuous, association between him and me on the night I was killed. As Carrie pointed out, Phil is tall and blonde. It could have been him in my car. He could be the Weasel's accomplice. *Gotcha*, I want to yell at him, before I've even discovered one iota of true evidence against him. This is how much I hate him, I tell myself, and it is important that I do, because my hatred is the measure I have used to rebut Carrie's accusation that I fancied him.

She is aware of my intention to tail him and the reason for it. She even protests his innocence.

How could I have married a serial killer? I would have known if he were a murderer. Do you think I could make three sons with a psychopath?

I only wish I shared her confidence in her taste in men.

It is one of those mild wet days of November, compensation for the stick bare trees and slush of rotting leaves, underfoot. The sky is a yellowy-grey bruise. It makes me long for the navy uniformity of night, the street lights gleaming like the polished buttons on a police officer's uniform. The guys I'm with are happy to hang. They are in no hurry to get home. None of them has a steady relationship, I imagine. Women have no doubt been attracted to less appealing specimens. But, they are so juvenile! They actually laugh at Phil's burps.

Their names are Jeff, Scott, and Brad, and like their boss, they are in their thirties. A difficult age, obviously, though not one I shall personally ever experience. Jeff has a doughy face which will be flaccid with alcohol abuse by the time he is forty, I predict, from the way he is knocking it back. Scott is the most handsome of the bunch: tall like Phil, but muscular, with rugged features that drain away slightly into the sides of his face, like the second facelift of a film star. Brad is a peacock. Everything he is wearing is the latest fashion. I don't see the point of it myself when his job requires him to put on overalls while he is working. I can only guess he finds it reassuring. It is self assertion, not self expression he cares about. Wouldn't therapy be cheaper?

They don't talk as such, they taunt and tease. The references are meaningless to an outsider. I have no idea in detail what they're going on about, except I am sure it is nothing important. There is one strange thing I do pick up. Scott asks Phil, how Maxine is. Who is Maxine? He isn't even divorced from Carrie yet. Could he have found someone so quickly? From the dewy-eyed look he gives, as he replies, he must have. *Fit*, he says, with a bashful grin. Fit? Fit for what? What does he mean? It's a northern expression, isn't it? So why is a Londoner like Phil using it? Five minutes away from Carrie and he is becoming a stranger.

I get into the passenger seat of his Audi, when he leaves the pub, for a mystery tour, which I hope is going to end up outside the place where he is living. He is over the limit, I shouldn't wonder with all that beer on top of an empty stomach. If I were still alive, I'd nick him.

As we set off, I try and recall the assortment of his relatives I've met over the years. One of his cousins must be putting him up because with the mortgages on Carrie's house and the garage, he can't be flush enough to afford a place of his own. He has put weight on since Carrie threw him out. He has been living on takeaways, no doubt. His clothes have changed for the worse too. She used to dress him in good quality suits, which she bought in a posh second hand clothes shop. Left to his own devices, however, he has reverted to being a department store man. Nothing fits properly, nothing matches. He is Mr Bland.

We come to a stop outside a Victorian terrace in Catford -

pebble-dashed with white PVC doors and windows. It has a tiny front garden which has been concreted over to take a car. He pulls onto it with the ease of someone who could do the manoeuvre in his sleep and, as he strolls up the front path, he rifles in his pocket for a key.

That you, pet, a woman calls, when he opens the door. *Supper is ready.*

I race ahead so I can find out who she is.

She is in the kitchen holding two plates which have been warming in the oven. She sets them on the kitchen table. There is an individual meat pie, mushy peas, and chips, on each one. I take this in while trying to moderate my disbelief. The woman performing these actions is so unlike my sister, I'm wondering whether Phil has an identical twin too, whom I've just followed home by mistake.

That's music to my belly, Maxine, I'm starving.

So this is Maxine. Well, I beg to differ but she isn't very fit, not in the Southern sense of the word, anyway. She is small and plump; very plump, with massive breasts which jiggle in her blouse, as she speaks. She is older than Carrie too. Older than Phil, I suspect; forty something, if she is a day. And, if not, she's had an incredibly hard life. She is not unattractive. She has light blue eyes, blonde hair, which is twisted back and up and secured, with a shiny black clasp, the ends frothing with curls on her crown like the milky head on a cup of cappuccino coffee. Her complexion is pale, and her face is chubby and jolly. Her smile reveals huge white slabs of teeth, even and smooth-cornered as tabs of spearmint gum. I like her. She is pleasing to look at and comes across as warm. Not so much a mumsy type, as the barmaid who turns casual visitors into regulars by remembering their name, as though it actually mattered to her. She is welcoming is what I mean. I can definitely see the attraction. But, she is the last woman I thought Phil would choose to shack up with. She is so unlike me and my sister, I feel slighted.

He kisses her on her cheek. *Had a good day, love?*

I can see from his face, he is interested to hear her answer. When did he look at Carrie that way? When was he that

147

attentive? How the hell am I going to tell her about this?

Busy as a blue arsed fly. My back's killing me, she tells him.

I'll run you a bath later.

A grin passes between them, the glimmer of a sexual encounter to come.

How about you, pet? What was your day like?

Well, I think I'll be sharing that bath with you, put it that way, he laughs, confirming their intention.

I can't bear to listen to this. I feel excluded, something I've never felt around him and Carrie. Their relationship was improved by an audience, which is probably why they had three kids. Phil and Maxine are an exclusive pair, however. They neither need, nor want, anyone else around them. How am I going to explain that to my sister? What strikes me as I tour their house, starting with the master bedroom, is the array of photographs. There are a dozen, at least, spread between the bedside tables, the dressing table, and the top of a chest of drawers alone. There they are, Phil and Maxine, saying cheese for unknown photographers at various parties and dinner dances. There are no holiday snaps but their nocturnal outings go back over a lengthy period of time, through a number of weight losses and gains for Maxine, and through a disastrous red headed period. Phil has aged in these photographs. This relationship must have been going on for most of his marriage to Carrie. I try and let this sink in. It is unbelievable. Yet, it is also true. It has to be. How am I going to tell her? The photographs reveal other things too. There was a flat, possibly rented, before this house. And, I am willing to bet my life insurance money on this being the reason why Phil took out a mortgage on the garage. He bought Maxine this house to live in. Could there be children? I scan the photographs here, before scurrying downstairs to check out some others in the living room. No kids. Oh dear, poor Carrie. Sam came along only four months after she got married. There has never been a time when her priority hasn't had to be the kids. Is that the attraction Maxine has for Phil? A childless woman who's prepared to make his sorry arse the centre of her universe?

I search the desk in the rear lobby, monitoring the couple's low murmuring voices for any change which would indicate they're about leave the kitchen and come in my direction. They couldn't see me anyway, I tell myself. Yet, I feel so guilty about searching through their private papers, under their noses, I can't rid myself of the sensation, they could. I find the deeds to the house. These are what I'm looking for. They are joint owners of the house. Another paper shows that Maxine took out her own mortgage to cover her half. It was purchased two years ago. Two years ago! I can only imagine Phil must have gone straight home to Maxine after work, returning to Carrie and the boys, after midnight, just to sleep. And, all those weekends he was supposedly working, he was here with her too. Well, at least I know there's no way he could be the Weasel's accomplice. I mean where would he find the time?

Carrie suspected there was someone else. For years, she accused him behind his back. I dismissed her instinct about his philandering, simply because it wasn't my own. I couldn't imagine anyone, apart from Carrie, being stupid enough to take him on. Does Maxine think his burping is funny? She must be the kind of woman I've never encountered before, if she does. There are no photographs of the boys in this house. Why is that? I can understand that he might not want to decorate his love nest with images of his ex, but why exclude his sons too? Does he have no feeling for them at all? Or does he see them as Carrie's now, not his? It is possible Maxine doesn't know about Carrie and the boys, I suppose. He might have lied to her too. Could he have made a bigamous marriage with her? I sift through the rest of the papers in the desk to see if I can find a marriage certificate. There isn't one. Surely, even Phil wouldn't be that daft. But, I still feel relieved. Why was he so dead set against splitting up with Carrie when he had Maxine stashed away? It doesn't make sense. What would make him go on with their marriage when he had this relationship which obviously makes him so much happier? Was it simply to make my sister's life a misery? Was it for the boys, or for money? Hells bells! How am I ever going to tell Carrie about any of this?

Gordon Richards is getting ready to make a move. He packs a few clothes in a canvas holdall, slides his passport into the pocket of the navy blue blazer he is wearing, and calls a cab. He leaves his white van parked in a street, around the corner from his house. Does he think someone might come looking for it while he is away?

In the centre of Leicester, he abandons the cab, and switches to a Skylink bus. This is when Bim and Kerry, who are with him, realise he is headed for the airport.

By the time I join them there, they are in the bag drop-off queue. In the flesh, he is not the terrifying monster I imagined him to be. He is below average height, and wiry, but muscular, like a weasel, exactly as Kerry described. His receding hair has been shaved close to his head since the photograph in our possession was taken, making it look darker, and also giving him a harder edge. He has grown a moustache again too, an old-fashioned droopy one. His face, at first glance, is unremarkable, which is as far as most people would get but, if they did linger a little longer on his features, they might notice that the veins beneath his white pulpy skin appear to be surfacing, dappling his face with shadowy stains, even in full light. His sunken blue-grey eyes are uncomfortably penetrating too. It is as though he is scrutinising every atom, around him, from a stronghold deep inside himself. He sees us, not consciously, but he does. He knows something new is present and this makes him nervous. I'm glad, because it is an ordeal for us to wait in line beside him too - for Kerry, particularly. She has to deal with her memories of being drugged and strangled by this man. To Bim, who can't recall what happened, he is probably a bit of a celebrity, although of the Sweeney Todd, Jack the Ripper variety, undoubtedly.

We distract ourselves by fretting over why he might be going abroad. If it is a holiday, why does he have so little luggage?

He could be off on a murder weekend, Bim jokes, darkly.

I hadn't even thought of that! He might have left a trail of corpses right around the world for all we know.

When we reach the desk we discover he is booked on a flight to Madrid, and from there to Granada.

Goody, goody, Bim chimes, immediately. *I adore skiing.*

There probably won't be much snow in the Sierra Nevada yet, Kerry warns her. *It's too early in the season. The ski station will have only just opened.*

She is having a geography moment; Bim makes a show of explaining to me. *I bet she knows the major industries of the region too. Won't that be a treat? I can hardly wait.*

I was hoping for a beach, myself, I fancy doing some snorkelling. Can we swim?

The other two examine me with curiosity.

Spirits, I mean. Can we move under water?

Ignore her. She is joking; Bim advises Kerry, before naming her top ten skiing destinations.

I assume she doesn't know.

We hear Gordon's voice for the first time when he starts to chat to the middle-aged couple behind us, in the queue to pass through Security. It is not high-pitched, exactly, but there is a thin querulous whine running through it, which gives him a nerdy feel. It is at once gratifying and mortifying to hear.

As Bim says for us all: *How could a berk like that kill us?*

I'm staying at my mother's house, he explains to his captive audience. *She spent her final years there until she died from a stroke, a few months back. I did wonder about selling it, after she passed, but I've fallen in love with the place. I feel closest to her there.*

Bim who is pretending to serenade him with a violin, comments: *They'll be ready to hand over their life savings to him, if he keeps this up. Do you think his mother's death could have changed anything, Kate? He said it was a few months ago. What if he has stopped killing? Does that happen with serial killers?*

Sometimes they do stop, either for years, at a time, or forever.

Would it make a difference to you if his killing spree were over?

I'd feel relieved but it wouldn't stop me wanting him to go to jail for the murders he has committed, already.

Kerry is looking agitated. *We don't have to sit with him on the plane, do we?*

No, not if you don't want to. Why don't we go up front with the pilots? That might be fun.

What will happen if we crash?

Just what we want - a nervous flier, Bim mutters. *And, better still, a dead one.*

What exactly are you worried about, Kerry?

If the plane exploded would we survive as we are now or would we be dispersed?

Triffid, Bim mouths at me.

I give her my I-know-how-to-handle-this-because-I'm-an-aunt look. *You will never have to find that out, Kerry,* I say, with exaggerated firmness. *Bim and I aren't going to let anything else happen to you. Okay? It must be frightening to be around the man who murdered you but you are completely safe from him now. I don't think it's possible for us to die twice.*

She's right, Kerry, Bim says. *It's him who should fear us now because together, we are going to stop him from harming anyone else.*

Do you think we could get him to crash the car? It would solve everything, if he were dead, Bim tempts, once we join the dual carriage way, after leaving Granada airport, in the Toyota Aygo the Weasel has hired - the cheapest car he could get.

She and Kerry are in the back but I drew the short straw so I'm riding up front, beside him. I can't decide whether she is serious, or not.

All we would have to do is scare him so he drives himself into the path of an oncoming car, she continues.

That would make us as bad as he is, Kerry says, disapprovingly.

Why? How do you know it's not what we're meant to do?

We could end up killing the other driver too!

Then, we'll drive him off the road into a tree. What about you, Kate? Are you up for a murderous experiment?

I have to admit I'm curious to see what would happen. As long as it doesn't affect anyone else, do your worst.

She leans over the Weasel's shoulder and almost immediately an image of her appears in the rear view mirror. Not the Bim we're used to but a putrefying approximation of her rotting corpse. Peels of bluish-grey skin hang from the cheek bones of her bloated face and her eye sockets are filled with two heaving globs of maggots. Her upper lip has decomposed, revealing a row of spindly gum-less teeth and fixing her mouth in a sinister Elvis Presley sneer.

The Weasel glances at the mirror and looks away without appearing to register what he has seen. It is only after his eyes have returned to the road, I notice him stiffen. Then, a rash of sweat beads explodes on his brow and his breathing quickens.

Given the stimulus, his reaction is shockingly muted. I can only imagine he has become immune to atrocities which would sicken the rest of us. I have the impression he is torn about what to do next. He desperately wants to check on his sanity back in that mirror. Is she really there? Or did he imagine her? But, he is worried he'll find himself out.

We watch as he struggles to get himself in check. Only then, does he look into the mirror, again. He stares, defiantly, into it and, as he holds Bim's wriggling orbs with his own eyes, I see him growing stronger, while she fades under the assault of the malevolence within him, until only his smug smiling face is visible in the mirror.

Enraged, I grab the steering wheel from him, forcing the car to the edge of the road. I can taste his shock but I am not powerful enough to stop him resting it from my grasp and bringing the car back under his control. Exhausted, I give up.

I wish Jackie were here. She could have finished him off!

Do you want to swop places so I can have a go, Bim volunteers.

I'm sorry but I think this should stop right now, Kerry tells us both. *We don't kill people. That's what he does and we're trying to put him in jail for it.*

Bim rounds on her. *What if we can't, Miss Goody-two-shoes? What if the only way to stop him is to kill him? Wouldn't that be better than watching him kill more women?*

His hatred is like a virus. Can't you see that? The more we are exposed to it, the more we catch it. He is dangerous to be around.
What are you talking about! I've never heard such twaddle.

I really think she could be right about this, Bim. He is so full of negative energy, it's as though he actually pollutes the atmosphere around him. Look at us. We've only been in his company a few hours and we're already falling out with each other.

The Weasel turns on the radio and sings along, even though the song is in Spanish. He makes as much noise as he can, as he tries to banish us from his head. This is how he understands us, I suppose. We exist only as figments of his imagination.

I stare out of the window but there isn't much to see. It is getting dark, already. The road climbs, steadily, as we turn away from the city of Granada, in the direction of Cordoba. Passing through a small town called, Pinos Puente, brightly lit, with the houses set back from the road, our path rises more steeply, and a natural balcony opens up to the side, from where we can look back over the lights of the city, and behind this, to the shadowy mass of the Sierra Nevada. We enter a tunnel of pine trees and the road becomes narrow and twisting, the Weasel sitting forward, the sooner to catch a glimpse of the headlights of an oncoming car. There are none. Eerie in the full beams of his car, there is only the pine forest and the road.

The trees part like a curtain a few kilometres further on and we find ourselves looking out over a small white village. Level with us, a ruin of a castle is perched on top of a craggy mount. It is lit up with large yellow spotlights and, immediately below, there is a church.

At the entrance of the village, the Weasel turns the car down into a warren of lanes, threading up and down, in and out, with seemingly random purpose. We pass through a small square dominated by a large ochre mansion, with three flags mounted in front. It reminds me of the opening in the centre of a maze. It should be our journey's end but we switchback further on, round two or more corners, before we come to a halt outside a three storied terraced house. I look up at it.

At a window, on the second floor, I spy a woman, small and thin, her black hair drawn back tightly into a bun at the nape of her neck.

Bim asks: *She's dead isn't she? Is it his mother?*

If she is, she's nothing like the woman in the photograph we have.

I think she is staring at us from a different era altogether, Kerry murmurs, softly.

I'm Maria de las Nieves.

Her face is in shadow when she meets us on the landing of the house. I can only just make out the bony profile of a hooked nose.

Mary of the snows, I translate. *What an incredibly beautiful name.*

She smiles at me, uncertainly. *It is late. I'll show you to your room, Señoritas.*

Bim asks her, in surprise: *Were you expecting us?*

I'm the housekeeper. It is my job to be ready to receive guests, she says, as she walks ahead of us down a narrow passageway, her starched long white nightdress crackling as she moves.

Reaching the end, she opens a door that leads into a bedroom. It has a window overlooking the street, which lets in enough light for us to see her more clearly. She is in her late forties, or early fifties, and is striking more than attractive. Her eyes are almond-shaped, with black irises, and her face is as long and narrow as the nose that overhangs it.

The room to which she has brought us is dominated by a double bed with a tall iron bedstead. At the foot of this, with barely room to pass between the two, there is a threadbare divan. The only other pieces of furniture are a bedside table, and a single coffin-shaped wardrobe. Above the bed, a plaster figure of Jesus Christ, nailed to a silver cross, hangs. He is wearing a crown of thorns and there are splashes of ketchup-coloured blood on his brow, with more oozing from the wound at the side of his groin. His lips

155

are drawn back in an expression of ecstasy, revealing his tiny white teeth. His eyes, a glassy maniacal blue, bore into the room, uncomfortably. They give me the creeps. There is no way I want to spend any time in this room.

We don't really need a room, I say to Maria.

Of course, you must have a room, she contradicts me, backing towards the door. *Now, if you excuse me, Señoritas, I have to see to the master.*

The master?

The wig maker, she says proudly, turning to go. *If you need anything, please call for me.*

The moment she has gone, Bim asks: *What's going on?*

I've no idea. She must just come with the house. It is obvious she knows nothing about Gordon Richards.

Who is the wig maker?

Another spirit? Maybe we should take a look around and see for ourselves.

We don't want to run into Maria though, Kerry says, quickly.

Bim nods. *She might not like us prying about.*

What neither of them is admitting is that the tiny housekeeper is a bit scary.

Maybe she disappears when she is not on call, I suggest, optimistically, in an attempt to reassure us all.

We wait until the house is quiet before stealing out of our door. We search every room, except the Weasel's, and a small one on the ground floor which we take to be Maria's since we can sense her presence there, but we discover nothing.

Disappointed, I leave Bim and Kerry in our room and go up to the third floor of the house which has been made into a roof terrace to take a look at the view. It is November, yet the night air is warm and there are crickets singing. The sky is clear and starlit; breathtaking, in truth, because it is so vast. I can't remember ever seeing such a multitude of stars, before.

Hearing a noise behind me, I turn around to see what has made it. I don't quite trust what I discover. The roof terrace has changed. There is a stone floor where there were tiles and it is no longer open to the stars but covered with a wooden roof. Strings of peppers, garlic, and cured hams, are hanging from the rafters. Maria is there too. Dressed in her nightdress, she is standing at the top of a rickety staircase which rises from the floor below. She hangs the lamp she is carrying on a hook and drags a small three legged milking stool to the centre of the floor. I'm less than fifteen metres away from her, yet she is oblivious of me. She climbs on top of the stool and, for the first time, I realise she is carrying a length of rope. This she loops over one of the beams and ties the end tight. With the other end she makes a noose, expertly tying the knot. Then, without hesitation, she slips it over her head and kicks the stool away from under her.

No, I shout, springing towards her.

Her hands catch at the rope around her neck, her nails tearing her skin, as she struggles to get her fingers under it. Her face is frozen in terror. She has changed her mind.

My God, how terrible, because it's too late, she cannot save herself. I reach out for her with the intention of grasping her legs so I can try to lift her up, enabling her to escape the pressure of the noose but, before I can touch her, she fades to nothing. Confused, I turn about myself to get my bearings. The sky is above me, again. The terrace is as it was. There is no roof. No wooden beams. No peppers hanging. No swinging corpse. I feel shocked, both by what I've seen and by my own gullibility in being taken in by it.

These things have passed, I say, firmly, to myself.

I follow the stairs down to the floor below, opening the door at the bottom which leads into the rest of the house.

Maria is standing there in her white nightgown about to ascend the stairs. She is carrying a lamp in one hand and a rope in the other. She looks right through me. I step back to allow her to pass.

Where are you going, Maria?

She doesn't answer me but continues up the stairs.

As I look after her, I see that they are made of wood and covered with loose flat stones. The sky at the top is black. There are no stars. No, that is not right, it is covered again. There is a wooden roof.

Maria is moving, slowly towards the top of the stairs.

Please don't, I call after her.

She says nothing in reply, but I stay listening until I hear the noise of the milk stool being kicked away from under her, and then, the dull thud of her falling the length of the rope, followed by the creaking it makes as she battles, vainly, to stop it from strangling her. Does this go on every night? And, for how long has she been re-enacting what I assume was the manner of her death? It is impossible for me to tell from looking at her in which century she lived and died, yet I'm consumed with curiosity about her. What drove her to want to kill herself?

There is an elderly woman sitting up in the bed, when I burst into our bedroom, in search of the others. Propped up by pillows, she is wearing a pink, knitted bed jacket. The room is untidy with an invalid's clutter - a dozen medicine bottles, a jug of orange juice, a box of tissues, and a women's magazine, are crowded onto the bedside table. The mess creates an impression of life but the woman in this bed is emaciated to the point where her bones look as though they might pierce through her skin, at any moment. Turning to face me, she smiles like a Death's head. She is clearly gravely ill. Her eyes, the irises milky, the whites yellow, are sunken deep into the shadowy hollows of the sockets. Her skin is drawn so tautly over the bones of her face she looks oddly youthful, despite her age. She has no hair, except for a couple of strands which spiral out of the top of her scalp like ectoplasm.

She beckons to me. *Come and sit with me, dear. I get so few visitors.*

I recognise one of the photographs in the room as I approach the bed. It is the same one we have in our possession. The man is Gordon Richards but the woman he has his arm around looks very different to the one lying now beside me.

Are you Mrs Richards?

158

Yes, dear but you can call me, Linda. I know what you're thinking. Nobody would recognise me now. I have cancer. It is bloody well killing me. She cackles like corn popping at her own joke.

Who takes care of you?

Gordon is here a lot of the time. He's my son. He's such a good boy. Well, I call him a boy but he is thirty-six, next birthday.

Is he married?

She laughs again. *There is still plenty of time for that.*

Why? Does he have a girlfriend?

He says I'm his girlfriend. He's going make me a wig now the chemo has made my hair fall out. He used to love my hair when he was little - long and blonde it was then.

Oh, I see. Is he the wig maker?

It is just a joke, dear. He likes to cheer me up.

What about your husband? Is he around?

He left us, dear. He went off with another woman when Gordon was nine years old.

And, never kept in touch?

No, dear, but we've managed just fine on our own.

What kind of child was Gordon? Did he like to play games?

Don't all children, dear?

Did he play that game...what's it called? Simon Says. Do you know it?

She lowers her eyes. *No, he never played that game.*

Never? Are you sure?

She looks towards the door.

Is it closed?

I nod.

His brother was called Simon, she whispers to me.

I didn't know he had a brother.

He died when they were seven, of cancer.

I pause, for a few seconds, as I try to assimilate this.

When they were seven? Are you saying they were twins?

Yes, that's right, dear. Poor Gordon didn't get much of a look in the year before Simon died. We tried to be fair. Well, I did. But Simon was always his dad's favourite. He named him after his

159

own brother, who'd died when they were children. Our Simon died at the same age - in the same month too. June. Imagine that. Steve, my husband, couldn't deal with it. She scratches her bald head. *He dressed Simon for his funeral.*

Your husband did?

No, Gordon.

But, you said he was only seven years old.

I know but he insisted on doing it. He put him in his own clothes.

I don't understand. Why?

I've no idea. I never understood it myself. They always had the same clothes because they were identical twins but they liked different colours. Gordon favoured beige but Simon preferred to wear blue. When he died Gordon swopped all his clothes for Simon's. I suppose it made him feel closer to him.

The Weasel rises and takes the mountain path down to the neighbouring village. He should be gone a couple of hours but to make sure he doesn't arrive back at the house, unexpectedly, Kerry follows him. As I look across the valley, from the balcony of his room, there they are - two specks in the distance against the pale blue sky. The sunlight is milky yellow, beautiful, but fragile, too sickly to give warmth yet, and there is a brittle chill in the early morning air; the first hint of winter approaching. Pine forest surrounds the village on two sides and, as the land on the other two falls away into a valley, olive trees march in line as far as the eye can see. The monotony is broken only by the occasional almond grove. On the banks of the river, which runs along the bottom of the valley, there are a few fields of arable farming and some grazing pastures for a ragged herd of goats and sheep. The whitewashed village houses, their garish geraniums, spilling from the balconies and sills, are shuttered to keep in the warmth. The village would look deserted but for the smattering of smoke coils oozing lazily from the chimneys. In the street, directly below me, two women wrapped in shawls jabber about the weather, the black olives which are due to be harvested before Christmas, and *La crisis,* the economic downturn in Spain. Inside, I can hear Maria busy cleaning in the kitchen. Her vigour rumours futility. When I looked in on her, she had the air of a woman who is inventing tasks to occupy herself.

Bim has been assigned the job of minding her so that I can search the Weasel's room in peace. She hovers at her back, attempting to bond with her by sharing the household tips she almost managed to pick up from Marigold, the woman who cleaned for her in Greenwich.

She used to swear by vinegar. I'm not entirely sure why but I do know if you drink an egg cupful before a meal, you eat less. An egg cup full of cider vinegar, that is. Well, everyone knows that. But, I'm not quite clear why it is good for cleaning too. Marigold definitely used to swear by it, though, she enlightens an unresponsive Maria.

As I listen for the sounds of anyone else stirring in the house, the only other presence, I'm aware of is Mrs Richards. She's asleep on the divan in her room.

Her son's room, across the landing from hers, is wooden beamed and white washed with a floor of matt brick-shaped terracotta tiles. There are two single beds, either side of a small pine night table, and opposite, a squat and solid chest of drawers. In the corner, an alcove has been curtained off to create a wardrobe, and next to the oak planked door, a tiny writing desk, with a pile of British newspapers and car magazines neatly stacked on it, is wedged. I open the chest of drawers. His socks and pants are in the first drawer, three long sleeved t-shirts in the second, and in the third, there is a jersey, on one side, and his folded pyjamas, on the other. There are no papers or personal possessions.

Looking down, I notice his holdall is protruding from under the bed. I set it on the duvet and search the side pockets. His passport is in one of them. The rest of the holdall appears to be empty apart from a folded windcheater but when I lift this, I discover a buff folder, underneath. Inside, there is an bundle of legal documents, including his mother's death certificate. She died of a stroke, before the cancer could kill her, exactly as he told the people he got chatting with, at the airport. The deeds of this house are here too and her Will. Gordon was her sole beneficiary. He inherited the house and her modest savings.

What are you doing here?

I spin around. Damn! This is all I need. How did Maria get past Bim? Where is Bim?

This is the master's room.

She is staring at the open holdall on the bed.

Maria, I wanted to talk to you, I say, in an attempt to distract her.

I asked you, what you were doing.

I was looking for you. I wanted to talk to you. I wanted to ask you why you killed yourself.

She looks confused. *I don't know what you're talking about?*

162

I'm...I'm...I'm the housekeeper. And, this is the master's room.

We are back to this again, and so soon. What do I do now? I don't know where the idea comes from but in the few seconds I have to turn it over in my mind I decide it just might work.

Maria, I want you to go downstairs and prepare some coffee for the master.

She appears to waver before returning to the same groove.

What you're doing in the master's room.

I'm the master's new wife and please go downstairs and prepare some coffee for him, I say in a commanding tone.

His new wife?

Yes, and I want you to...

She starts to wring her hands. *Where will I go?* She looks devastated. *He won't need a housekeeper if he has a wife.*

I'm so stunned by her response, I forget what I'm doing there myself.

Is that what happened, Maria? Did the master marry?

What master? There is no master. He is a figment of her imagination, Bim says, appearing beside me.

Where have you been? You were supposed to be watching her.

I was but I heard a noise in the room above. You have to hurry, Kate. I think the old lady is dying. I know she is his mother, but...

Bim, she's already dead!

But her suffering seems so real?

She's like Maria. She'll die and then, she'll go through her illness, until she dies again.

It's a bit weird, isn't it?

I smile, wearily, at her.

Maria is backing out of the door, making a low gurgling wailing noise.

Stop that at once, I say, sharply, making Bim jump. *I want you to prepare some coffee for the master. And, I want no more talk about having to leave this house. You are the housekeeper here, and always will be.*

As she passes through the door on her way to the kitchen, I call after her: *Maria, why did you say the master was a wig maker?* I don't catch her answer. *What did she say, Bim?*

163

I think it was something about the alcove.

I pull the curtain covering it back. There is a rail inside, groaning with women's clothes.

These must be his mother's. Why has he kept them?

Bim points to something on the floor which is partially hidden by the hem of a silken dressing gown.

I bend down to pick it up. It's a plastic skull cap, the kind hairdressers sometimes use to do highlights. It is covered with tiny holes, through which strands of hair have been pulled and glued on the inside to create a crude wig. It is blonde hair; human by the looks.

Do you think he is a transvestite?

That is mine, Bim exclaims, grabbing at it. *I'd recognise Jacques' highlights anywhere. I should do, they cost enough.*

Actually I think there's a mixture of hair here, Bim. See? That bit there looks like Gerte's.

Why have only half the holes been filled?

He seems to be taking just a small chunk from each woman he murders.

So he is going to need more victims to finish it?

I nod.

I don't understand why he is doing this?

He is sick, Bim.

Well, he is not having my hair. I'm taking it back.

You can't, he'll notice.

Why should I care about that?

He might destroy it. It's evidence, Bim. It proves the connection between him and all the women he has killed.

Why don't we just give it to the police then?

I doubt the Spanish police would be interested. He hasn't murdered anyone here. Well, not as far as we know.

We could always take it back to Britain with us and give it to the police there.

It wouldn't work. They would have to find it in his possession for it to count.

Then, we could hide it in his suitcase and try and get him searched at the airport.

164

But, they'd have no reason to think it was anything more than a bit odd. They're not going to bother to try and find out whether it is human hair, let alone whose it is, unless they suspect he has done something wrong.

Kerry appears just as I'm putting the wig back.

What is that you've got there?

I can hear footsteps, below. *Is he back already? Did he change his mind about going to the next village?*

Kerry ignores my question. *What is it?*

It is a wig for his mother, I think. It's made from the hair of his victims.

Gordon begins to mount the stairs. I manage to put the wig back where it was on the floor of the alcove before he enters the room, but I don't have time to slide the curtain across. He spots it, immediately. He checks inside to make sure the wig is there and looks under the bed where I have returned the holdall. Then, he turns and goes straight to his mother's room. His eyes comb it for anything out of place. Next, he tours the rest of the house, room by room, finishing up at the front door where he inspects the lock, pulling anxiously at his lower lip as he does so, the only leak of emotion to escape him. After he has finished checking it, we follow him back to his mother's room.

She is lying on the divan. She appears to be dead.

I sit on the bed and Bim stands beside me as we watch Gordon looking about her room. Kerry goes to the window and in the doorway I see Maria hovering. I'm sure Gordon senses us there with him. He knows somehow that he is not alone.

He smiles to himself. *Hello Mum*, he coos, softly. *Is that you?*

WINTER

The Weasel is in love with routine. Each day is meticulously the same. Nothing spontaneous is allowed to interrupt his need for repetition. The only variance is a different but intersecting pattern of behaviour, creating a Venn diagram of habitual paths: once a fortnight, he returns to his house in Leicester for the weekend to clean, collect his post, and change items of clothing.

We follow him, back and forth, waiting and watching for something to occur, which will enable us to trap him, just so we can escape the annihilating tedium of our vigil. It is as though he doesn't quite exist. He is more ethereal than us. It seems incredible that there should be nothing interesting to note in the life of a serial killer but this is exactly how it is. He is a bore. There is a complete absence of the personal about him. He has no relationships, keeps no diary, and writes and receives no letters of any significance. His mobile phone doesn't have a single contact listed in it. Nor are there emails from anyone who could remotely be described as an acquaintance on either of his computers. The man is vacuous with mystery. Yet, at the same time we sense a light has gone on deep within him. He too is waiting. No, it is more that he knows something is on the way. There is a dull but persistent drone of anticipation inside him. Slavish to a fitness regime of his own devising he walks and jogs daily, and has rigged up some weights which occupy a good two hours of his time, each afternoon. In the evening, before he goes to bed, he does more exercises. It is not easy for us to think clearly around him. The way he bores is soporific, dulling our mental capacity, but in the fleeting moments in which the fog dissolves, one single conclusion is beginning to form in our minds: the Weasel is preparing to kill again.

The first blip in his rigid curriculum happens in Spain without warning when he gets into his hire car, one morning after breakfast, and drives out of the village.

166

Huddled together on the back seat, we assume he is making an unscheduled visit back to the UK, initially, but he misses the turn off for the airport, and heads in the direction of the city of Granada, instead.

Bim is ecstatic. She wants to go window shopping for a new cocktail dress.

Reece always hosts a party at the ski-lodge he rents, over Christmas. I shall need something stunning to wear, this year.

Particularly, as nobody will be able to see you, I attempt to reality test.

Exactly!

But, Gordon confounds her by driving past Granada and taking the road towards the coast.

The olive and almond groves slowly give way to orchards of lemon and orange trees, and then to a vast chequer board of makeshift greenhouses, which stretch as far as the fields of sugar cane that hem the sea.

They call this the tropical coast because of the range of fruit and vegetables grown here but it used to be known as the windy coast, Kerry informs us.

Aren't we lucky to have a geography student with us, Bim remarks, dully.

I wish I'd done more travelling when I was alive, I confide to them both.

Really? My biggest regret is not running up a massive credit card debt. Think of the fun I could have had before I died.

I would have liked to have gotten married and had children, Kerry says, softly.

That silences us all.

As the sea comes into view, Gordon remains a blank. He could be driving through a tunnel for all the impression his surroundings make upon him. He turns in the direction of Almeria, but almost immediately takes the road for the port town of Motril. We're all for going to the beach, but he ignores our raucous demands, and takes us towards the commercial centre, instead.

He leaves his car in a subterranean parking lot and walks

167

briskly through the streets with the air of a man who is looking for something.

Twenty minutes later, during which we've had to prise Bim away from every dress shop we've encountered, he enters an internet café. The place is empty and the manager motions him to choose whichever booth he wants. Gordon sits down at the one furthest from him, and logs in to an email account, but not the one in his own name which we've seen him check on his laptop, back at the house, or on his desktop computer in Britain. The address of this one is *xxxsayssimonxxx*.

There's one email in his inbox. It says: *I've found a candidate*. The sender doesn't give a name, but the email address is: *Dead-gorgeous*.

We're slavering with curiosity but the message causes no ripple in Gordon. He simply reads and deletes it, twice; once from his inbox, and a second time from the list of deleted items. Then, he pays for his computer time, picks up his car, and drives us back to the village.

I don't understand. He has had no contact with anyone, Kerry says. *How did he know there was an email waiting for him? Did we miss something?*

I'm not sure. I don't think so. He must have known it was going to arrive on a pre-arranged dat that was set before we started tailing him.

We all look at each other. What else don't we know about him? What other surprises are laying in wait for us?

When the Weasel returns to his house in Leicester for his cleaning weekend, he finds a large brown envelope lying among the usual utility bills and advertising fliers, on the front doormat. It has a central London postmark and the address has been typed - badly. Whoever sent it doesn't do this for a living. Gordon shows little interest in it. He picks it up and places it on the kitchen table, where it remains, unopened, as he unpacks his bag, showers, shaves, changes his clothes, sets the washing machine, waters his spider plants, and cleans the house, from top to bottom. I find myself thinking of Gail Martos while all this is going on. She and the Weasel seem to share the same need to control how something enters their space, but their motivation is different. Gail is dominated by fear, generated by his attack on her. But, Gordon is moderating pleasure, and not pain, through his prevarication. He wants to open that large brown envelope so badly he forces himself to wait. It is the mastery of his desire, not the satisfaction of it, which pleases him most. It is perverse. But, then, what else could be expected from a serial killer?

After he has finished his chores, he makes himself a cup of tea and sits down at the kitchen table to drink it. He eyes the envelope, while he does so, but he doesn't reach for it until he has finished his tea. Pushing the empty cup and saucer away to create a space in front of him, he slits open the edge of the envelope with a pen knife and shakes the contents out. A dozen photographs scatter across the surface of the table. They all depict the same woman.

What I notice first about her is the obvious, she is a petite blonde. But, close behind this is the realisation that these photographs appear to have been taken without her knowledge, as she leaves a house, walks along a street, and gets into a car. On the back of one of the photographs there is a typed caption. It gives a woman's name, Cheryl Tinsdell, the make, model, and number plate of a car, and an address in South London. Then, it says: *She is away from home for the next week.*

169

This must be the candidate. And, Dead-gorgeous is the accomplice. I feel oddly triumphant about this. I've sensed him waiting in the shadows like a thought I couldn't quite grasp, from the very beginning and, now, finally, it looks as though he is getting ready to reveal himself. As usual, the Weasel's demeanour gives little away. He examines the photographs, minutely, and puts them back inside their envelope. This, he throws into the fire place in the living room, douses it with paraffin, and sets light to it, watching it burn to a fine smouldering powder.

He doesn't go back to Spain, as expected, on the Monday. He drives to London, in his white van instead, with us in the back. To Peckham, in South London, to be exact; a tree lined avenue, bordering a park there. He stops the van adjacent to a large Georgian house, which has been converted into flats. It has three floors and what looks like a basement, down a short flight of steps to the side. A black and white tiled path cuts through the middle of a handkerchief of lawn, at the front, on its way to an imposing double-door entrance. The car that was in one of the photographs is parked a few doors up. It is a white BMW, several years old, but still in gleaming condition. Nobody enters the building, during the entire two hours, he stays sitting there, watching. Hardly anyone passes by on the pavement either. It seems to be a quiet residential street, populated with well heeled young singles out working during the day.

The flat number, he was sent, is 4B. Kerry goes off to find out where it is.

It is the basement flat, she informs us, when she returns. *There is only her name on the doorbell, C. Tinsdell. It looks like she lives alone.*

The Weasel finally gets out of the car. He walks briskly across the road, but instead of stopping at number 4, he continues past it. Then, when he reaches the corner, he turns and retraces his steps. This time, as soon as he is level with the door, he darts up the front path, checks the names on the doorbells and disappears down the steps to the basement - with the three of us hard, on his

170

heels. The front door and a small window are both covered with security grills. The glass is opaque too. There's no way he can see, inside the flat.

Good move on Cheryl's part, Bim comments. *Security is a priority for a woman living alone.*

I nod and smile. She is preaching to the cremated.

Gordon searches the tiny patio which surrounds the door, lifting pot plants and the door mat, before sliding his hand along the top of a half porch, but there is no hidden key.

Kerry watches him, perplexed. *Why does he want to get inside the flat when we're still months away from June?*

He is checking out her candidature, I imagine.

That can't be right, Bim says.

Why can't it?

Well, he has never done it before.

How do you know he hasn't?

Not, with me, anyway.

Why not? It seems pretty obvious Jackie was randomly selected. It was simply her misfortune to cross his path on her way to Sheffield that day and he seized the opportunity. Kerry too was probably pounced on randomly, although he must have gone out with the intention of abducting someone, otherwise he wouldn't have been able to drug her. But, what if things took a new turn with Gerte, and you, Bim? It is possible one or both of you could have been selected in advance.

You mean he was stalking me!

His approach may have been changing all along as he perfected his technique. But, choosing the women he is going to murder in advance may also indicate the arrival of Dead-gorgeous as his accomplice. There would be more need to plan in advance, if there were two of them.

But, selecting his victims randomly has been the Weasel's strength up until now, Kerry says. *It has helped him to go undetected. If he and this accomplice are putting more forethought into who they kill, they're far more exposed, aren't they? The chances of something connecting them to their victims, or of connecting their victims, one to another, must increase.*

Bim looks from her to me. *Do you have any idea what she is going on about?*

Yes, and she's right. We are going to have to investigate Cheryl, and everyone who comes within her orbit, very carefully indeed to see if we can find a link between her and you.

Why only me?

You and Gerte then; the London victims.

Kerry starts to look around us, agitatedly. *Where has the Weasel gone?*

We've been so absorbed in our conversation we've managed to lose him. He has given up on his search and left. We dash up the basement stairs after him, only to find him sitting in his van, already, gunning the engine. He is about to drive away without us. We only just make it inside in time as he pulls away from the kerb.

The next day, he misses the Skylink bus to the airport, on his way back to Spain. There is time to kill before another one arrives and apparently he already knows how he wants to spend it. He doesn't hesitate. He sets off walking purposefully until he reaches an internet café. It is a dingy student hangout, not the kind of place I'd have expected him to frequent, but he greets the manager as though he is familiar to him so he must have been here before. I bet he always uses the same computer. That would be typical of his type. He goes to an internet café to make sure there is no evidence against him on his own computer, and then establishes the comforting, and potentially incriminating, routine of using the same internet café and the same booth. It is good to realise the man isn't as smart as he likes to think he is.

We watch him set up a new email account, this one in the name of *Peterpiperpip*. The message he sends, reads: *It is early yet. There may be others.* The recipient is Dead-gorgeous.

Bim is frowning. *So why is he so lukewarm about Cheryl? Is it just because he couldn't gain access to her flat? Did that give him a psychopathic bad vibe or something?*

Maybe the impetus to plan their next victim so far in advance comes from Dead-gorgeous, not the Weasel, Kerry suggests.

172

I did a three-day course on psychopaths once. I wish I could remember more about it but I think you might be right. There are sometimes differences between the ones who kill in pairs. Their fantasies overlap sufficiently for them to cooperate, but they're not identical.

So Gordon has found another twin, who wears the same clothes, but who prefers them in a different colour.

Bim rolls her eyes and mouths: *Triffid.*

Kerry laughs at her. She is completely mud free these days and she has ditched the wedding dress. Her new eternity clothes are a pair of faded sky-blue jeans and a blue t-shirt, with the slogan - THE MEEK DON'T WANT IT - emblazoned across the chest in sapphire-coloured diamante.

I wonder how he found Dead-gorgeous, she says. *I mean how does a man find out whether some else enjoys killing women as much as he does?*

The dark side of the internet, where else, I reply. *There are probably thousands of websites there where perverts swop fantasies.*

Please don't tell us we are going to have to monitor any of them, Bim says. *There must be another way to find out who Dead-gorgeous is.*

Cheryl is our only lead. If he still likes her as a candidate, he might go on stalking her. We have to immerse ourselves in every aspect of her life in the hope that sooner or later we'll get lucky and stumble across him, before your powder blue satin high heels turn up on another corpse.

Kerry is looking anxious. *How can we do all that and keep Gordon under surveillance too?*

We'll have to ask Gerte and Jackie to help out.

Jackie is a nutcase, Bim exclaims. *What can she do?*

She has a point. *Okay why don't you two stay with Gordon?* Kerry groans. *You already know his little routines so you'll spot anything different happening more quickly than the others would. Gerte and I can shadow Cheryl.*

And, Jackie?

Well, she can fill in for anyone who needs time away.

173

Bim and Kerry glance at each other. From their expressions, I anticipate that they will not be spending any time away from each other for the foreseeable future.

And, there is our financial controller too, I suddenly remember.

What financial controller?

Denise Boulay. She can act as the link between us all.

Cheryl Tinsdell is the outdoors type. She rides a horse at weekends and on three evenings a week she practices hockey with a local women's team. She is petite but athletic. She won't be a push over for anyone trying to abduct her. By profession, she is a food photographer, with her own tiny studio around the corner from where she lives. She works mainly for a string of high profile women's magazines, aimed at the more mature end of the market but, recently, she has been approached by a publishing company about managing the photography for a cookbook they're intending to commission.

Her flat reflects her skill in dressing a scene to be seen. It is very stylish. The interior is straight from Marrakesh. The floors are covered with hand painted tiles and the furniture is heavy, ornate, low, and sparse. There are opulent floor cushions scattered around to break up the space and entertain the eye and, on the white walls, vibrantly coloured rugs and tapestries are hung. Only the kitchen is situated in different continent. It is high-tech American; a stainless steel laboratory - the antithesis to the relaxed exoticism of the rest of her home.

Her preoccupation with the visual extends to her appearance, naturally. Her hair is sculpted into a short sleek bob. Her makeup is expensive and discreet and she dresses like a model from an old Biba catalogue. Gamine is the word which comes to mind as I watch her. I like her. She is a woman's woman, the kind of mate to be counted upon in a crisis. She'd actually make an excellent addition to the team; although, since we're supposed to be doing everything we can to prevent this from happening, I keep this opinion to myself.

There are men in her life but nobody special. She has frequent dates with three regulars, a dentist, an architect, and a journalist. They're all tall, with dark hair, which assuming the fair-haired man recorded driving Bim's car is Dead-gorgeous, does rather rule them out as suspects. They are courting her in a warm, friendly, but dispassionate manner. All three are of an age when they're ready to settle down and they're engaged in the serious business of evaluating her potential as a life partner. (Not good, at this moment, I would have thought.)

I believe they've misjudged her. She is not waiting for a merger proposal. She wants to be swept of her feet.

She has so much going for her, this woman, Gerte comments to me one night. *How can those bastards take it away from her?*

She doesn't have to marry any one of them, if she doesn't want to, Gerte.

She examines me, quizzically. *Not the boyfriends, Kate, the killers!*

Oh, the killers.

You don't think your sister's experience of men has soured you against them a little, do you? Or did that happen before. Your dad died when you were ten years old, didn't he? Maybe that is why you took against, my Karl.

Another possibility is that I have been a murder detective for too long, Gerte. Statistically, young men are far more likely to be murdered than women, but the sickest psychopathic killers always seem to be men who prey upon women. It's probably because Cheryl's life is so full that Dead-gorgeous wants to snuff it out. Him, not the Weasel - I doubt Gordon cares how his victims' lives are, as long as they have the right physical characteristics and a pulse. Well, initially, at least.

Tell me we are going to stop them from harming her.

Well, it won't be for the want of trying, if we don't, I reassure her.

We spend hours studying the people who weave in and out of her life hoping to discover someone else who is doing the same as us. There is nobody. Or, nobody we notice; nobody as amateurish as the Weasel, sitting outside her house in his car, two hours at a time. The more familiar we become with the circles in which she moves, the harder it gets. Everyone starts off as a suspect but then, as we get to recognise the neighbour going to the shop at the end of the road and the colleague walking his dog, morning, noon, and night, in the park opposite from where she lives, the threat of them evaporates. We can't help dismissing them, despite our sworn intention not to. *Oh, it is him or her again,* we say, uninterestedly. Yet, we also realise, it is precisely these people who are the most dangerous to her, because the skilled stalker would hide among them. The problem is that, over time, there are simply too many of them. The more people we recognise, the less effective we are. It is hopeless. We can identify so many opportunities to abduct her within her daily schedule we would have to wall her up in a tower to protect her. Not least, because it turns out she isn't as security conscious as we would like. It is Gerte and I who lock the windows and slide the bolts across on the front door at night. If they want to get at her, they probably will. Our best hope of saving her is to stop them, first.

On one of our evenings in together - Cheryl, Gerte, and I, snuggled up together on the sofa, watching a film - Bim shows up, unexpectedly. She is in a state.

Reece is going skiing with a blonde bimbette he met at MY memorial service. Can you believe that! I used to go to school with the witch? How could they do this to me?

Bim, they're supposed to get on with their lives without us, Gerte attempts to reason with her.

Oh, is that right? So if Karl went off with someone else, that would be okay with you, would it?

Someone like a prison warder, you mean? Karl is still in jail for a murder he didn't commit. She doesn't actually add, *where Kate put him,* but I hear it anyway.

It's only a question of time, Gerte, I reassure her, defensively. *Now, they know they're looking for a serial killer they'll let him go.*

So you keep telling me. But, they don't seem to be in any great hurry, she replies, tartly. *Anyway, to answer your question, Bim, if Karl was free and did find someone else, I'd be happy for him. After everything he has been through I think he deserves someone to love and maybe one day to have children with.*

Bim examines her with scepticism. *Well, I'm not the least bit happy for Reece and the bimbette. I'm going to make their lives a living hell. Jackie has been giving me lessons.*

Jackie? When did she show up in Spain?

She ignores my question. *This relationship is definitely not going to last.*

Cheryl gets up from the sofa, startling us all. She goes into the kitchen and opens a bottle of Chardonnay.

She is probably sensing all this negative energy about Reece and the bimbette, I complain.

Are you accusing me of driving her to drink? Because, I'm not the one living with her, am I?

We were wondering whether there could be a professional link between the two of you, Gerte rushes in, before I have a chance to retaliate. *You worked in PR and she's in women's magazines. It is possible you knew some of the same people. Dead-gorgeous could be one of them. Maybe you could stick around to see if there is anyone in her life you recognise. It might help to spend a little time away from Gordon too.*

And, Jackie, I put in.

Yes, they do seem to be stirring you up a little, Bim, Gerte adds, gently.

Okay, but I'm only free until the weekend, she informs us, airily. *After that, I'm spending Christmas in a luxury ski lodge in the French Alps with my boyfriend.*

What about the bimbette?

She is going to break both her legs on the first day and be flown home to Britain for emergency surgery.

I can't gage whether she's serious or not.

Won't Reece want to go with her, if she's injured?

Not if she's unconscious until New Year. What would be the point?

On Christmas Eve, Carrie sets me the task of marshalling the boys to dress the tree for her, while she retreats to the kitchen to check on the sausage rolls and help herself to eggnog. I anticipate she will be gone for some time. In her wake, I am counting, silently, and slowly, in an attempt to keep control of my temper. I only arrived here a few hours ago, and my argumentative nephews have already exhausted my patience. Spat 999 has been caused because Sam wants to choose a colour scheme for the Christmas tree but Jethro and Caleb favour the dolly mixture approach to bauble decoration.

It will look like you've been sick all over it, Sam shouts, in disgust.

Sick isn't colourful. Sick is brown or yellow, isn't it Auntie Kate?

I smile, wanly. What do I care? It is Christmas Eve, and I am not in a festive mood.

Not if you're sick just after you've eaten, Caleb suggests.

You're supposed to be on our side, Jethro complains to him.

Sam whines: *Auntie Kate, it will look like sick, won't it?*

I say nothing. Instead, I pick up the Christmas tree fairy from the cardboard box where she has rested all year and make her wings flutter, as though she is actually flying, until she reaches the top of the tree. Once there, I rudely push a pine branch up her skirt to secure her. I am hoping this might move things along. Sam appears suitably wowed but the younger two can see the strings, of course.

I wanted a star on the top, this year, Jethro grumbles.

I am on the point of shouting at him, when I remember something. *You used to do the tree with your dad, didn't you?*

They all stare into the distance. This is their first Christmas Eve without him. They're not going to see him until Boxing Day, when Carrie is allowing them to spend the day with him and Maxine.

I was shocked by this when I found out about it. But, Carrie seems to have gotten over her rage towards Phil, in exact proportion to her deepening involvement with Nigs. It is no doubt thanks to him that a day without the boys around has its attractions. It must be hard for the boys, though. I'm not sure I am up to inventing a new Christmas ritual to replace the old familiar one, they had with him. Gaining a dead aunt can't be much solace, if you've just been separated from your dad.

Why don't we toss a coin? Heads for colour coordination and tails for dolly mixture, I cry.

I check to see if the boys are with me on this. There is a low squawking assent. Throwing the coin high into the air, I allow it to fall on the rug, where we can all inspect it for tricks and tampering.

Tails! We win. We win, Jethro yells, excitedly.

It will look like sick, Sam growls, surly in defeat.

Dolly mixture it is then, I say, briskly.

I have to toss the coin several times more before the tree is finished and we can invite Carrie, our tipsy guest of honour to turn on the lights. The sparkle silences us as a collective *ahhhhh* oozes out like slow pouring honey. A couple of carols and a plate of warmed up sausage rolls, later, and the boys are almost ready for bed. Well, they're in their pyjamas.

I read them a story from the Bumper Book of Christmas Ghost Stories for Children which is so frightening Caleb is soon asleep in his mother's arms, Jethro's eyes are drooping, and even Sam seems to have entered a pre-sleep inertia.

Jethro asks me, sleepily: *Now you are dead Auntie Kate, do you know Santa Claus?*

Carrie stifles a giggle.

No, I haven't had the pleasure yet. Maybe tonight, though.

We carry the two youngest ones upstairs to bed. Then, we go and say goodnight to Sam. Downstairs, again, by the fire, Carrie pours herself another glass of eggnog. When we're sure the boys are asleep, we will take up their presents in three pillow cases and place them by their beds.

You've done a good job with the boys, I tell her. *Despite the bickering, they seem much more steady, particularly Sam.*

180

Settling things with Phil was the secret. We have been working together rather than against each other, recently.

Don't tell me you have dropped the court case against him?

The Crown Prosecution Service has. The police gave him a caution, instead.

That's outrageous. He could have killed you.

She shrugs. *His lawyer found out about my relationship with Nigs.*

What does that matter when he has had Maxine stashed away for God knows how long?

That's what made him more cooperative over the financial settlement, and he has agreed to me having sole custody of the boys, as long as he can see them. I could get all bitter and twisted about what he did. But, I'm not sure it is in my interests, nor the boys.

What I don't understand is why he stayed with you, when he had her.

Thanks! The joke is, if he hadn't had me to bully, he might not have had such a good relationship with Maxine. And, a cynical part of me thinks that the only reason we're getting on better now is that he has her at home to help him ventilate his rage. We met when we were so young, Kate, the dynamic between us was forged in immaturity, and that is pretty much where it stayed.

Why does everything have to be so complicated with you?

Human relations are complicated.

No, they're not.

How can you of all people say that? Our Dad was murdered when we were ten years old, Kate. Shot in the head while he was on duty. Don't you think that complicated our ability to relate with other humans just a tad? My counsellor says...

When did you start counselling?

A few months ago, anyway as I was saying my counsellor reckons it was Dad's death which made me cling on to Phil.

I'm fed up with your counsellor, already.

Why do you have to do that? Why do you have to be so flippant about anything that is important to me?

Okay, okay, so your counsellor says you're a cling on. Well, I'm a Vulcan.

You're emotionally autistic!

Isn't that what I just said? By the way, while we're sharing confidences, are you and Nigs getting serious about each other yet?

She blushes. *You could say that.*

How would you feel about giving a message to him for me?

A message... from you? Oh, no, Kate, I'd rather not. He doesn't believe in all this stuff?

In all what stuff?

In...you know...ghosts.

How many times? I'm not a ghost I'm an earth bound spirit.

Take it from me, Kate, the living don't appreciate the distinction.

Make him.

No, I don't want to.

Not even with another woman's life at stake? He can't be that hard to convince. He used to think he could smell my perfume.

That was in the first weeks, after you died. He has rationalised it now.

Fine, forget it. I shall have to find some other way to communicate with him.

You're not going to do anything to frighten him off me, are you? Or give him a heart attack?

I'll try not to but I can't promise.

She drains her glass. *What is it you want me to say to him?*

I want you to give him an envelope.

With what inside?

A tip off about his murder investigation, that's all.

After we've taken the children's presents to their rooms and Carrie has gone to bed, I sit up watching a twenty four hour news channel. I have nothing better to do. Most of the stories are the typical Christmas fare: lots of international items bought in from news agencies because the regular channel reporters and production staff want to have a Christmas too. The few national news stories they've carried so far have been tinsel. Sentimental

182

pap filmed in advance and designed to produce some seasonal cheer in the collective unconscious.

I'm so bored and fed up I'm beginning to wonder what I'm doing here at all. I can't eat, I can't drink, and I have no use for presents. To date my afterlife hasn't yielded any of the answers I was led to believe it should. I'm beginning to suspect post-death experience is like collection of Russian dolls. All will finally be revealed in the after-afterlife, or failing that, the after-after-afterlife, or even, the after-after- after- afterlife.

I catch a glimpse of a photograph I recognise on the television screen. It's Jackie. They've used the skull they found in Oxley Woods to build up a computer image of what her face must have looked like when she was alive. If her presence in the spirit world is anything to go by, it is an amazingly accurate likeness. The reporter explains that the police are hoping someone will be able to put a name to her face. I stare back at Jackie's dead eyes, feeling useless. Maybe I should make an addendum about her identity in the letter I'm already planning to write to Nigs.

The presenter moves on to the next story. *Karl Grüner who was convicted last February of the murder of his girlfriend Gertrud Weiss was released from prison, earlier today, pending a judicial review of his case, in the light of new evidence linking his girlfriend's murder to the deaths of three other women.*

They have finally set him free then. I was beginning to think it would never happen. I wonder whether Gerte knows. Maybe now she'll stop giving me a hard time for believing he killed her in the first place.

Take a look at this envelope. *It was pushed through the door today. See? It's addressed to D.I Kate Madding.*

Nigs stares at Carrie, blankly. *But, there is no post on Boxing Day.*

Can't you just tell he's a detective, I whisper in her ear.

Scowling in my direction, she says to him: I *thought you should open it in case it's from one of her informants.*

This wasn't in the script we agreed beforehand. I dig her in the ribs. *Why would an informant be sending a letter to me here, you dunce!*

Fortunately Nigs isn't as quick on the uptake as me. He accepts the envelope she is proffering, and slits it open, emptying the contents onto the kitchen table. There are three press clippings and a note.

Do you have some gloves? The sort you use to dye your hair would be best.

I only put henna in my hair, she tells him, defensively.

Carrie, go and get him the gloves.

She goes to the bathroom, muttering under her breath. *I was just telling him that I don't put dye in my hair. I use henna.*

Maybe he noticed the lowlights you had done for your first date, I quibble, following her.

I didn't do them myself though, did I?

Fine! Please, let's not argue anymore about this. Just fetch the ruddy gloves.

Returning to the kitchen, she leans over Nigs shoulder and asks: *What do the cuttings say?*

He puts on the gloves, and scans the story, with the headline: BRIDE GOES MISSING ON HER WEDDING DAY.

I'm not sure. This one is about a missing bride. But, I don't understand...

He turns to the next cutting: CAR BREAKDOWN PATROLMAN WAS THE LAST TO SEE TRAGIC BRIDE. He is looking even more confused by the time he has finished.

Tell him to read the damn note, I instruct Carrie.

What does the note say, Nigs?

He uses a pen to slide it closer and reads it aloud.

Dear Kate, I thought you should know, Jackie Brand, the missing bride, is the unidentified woman whose body was found in Oxley Woods. Her car was abandoned by Humber Bridge in what was believed to be a suicide but in fact, she was murdered by Gordon Richards, the motoring association patrol man, who was sent to help her, when her car broke down. His first victim, Gail Martos is still alive and can identify him.

Do you think it could be true, Nigs?

He shrugs and rereads the first two cuttings. Then, he starts on the third: LEICESTER WOMAN ATTACKED WAITING FOR ROADSIDE ASSISTENCE. This produces a low, flat whistle.

He looks up at Carrie. *Did you see who delivered this?*

She notices something on the floor which must be picked up, immediately. I am willing to bet inside her head she is cursing me. My sister likes to think she has scruples. Lying to him by omission is one thing but I know she won't want to make it any worse by telling the new man in her life a direct lie. She slips into the seat across the table from him, avoiding his eyes all the while, and smiles, enigmatically. *What do you think it means?*

He must be in love. A half-wit could tell she is hiding something.

I don't know but he seems to know her, doesn't he? He calls her Kate.

My lodgers, Jaswinder and Jitendra, and their son, little Surinder, have moved back to Richmond. They were supposed to stay another three months but Jas told Carrie their house had been finished ahead of schedule and she wanted to live there while she decided how to decorate it. I'm trying not to take their departure, personally. It is true I've neglected them of late. I've barely been able to make dinner with them, for weeks. But, I've still called in to say hello whenever I could. Carrie claims it was this which scared them off. *They kept smelling that perfume of yours!* I take no notice. She is just sore because she has found out it was Nigs who gave it to me for my last birthday. Whatever their reason for leaving was, the flat feels like a wasteland without them. I hate being alone. In desperation, I'm thinking of moving into the spare room in Bennett and Chelsee's place, next door.

It is New Year's Eve and I've been deserted by my sister who is spending the night at home with Nigs while the boys have a sleepover with their father. My clients are all busy too. Bim is still in the Alps with Reece. Kerry and Jackie are watching the Weasel, in Spain. Cheryl is safely ensconced with her parents, in Wales, and Gerte is with Karl.

The clock has already chimed three in the morning when I hear a key turn in the lock. For a moment I think my lodgers may have returned and I approach the door with excitement. But, as it opens I see the figure of a tall man. I recognise his silhouette, immediately. What is he doing here? Why isn't he with Carrie? I knew she'd given him a key so he could stop by and fix a leaky radiator but this seems an odd time for him to be doing it. Besides, he has no tools with him.

He goes straight to my study. Carrie has locked all my personal possessions in a large cupboard there because she still can't face sorting through them. He has no key to this but by the light of a torch, he holds in his mouth, he picks the lock.

This is when it dawns on me: he is conducting an illegal search of my flat. How dare he?

He unpacks the cardboard boxes and stands at my desk painstakingly going through the contents. His movements are clumsy as though he's been drinking. He is about half way through his search when he drops a file of papers and they scatter across the floor. Instead of trying to pick them up, he sits down in the midst of them. He makes a strange noise deep in his chest and the next moment his whole body is convulsing.

I think he is having a heart attack at first because, in the false gloaming of the torchlight, I can't see him, clearly. It is only when I hear a wet snuffling sound escape from his mouth, I realise he is actually sobbing.

Look what you've done to *me*, he gasps, before he is overwhelmed by tears again. *Who was he? He called you Kate! Was he a friend?*

There are so many emotions avalanching through me, it is hard to separate them. A wild searing love for him predominates but there is a glimmer of fear for my sister too. She doesn't need another secret love triangle in her life and certainly not one with her dead twin. But, yes, if I'm honest, there's also guilty stab of satisfaction that it is me who still has his heart and not her.

Marry me, I say only half ironically.

In France, the law permits a living person to marry a dead one, if the deceased expressed a wish to be wed before his or her untimely death. That is what I read somewhere, anyway. It seemed a pretty silly law, at the time, but now I begin to see the wisdom of it.

I put my arm around his shoulders and whisper to him. *Go home Nigs. I love you, I really do, and I regret so much not telling you that before it was too late for me to do anything about it. I regret not acknowledging it to myself. But, you have to let me go. It's not fair on you and it's not fair on Carrie either. She has been through enough.*

Leicester is cold, cold, cold. There is still snow glistening on the pavements a week after it fell. Gail Martos is at home recovering from a nasty bout of flu. She is feeling irritable because Nigs and Fester have arrived on her doorstep unannounced, forcing her to get up from her sick bed.

It's about time, she complains, after she has checked their warrant cards and phoned Bixby to confirm they are who they say they are. *I've been waiting for someone to contact me, ever since I posted back the questionnaire you sent in the summer.*

Nigs raises his eyebrows, questioningly, at his partner.

Neighbourhood watch, probably, Fester whispers to him.

She ushers them into the living room and motions them towards the two armchairs, while she takes the sofa, opposite. She is wearing a snoopy dressing gown and furry slippers.

Surrounded by the cuddly toys huddled on the arms of the chairs where they are sitting, I sense my former colleagues may be re-evaluating her as a credible witness.

Then, she turns the tables on them and produces the photograph of Gordon Richards that we sent her through the mail.

Nigs examines it and the accompanying letter and passes them to Fester. They exchange a glance.

And, you're sure the man pictured here is your attacker, Ms Martos?

I'm certain. Is he in custody yet? Do you want me to testify against him?

Possibly, in due course, he says, hesitantly. *Do you know his name?*

No. She examines Fester's and Nigs' faces. *But, you do, don't you?*

Nigs smiles at her, reassuringly. *Can we take the photograph with us?*

Yes, of course. Oh dear, was I supposed to return everything? I didn't realise. I just thought you wanted the questionnaire back.

I don't suppose you remember the address where you were

188

asked to send it?

It would have been the same as the one on the letter, wouldn't it?

Nigs clears his throat. *There isn't actually one on the letter.*

But, you did get my reply, didn't you?

Nigs turns to Fester, silently appealing for help.

We are sure someone did, Ms Martos, Fester answers. *But, my colleague and I are from a different squad.*

Oh yes, of course, you are, Gail agrees, uncomprehendingly.

After they have made their excuses and left, the detectives sit outside the house in their car.

Fester scratches his bald head.

So what the hell was that about? Who sent her that photograph?

The same person who sent Kate the envelope? He has to be a private detective, don't you think? Maybe one of the victims' parents hired one.

He is way ahead of us, if that's true.

Did Kate ever mention to you, she was friendly with a private detective?

No, and they can't have been that friendly, if he doesn't know she's dead

Nigs shrugs. *Whoever he is, he's obviously conducting his own investigation – that's what makes me suspect he's a private eye.*

Or he could be just toying with us. It might be the killer, mightn't it?

But, the info he sent Kate about Jackie Brand was correct.

So? Who better than the killer to know that, mate?

Nigs looks at the photograph. *It's a bit of a mystery, that's for sure, but one thing seems clear, Gail Martos was attacked by a man offering roadside assistance, and the last person to see Jackie Brand alive was a man paid to offer roadside assistance. The sixty four thousand dollar questions are whether they are one and the same man, and if they are, whether our killer could really be Gordon Richards.*

The corridors of Leicester police station smell of air-freshener, the sickly sweet fragrance reminding Nigs and Fester of rotting flesh.

I think it is him, Nigs whispers to Fester, although there is nobody there to overhear him.

Fester gives him a sceptical look. *Because the artist's impression, based on the description that Gail Martos gave, five years ago, vaguely matches him? That'll be an interesting case for the CPS to prepare.*

She positively identified the man.

From that photograph? Least said about that the better. We've no idea who sent it to her. A good lawyer is bound to infer we did it ourselves to lead her in the direction we wanted her to go. We're going to need more than her being able to identify him to get this guy into court.

She put in her statement that her attacker drove a blue Renault van and he used to own one.

Him and thousands of others, mate. It proves nothing.

Nigs clears his throat. *How should we play this, then?*

Real friendly, Fester counsels. *We have to be very careful. Nobody except Bixby knows what we're about and we don't want to blow it. Mr Richards is here of his own volition to go through the statement he made when Jackie Brand went missing. That is all. We have no reason to suspect him of anything. It is just a formality.*

Do we both go in?

No, that might make him nervous: one in, one watching.

You go in then; you've got a better poker face than me.

You reckon? Kate was the one who was the best at the wolf in sheep's clothing stuff.

She should be here, shouldn't she? He punches Fester playfully in the ribs. *It's all down to you now. Go get him, big guy.*

Good morning, Mr Richards, Fester says, as he enters the

interview room. *Thanks for coming in to see us, today. I'm sorry to have kept you waiting. Would you like a cup of coffee, or anything?*

The Weasel has risen from his chair to greet him. The two men shake hands.

No, don't bother. I'm fine, thanks.

They sit down opposite each other and Fester places a buff folder on the table in front of him. Looking up into Gordon Richard's eyes, he smiles. *I just want to go through this statement with you and then we're done.*

I'm happy to help, Detective, but it was a few years ago now. He leans forward. *I'm not sure I can add to whatever I told you back then.*

Did you know Jackie Brand's body has been found?

Richards holds Fester's gaze, steadily.

Yes, I read about it in a newspaper. Her poor parents, it must be terrible for them.

Do you have kiddies, Mr Richards?

No, no, I'm not married. But, I can imagine. Or maybe I can't. It must be the worst.

Yes, well, if you read about it in the papers, you'll know she was murdered. So anything you can give us will be a help.

I think you already have everything there. He nods at the statement.

Let's just go through it then. Okay?

Sure.

Your control room received a call from Jackie Brand at 12.30 pm that Saturday. She'd broken down on the M1, near the Leicester turn off. You were the nearest patrol man.

Fester looks up to confirm this with him.

Yes, that sounds right. Although, I wouldn't have known what time it was now without you telling me.

Do you remember what was wrong with the car, Mr Richards?

He blows his cheeks out and scratches his head. *Sorry, I don't. Does it say what the problem was there?*

It says the engine died because the air filter hadn't been changed to the summer position.

Remind me what car it was?

A Renault 5.

Yes, that's right. You don't seem many of those anymore. Nice old cars. They have two positions, one for summer, and one for winter. They regulate the amount of air coming into the engine. If the tube is in the wrong position, it can cut out at speed. It just loses power.

How long would it take to fix something like that?

Richards looks over Fester's shoulder at the wall behind, as he appears to consider this. *Oh, seconds, I would think?*

On your time sheet, you said it took forty five minutes to get Miss Brand's car going.

He widens his eyes and shrugs as though he can't figure out why that should be. Then, something occurs to him.

I probably checked a few things, before realising what it was. I may have thought it was something more serious at first. And, the car won't start until the engine cools down. So I would have had to hang around until it did to make sure it was okay. Yes, that must be it.

Can you remember what you and Miss Brand talked about?

The car, I guess.

Nothing else?

I'm truly sorry, Detective, but it was so long ago I don't remember.

In your statement you say Miss Brand told you she was on her way to Sheffield.

I'm sure that must be right then.

Do you remember how she seemed?

He shakes her head. *She was wearing a wedding dress, I remember that. It was strange to see a bride driving herself about like that.*

Did you talk about that?

Is there anything about that in the statement?

Fester's mobile phone buzzes. He picks it up to read who is calling. Then, he gets up, abruptly.

I'm sorry Mr Richards, I have to get this. Will you excuse me? I'll just be a few moments.

Sure, go ahead.

Fester heads for the door, muttering into his phone. Once outside, he makes his way to the office next door where Nigs is waiting.

He comes across as a pretty ordinary bloke, doesn't he?

They usually do at first, that's what makes them hard to catch.

How does he seem when you're sitting opposite him?

I noticed one thing. He's wearing loose clothes and, at first glance, it looks like there is nothing of him but, when he put his arm up to scratch his head, I caught sight of his contour. He works out, this guy. He has got muscles. That fits the forensic psychologist's profile of the killer.

Nigs rubs his forehead. *Okay, why don't you try giving him a surprise? Mention Gail Martos. Not her name, we don't want anything happening to our only witness - just that we know of a witness. Let's see if he reacts.*

Fester goes back into the interview room.

Sorry about that. Now, where were we? He sits down. *I think we're almost done here. Just a few more details. Contact details, really. Where are you living now, Mr Richards? We called at the house a couple of times and one of the neighbours said you were away.*

Which neighbour? A surly note enters his voice for the first time, taking Fester by surprise.

I don't remember. Is it important?

No, no, of course not, Richards assures him, recovering his neutrality. *I'm living in Spain. Well, I'm not an official resident, I go back and forth. It used to be my mother's house. She moved there when she retired. She died earlier this year.*

Fester smiles, sympathetically. *Was it sudden?*

She had cancer. I gave up work to spend as much time as I could with her so I haven't been in Leicester much. I've really fallen in love with Spain. And, now my mother is dead, the house is mine.

How often do you come back?

Once in a while, just to keep an eye on the house here and my tenant.

You must have missed a lot of the furore over this serial killer then.

They call him the June Killer, don't they? There is a faint smirk on his lips.

The newspapers do. Our psychologist says he is a bit more pathetic that that, some type of inadequate.

Richards looks down at his nails. *He must be to do that stuff,* he says, equitably. Still studying his nails, he asks*: You any nearer catching him?*

Yeah.

He glances up, searching Fester's eyes. *Really?*

We've found a witness to his first attack.

Gordon turns to look at the clock on the wall behind him, yet not fast enough to stop Fester noticing the frisson of surprise in his dead eyes.

He enters the house by knocking out the air vent for the water heater downstairs. He gets a wire through and uses this to open the latch of the rear lobby window. It is a small window, but he manages to wriggle through, worm-like, into the house.

I feel his presence, immediately. The atmosphere is dulled by him. It is like a curtain falling. It has taken him less than four minutes, from beginning to end, which is the last underestimation I can afford to make.

I glance down, nervously, at the woman who's sleeping beside me. She is snoring, lightly, one arm wrapped around a cuddly toy and the other beneath her pillow, resting on the steak knife she has placed there every night since she was first attacked by Gordon Richards.

Bim and Jackie appear at the foot of the bed. They've been at the front of the house, waiting for him.

He must have walked here. Nobody has driven into this road, Jackie says.

No, he is too cunning for that.

Gerte and Kerry arrive, next. They've been watching the back.

He came across the gardens. He must have parked his car a couple of streets away, Gerte says.

The five of us listen to the house.

Did the police waiting outside see anything?

Bim shakes her head. *They're just sitting in their car, chatting. They think the whole thing is a waste of time.*

Your old colleagues should never have mentioned there was a witness, Gerte says, angrily. *They had no right to put Gail in danger. The Weasel was bound to make the connection.*

At least, they alerted the local bobbies so they could protect her, I say, without conviction.

He has reached the foot of stairs, already, Kerry warns us. *What are we going to do?*

I'll go and make a 999 call. That should send the uniforms outside running in here.

I get off the bed and cross the landing to the upstairs telephone. As I lift the receiver, I look down into the darkness of the stairwell.

A man, dressed in black, is crouched low at the mid-point of the staircase. His head is covered by a leathery mask which has three slits, two for his eyes, and one with a zip for his mouth. It would look absurd, if it didn't proclaim the sinister intent which has brought him to this house, at three o'clock in the morning.

The telephone line is dead. He must have cut it downstairs. No matter. I have Carrie's mobile. When the operator answers I start the tape she has recorded for me. *I've just seen a man breaking into a house where I know there is a woman living alone.*

I turn the volume up, hoping to frighten him into running away but he doesn't hear through the mask. I watch him crawling like a reptile up the remaining stairs, the handles of a holdall looped over one of his shoulders.

...Her name is Gail Martos and her address is 14 Blackwell Road. Please hurry. It is an emergency.

I hang up. *That should do it,* I reassure the others, as I return, but I can tell from the energy in the room, no one is convinced the police are going to get here in time to save her.

The man in the leathery mask straightens up and as he passes by me I realise for the first time how tall he is.

It's not him, I exclaim to the others. *It must be Dead-gorgeous.*

He stands in the open bedroom doorway. I can't see his mouth through the mask but I bet he is smiling. He thinks this is going to be easy. Placing the holdall down by her bed, he bends over to extract something.

Hell, it is a stun gun, Gerte says. *He is going to abduct her.*

None of us react. We've become hypnotised by the horror of what is unfolding before us.

He puts the gun against her thigh and Jackie breaks the spell that has fallen over us. She knocks it from his hand. It clatters to the floor but he can't see it. He is going to have to feel around on his hands and knees if he wants to retrieve it.

The commotion awakens Gail. She sits bolt upright and screams, holding the steak knife in front of her chest. She understands what is going on in a blink of an eye. She has been expecting this, every single night, for the past four years.

Dead-gorgeous stares at her in disbelief. Then, he makes a grab for the knife, but she is too quick for him. She lunges the blade upwards towards his torso.

Instinctively, he puts out his hand to protect himself and she slashes through his leather glove, splattering the duvet with blood.

Bitch, he curses, in pain. *Bitch, bitch, bitch!*

Making a fist with his injured hand, he brings it down hard against her head, knocking her sideways.

Her shoulder is rammed against the wooden headboard so forcefully one of the knobs hits the wall and splinters off. The blow disorientates her and he easily prises the knife from her hand.

He pushes the blade towards her throat but before it touches her, Gail draws herself back, and swings herself away from his hand. The move is as quick and graceful as a yoga exercise which makes what happens next more astonishing. As soon as she is clear of the knife, she hurls herself at him, biting and scratching like a rabid dog.

He staggers backwards and drops the knife as he tries to protect himself.

I hope he is thinking the same as me. He is fighting for his life now, and not for hers.

Turning to look towards the door, he checks his retreat before throwing Gail down onto the bed and running onto the landing.

He is trying to get away. Get his mask off, we need to see him, I call to Jackie.

She follows him onto the landing but he suddenly spins around and doubles back on himself, passing through her on his way back into the bedroom. He has taken all of us, including Gail, by surprise.

Grabbing a handful of her hair, he yanks her head backwards and, before she can recover, he places a thumb over her wind pipe and starts to press.

Jackie is still reeling from having felt him move through her.

197

Do something, Bim calls to her but I can see she is struggling to stay in the room.

The rest of us look at each other, paralysed, by indecision.

The gun, Kerry mutters. *Where is it?*

We search the floor.

Here, under the wardrobe, Gerte cries, tossing it to me.

Gail's arms are flailing and I can hear her gasping for breath. I put the gun against the Dead-gorgeous' ankle to stop him killing her and I hit the button. Nothing happens.

Let me try, Bim says, taking the gun from me but it makes no difference.

It must be broken. What are we going to do?

Gail's body is becoming limp. She is losing consciousness.

Fix it, fix the gun, Gerte screams at me.

Suddenly, Kerry flings all the bedroom windows wide and the room fills with wind.

Dead-gorgeous looks up, startled and, as it dawns on him they have opened on their own, he turns to stare at them in amazement, leaving Gail lying on the bed.

She is making a low gurgling noise. I turn on the light in the bathroom, across the landing from her bedroom, to draw her attention.

Come on, you have to run to the bathroom while he is distracted.

Lifting herself up, she slides her legs over the opposite side of the bed from where Dead-gorgeous is closing the windows.

He steps backwards and reaches out to catch her but she is a fraction of second ahead of him. She staggers across the landing and, as she crosses the threshold of the bathroom, the door slams behind her in his face.

He uses his body as a battering ram against it, but Jackie has already slid the bolt across.

The door won't hold, Gerte warns. *It opens, inwards. We need to put something against it to stop him from breaking it down.*

There's a wooden towel cupboard which might do the job, Jackie says.

Do you need any help?

198

Her answer is the sound of the cupboard escaping the brackets securing it to the wall, followed by a loud thud as it falls heavily against the door.

Gail has fainted from fright, Jackie says, passing back through it.

She'll feel better when Dead-gorgeous is in jail where he belongs.

Bim taps him on the shoulder.

He freezes while he tries to evaluate what he has just felt. Then, very slowly, he turns around to look. His eyes widen with terror as he recognises Bim standing before him in her blue satin cocktail dress and matching handmade shoes. His mouth appears to moving silently under his mask but no sound escapes him.

She smiles, seductively, at him, her face bloated with decomposition, her skin peeling off her bones.

Aren't you dead gorgeous, she mouths at him. *Fancy a shag?*

A whimper finally forces its way through his lips, as he backs away from the bathroom door and tries to slide along the wall to escape her.

What's the matter? Don't you like dead girls? Putting her hand in her mouth, she pulls out some of her teeth to show him. They still have the gums attached to them. *Go on. Give us a kiss,* she begs, as he retreats towards the stairs, unable to take his eyes from her.

Feeling behind him with his foot, he miscalculates and misses the top stair, tumbling backwards, head over heels, all the way down to the bottom. He scrambles to his feet, groaning with pain, and hobbles towards the window through which he entered. All thought of abducting Gail appears to have evaporated. He only wants to get away from this haunted house.

When he realises the window has been mysteriously jammed shut, he starts to panic. He runs to the back door but it is locked. Next, he tries the front door but that won't budge either. As fast as he slides the bolts back, they flip across again into position. Panting wildly, he hurries into the dining room, picks up a chair and uses it to shatter the window pane, hurling himself after it.

It is only when he picks himself up off the ground, he notices the two uniformed policemen hurrying up the front path, towards him. There is a mixture of indecision and resignation in his body language, as he shifts his weight from foot to foot. He wants to give up. Perhaps, he is relieved to see the reassuring presence of two living policemen. But, as they near him, he rallies again. He lowers his head and barges into the middle of them like a rugby player. Startled, they let him pass and he vaults over the garden gate.

He stumbles as he lands and one of the policemen leans over and makes a grab at the back of his mask. He is hoping to stop him in his tracks, but it tears and comes away in his hand.

Dead-gorgeous turns his face away, but he can do nothing to hide his blonde hair, as he races full pelt to the corner of the road.

Reaching the next street, a car pulls in front of him and the policemen chasing after him are blinded by the full beam of the headlights. They hear a door slam, the engine scream and the next thing they know the driver is accelerating the car towards them. They don't see what he looks like. They are too busy trying to save their lives.

Inside the house, Gail is sitting on the bathroom floor, hugging her knees and crying.

You were asleep, and when you woke up, a man was standing over your bed, holding a stun gun. You tried to get away but he grabbed you by your hair, and started to crush your wind pipe. Somehow you struggled free and you managed to lock yourself in the bathroom, where you fainted. The man must have seen or heard the police arrive. When you came to, he'd fled.

I repeat this version of events in her ear several times to make sure she has got it. She is so close to passing out, the odds of her taking it in, unquestioningly, are good. Maybe now the police will do what they should have done in the beginning and move her to a safe house.

I blame myself too for placing too much reliance on them. I need to stop thinking like D.I. Kate Madding, and start being who I am now - D. I. Ghost.

The front door opens and a tall, elegantly-dressed man walks down the stone steps, along the path, and out of the gate. It is a sunny morning but a shrill blast of air hits him as he reaches the pavement, forcing him to pause for a second in his stride. The March winds have arrived early, this year. It is still only February. He pulls up the collar of his camel-coloured cashmere coat and crosses the road, swinging the brown leather attaché case he is carrying. He is about to unlock the dark green, top of the range, Audi parked there, when he senses someone behind him. He turns around, quickly, and freezes. He is face to face with a man in a black woollen mask. His mind is racing. Is he about to be mugged in plain light of day? What is Blackheath coming to? Then, he registers the navy blue police bullet proof vest. He should feel relieved and, if this masked man wasn't holding a gun to his head, he would be, but as it is, he starts to shiver, uncontrollably, while he fights the urge to release his sphincter so the contents of his bowel can pour into his pants.

He is guided by the masked man along the road, out of sight of the large detached house he has just left.

Could you show me some ID, please, sir, the officer asks,

It seems incongruous to hear such courteousness in the voice of a man who is pointing a gun at him. He fumbles in his pocket, noting a slight stiffening in the body of his companion, as he pulls out a leather wallet with his driving licence inside.

The policeman takes it from him, before it is offered, not rudely, but impatiently. *It says here you are Basil Mountford.*

Yes, he whispers, his life is flashing before him while he wonders what he could have done to warrant this.

And, that's your car?

Yes.

And, you live in that house? The officer points to the house he has just left.

He glances at it. Up until this moment, living there has made him feel sure of himself. That's what six bedrooms, four en suite, and an indoor swimming pool, on a private estate in the posh part of South East London can do for one. It gave him the assurance that he was unassailable. How has he arrived here then - being treated like a common criminal?

That's right, officer, he answers, beginning to find his voice. He hasn't done anything! This is obviously a terrible mistake. Why should he be cowered by the presence of the police? He'll sue them for humiliating him when this is all over. How dare they treat him so shamefully! He is no lawbreaker.

I'm a barrister, he says out loud as though he needs to remind them both of his status. He feels a sense of substance trickling back inside him. He has deliberately omitted to mention that his specialism is corporate and not criminal law. They don't need to know that yet. He wants them to sweat a little first.

What can I do for you, officer?

The armed policeman lowers his gun from his head to his stomach and takes a step backwards, cursing, silently. He glances to his left at the senior officer in charge of this operation, Chief Inspector, Ray Barley.

Barley coughs, in acknowledgement. His chest has the wet rattle of a smoker and actually he is dying for a fag. He takes off his own woollen mask so Mr Mountford can see his face and lights up. He is several years younger than the suave-looking man in front of him, yet he feels decades older, this morning, after being dragged before dawn from his bed.

We have reason to believe your car may have been used in a serious crime, he explains.

Mr Mountford's ebony face creases with incomprehension. *A serious crime? What serious crime? When?*

Does anyone have a spare set of keys to this car?

No, he answers, emphatically.

You haven't loaned it to anyone?

No, absolutely not. Would you mind telling me what is going on?

Barley draws deeply on his cigarette to stop himself coughing again. He exhales to the side to keep the smoke away from Mr Mountford.

This car was used in the attempted murder of two police

officers in Leicester, in the early hours of this morning.

Mr Mountford laughs. *Well, I know that's impossible. This car has been parked here all night.* He is aware Barley is studying him, silently. *Someone must have copied the plates,* he suggests, offering them both an honourable way out of this.

Barley shakes his head, the sudden movement freeing a mousy forelock, which falls across his forehead.

Perhaps, you could come with me for a moment, Mr Mountford, he says, smoothing his hair back into place as he leads the way towards the car.

He points at the front wing. *Can you tell me how and when these scratches and this dent were made?*

Mr Mountford's brown eyes widen. *How did these get here? I have never seen them before.*

Barley believes him. Mountford has been duped. Indeed, he is pretty sure by now somebody is making a fool out of them both.

Did you happen to look at the mileage of the car when you last used it?

No, why would I? Mr Mountford sounds exasperated. *Listen, officer, there must be some mistake. I left this car here at ten o'clock, last night, and now it is nine o'clock, the following morning, and it is still here, in exactly the same spot.*

With scratches and a dent, you have never seen before?

He opens his mouth to object but Barley raises a hand to quieten him before he can suggest that someone must have hit his car, while it was parked here, or some such nonsense.

Feel the bonnet, sir.

Mr Mountford puts his palm gingerly on the polished surface. It is warm. His mind spins. *I-I-I don't understand, officer. How can this be?*

That's what we aim to find out, sir, Barley says, quietly. *Could I have the keys, please?*

He hands them to him.

We are going to have to check it for explosives first, he tells him.

Mr Mountford shakes his head. *I can't believe this is real.*

It won't take long, sir. Please bear with us. It's just a

precaution.

Two men in overalls move in. One has a sniffer dog on a leash.

Mr Mountford turns away. He has no interest in watching this. He prefers to pretend it isn't happening.

It's clear, Gov, one of the men shouts, a few minutes later.

Barley dons a pair of latex gloves and opens the passenger door.

Mr Mountford gasps when he looks, inside, over his shoulder. There is blood on the glove compartment.

Get the SOCOS in here, Smith, Barley calls to one of his masked men.

The car's owner is feeling queasy.

I'm sorry Mr Mountford but, when the scene of crime officers have finished here, we are going to have to take your car away for further forensic tests.

He is certain he has aged a lifetime since he left his house to travel to his chambers in Lincoln's Inn, less than ten minutes ago. His hand strays to his black, curly hair. *Yes, of course,* he mutters, wondering whether this police officer is judging him for not dealing with this more robustly.

Barley places his arm gently behind his back to guide him. *Could we go inside and talk, sir?*

Yes, of course, he repeats. *That would be better.* He is acutely aware by now that his neighbours are staring at him.

His wife, Hazel, a well groomed red head, a thousand beauty treatments younger than her husband, opens the door before they reach the gate.

What's going on, darling?

Mrs Mountford, could we all sit down? I need to ask you and your husband a few questions.

Mr Mountford and his wife lead the way into their living room. They sit side by side on the edge of a brown leather sofa, one of three in this long airy room.

Barley takes the one opposite them. He covers the same territory, as before. Does anyone have a spare set of keys? Have the couple loaned the car to someone recently?

They shake their heads.

Is there anyone who might want to try and involve you in this, Mr Mountford? An ex-client? Someone who might have a grudge against you or your wife?

I can't think of anyone.

Mrs Mountford? Have you seen anything suspicious over the last few days; someone hanging around, perhaps?

There has been nobody, she assures him, quickly.

He smiles back at the couple. He will need them to examine every corner of their lives to see if the faces of these two men become visible.

Please, it is important, he tells them. *The men who did this are suspects in a series of murders. They visited a woman's house in the early hours of this morning and tried to kill her. Then, they almost mowed down two police officers as they got away. They're extremely dangerous. We want to make sure we catch them, before anyone else gets hurt.*

SPRING

We've been watching him pacing up and down the pavement, outside the house, for the past half an hour, all the while talking to himself, urgently, firmly, as though needing to persuade himself of something. Blind to the flurries of cherry blossom stirring around him in the wind, his raincoat gapes open to reveal a baggy grey-green suit and khaki knitted tie, as he keeps his eyes firmly on the ground.

Carrie asks me: *Do you think he is a schizophrenic?*

Don't you ever read a newspaper? He is Karl Grüner, Gerte's boyfriend, I enlighten her.

What is he doing here?

I shrug. *There's only one way to find out. Call him over.*

We open the front door.

Excuse me, she calls to him across the garden, from the porch steps. *Are you okay?*

He starts at the sound of her voice but he approaches, walking slowly, reluctantly, even, up the path to the door.

I saw you through the window, Carrie continues, as he draws closer. *You were looking a little lost. Why don't you come in for a moment?*

I have no idea what I'm doing here, he says, staring up at her with a helpless expression. His arms are thrown wide, palms up, to emphasise the point he is making. He speaks slowly, deliberately, enunciating every syllable with care. Mounting the front steps, his eyes widen with shock when he focuses on Carrie's face.

Yes, Kate Madding and I were, no are, no were, identical twins. She smiles, nervously. *I suppose that just about sums up the difficulty of losing your identical twin.* She steps back for him to enter. *She's dead.* The word ricochets around the hallway where they are both now standing. *You did know that?*

Yes, I read about it in the paper, he says, softly. *I'm sorry for your loss.*

Do you want a coffee?

He follows her into the kitchen, a perplexed expression worrying his thin stain of a mouth. The rest of his face appears featureless, at first glance; a bland expanse of skin paling into mildew and stale milk-coloured coils of hair. His eyes should be startling to make up for this, but although unusual - they're green - it is such a watery shade, they're all but missed behind the steel rimmed glasses he wears. The red slash of his mouth is what calls attention to him but his lips are too wiry to really attract. They carry the asceticism of learning. Or is it moral rectitude? Both, maybe. He would be kind but not passionate, thoughtful but not spontaneous, this man. A lousy snog if ever I saw one!

The thought makes me feel guilty for fear that Gerte might come flying to his defence but she doesn't materialise. I am relieved but not entirely surprised. She has shown less and less interest in him during his first few months of freedom. She has other matters on her mind. She wants to walk into the Light. She claims to have seen it, and really I have no reason to doubt her word. The only reason she hasn't is because we need her to stake out the Weasel's Spanish house, in case he returns there. We have lost him, us and the police - lost them both, him and Dead-gorgeous. So, now in Spain, Leicester, and London, we wait; Gerte and Kerry, increasingly impatient with their earthly duties; Bim, Jackie, and I equally restless but still determined to shun the Light which has so far shunned us.

Carrie fills the kettle and sets two mugs on the table. *Is instant, okay?*

Karl laughs to himself.

Did I say something funny?

No, no. Instant is fine. It's just that...

What?

How did you know who I was?

My sister said it was you.

He nods as though this makes sense to him. Then, the muscles in his face tighten as the meaning sinks in. He avoids looking at her.

Carrie pours boiling water into their mugs and places a jug of milk, a bowl of sugar, and a plate of digestive biscuits on the table.

Please, let's sit, she suggests, pulling out a chair herself.

Karl sits down heavily opposite her and stares into the coffee in front of him.

You must think about her a lot...Gerte, your girlfriend, I mean.

His head shoots up, his eyes searching hers.

I used to dream about her all the time when I was in jail but not now. She has gone. It is a dead zone. His mouth slackens. *No pun intended.*

Kate really believed you'd done it, you know.

Well, I hadn't.

Yes, yes, of course, we know that now. I can't imagine anything more terrible than being convicted of a murder you didn't commit.

You said she told you it was me, outside on the pavement. How could she? If she is...

Carrie grimaces. *I told you - identical twins.*

He eyes her, uncertainly, sizing her up; assessing her mental state, probably.

Ask him if he knows something which might help catch Gerte's killer, I prompt Carrie.

I was wondering whether you know anything which might point to your girlfriend's killer.

No, nothing.

He sits back and runs his fingers through his hair.

So what does he think happened?

Do you have a theory about the murders?

Nothing that the police wouldn't have thought of, already.

Oh, for heaven's sake, Carrie! Get him to spit out whatever it is that has brought him here before I lose my patience.

Would you mind telling me your theory? I'd really like to hear it. Carrie smiles at him, encouragingly.

It is so weird sitting here talking to you. It is like talking to her but you're different. Identical, but not. I don't know your name?

Carrie Hamilton. She holds her hand out to shake his and he

208

grasps it, briefly.

Karl Grüner.

He sips his coffee. *The key has to be the cars, don't you think? There's always a car involved. The bride's car is found by Humber Bridge. The other car disappears. Gerte is found in a car. They are all abducted while they're out driving.*

The police think he is a mechanic.

Does he know the cars? Or does he choose them at random?

He works for a motoring organisation.

Karl slaps his forehead with his hand. *That's how he does it then. I knew the cars were important. But, the cars are always okay. Does he fix them?*

I don't know.

But, the police know who it is?

Yes. Well, one of them. They think there's an accomplice.

And, they will catch them?

I imagine so, with any luck.

He sighs, deeply, his body sagging in his chair as he exhales. *Then, it's over. I think that is what I came here to learn. Now, I can go back to Austria and live my life.*

He doesn't even finish his coffee. He rises from the table and walks to the door, apologising for taking up Carrie's time. He waits for her to open the door and bolts down the stairs.

I watch him walk briskly down the front path and onto the pavement, his shoulders hunched inside his raincoat. He is fooling himself. He won't get on with his life. Not, as before. I turn away.

Carrie asks me: *What did he come for?*

He couldn't keep away. He is as much a victim of this as Gerte and the others are, I tell her, bitterly. Then, I disappear, chased away by the sadness I feel for him.

I go to my office, the quietest place I can think of, during the daytime. Denise usually only comes there at night to work.

The key is the cars, I repeat to myself. But, the Weasel was no longer a breakdown mechanic by the time Gerte and Bim were killed. He wasn't working in the UK, at all, as far as we know. He was in Spain. Well, coming and going to Spain. He still had the uniform though. Could he have pretended to be one? No, that's not it. Karl's right. The key is the cars. Not, the Weasel.

Damn! Why didn't I think of this before?

Did you have any work done on your car in the month before you were murdered, Bim?

She considers my question, carefully, I hope.

No I don't think so, why?

Think, Bim, please, just think. This is very important.

I am, I am. It was a company car. They took care of everything. I never had to do a thing.

Did they use a particular garage to service their vehicles?

I don't know. I guess so. Mine was still under the manufacturer's warranty. It would have gone to an approved garage; somewhere with a concession for that brand, I suppose.

You never dropped it off, or picked it up, yourself?

No, it was picked up and delivered by the garage.

Picked up, and delivered, where?

Work. Home.

Which?

Both.

So the garage knew where you lived and where you worked.

Yes. Is that significant?

When was it serviced last?

I don't know.

You must do. Come on, Bim.

It must have been....

Yes?

I think it was a week or so before the party.

Are you serious? But, you said it hadn't been worked on.

It wasn't. There was nothing wrong with it. It was just a service.

And, you're sure this was "a week or so" before you went missing?

Yes, but I don't see what you're getting at. Are you saying there's a connection?

Where did they drop it off?

At work.

Did you see who brought it?

211

Let me think. Yes, I must have. I seem to remember giving him a tip.

What did he look like?

I don't recall.

What was the name of the garage?

I don't know.

We're watching Cheryl dress a photograph she has been commissioned to take of a picnic for one of the women's magazines. I am tempted to send the whole lot flying from the table onto the floor with frustration.

It's no good being angry with me, Kate. It's not my fault. I just don't remember.

It's nearly May, Bim, do you know what that means? We are six weeks away from gaining a new member of the team.

Okay, okay, let me concentrate. Don't move around so. You're making me nervous.

I stay as still as I can and wait, impatiently. *Well?*

I'm getting something. He gave me a calendar, one of those washable plastic pocket ones. I think it had the name of the garage on the other side.

What did you do with it?

I probably threw it away. It was really tacky. And, it was already half way through the year. I didn't need, or want it.

I resist the temptation to scream. *Someone in your company must keep a record of the garages they use, surely.*

Our team assistant. And, actually, I think I may have given her the calendar. I mean, she probably threw it away but I believe I may have dumped it on her desk.

Right then, here is what we are going to do. I am going to stay here with Cheryl, while you go off and take a look at this assistant's desk.

Now?

No, tomorrow. Yes, of course, now.

Sophie won't like it. She really hates people going through her desk.

It is not like she's going to know, Bim. You're dead, remember? I won't tell her, if you don't. Okay?

She is very intuitive.

Just do it, please Bim - for me.

She disappears. I expect her to come straight back but she doesn't. By the time she eventually does return, I am on the point of abandoning Cheryl to go looking for her.

Where have you been?

You know where. It took longer than I thought. They have reorganised everything. Sophie is working for a different account team now. They have disbanded mine. How could Reece do that? It is as though I never was. I feel like I made no impression at all.

I'm sure you did, Bim. But, that is how life is. Those who are left are supposed to move on without us.

Then, why are we so concerned with them, when it is obvious they don't give a damn about us?

I don't know. We just are.

I don't think I want to stick around, if everything is going to change like this, Kate.

Why? Have you seen the Light?

No. Have you?

No.

We examine one another, glumly.

Kerry and Gerte have, Bim reminds me.

Yes, they told me too.

Do you want to stay here, Kate?

I'm not sure what I want. I never was sure, except about work. That is the only thing which meant anything to me while I was alive. And, that is all I have now I'm dead. Trying to catch these killers is what gives me definition. It allows me to recognise myself.

Is it enough?

Yes. For me, it is.

She comes closer to me. *Can I stay with you, Kate?*

If you want to.

I think, now I've seen the bimbette off, I shall wait until Reece passes, she says, wistfully. *It won't be long now. Another year, that's all.*

How the hell do you know that?

213

I haven't a clue. I worked it out the other day. I'm not sure whether it's a new trick I've learned, or one I have been able to do all along without realising it. Am I the only one? Can't you tell by looking at someone when they're going to die?

I can't, but my thoughts have already run on from *why didn't you say something about this sooner*, to what I say next: *What about her, Bim?*

We both look at Cheryl, who is busy taking photographs of the picnic.

Bim beams at me. *Kate, do you know what this means?*

I nod. *We are a few weeks away from another murder and we have no idea who the victim will be.*

Nigs' flat at the top of Forest Hill in South London is a mixture of ancient and modern furniture. Some pieces are family heirlooms which he has had restored, while others were made by one of his sisters who is a carpenter. An entire wall in his living room is covered by shelves full of records, CD's, tapes and DVD's. He is not one for reading, Nigs, but he is passionate about blues and jazz. The décor is perhaps a little unadventurous - the whole flat is painted white - but with so much gorgeous wood and some striking sofas and cushions, it manages to look stylish compared with the average policeman's bachelor pad.

He has invited Fester over for dinner. This wouldn't have happened when I was alive. Socialising was always conducted in bars and clubs. Since my death, however, a more intimate friendship has developed between the two men.

Inevitably, their conversation turns to work. Their investigation into the June Killer as they call him has stalled. The only forensic evidence found in Mountford's Audi was the blood of the mystery accomplice. They have no proof whatsoever that the driver who picked him up was Gordon Richards but he does appear to have dropped off the face of the planet since then.

Nigs sets a beef and vegetable stir-fry and a dish of coconut rice on the kitchen table. He and Fester demolish both in under fifteen minutes while I try and convince myself that watching them is just as much fun.

Fester takes a slurp of beer. *Where could he be?*

We have no reason to believe he has left Britain. He certainly hasn't turned up at his house in Spain. It's not that difficult to stay out of sight as long as you're smart enough to avoid using a credit card, cash card, or mobile phone.

I wish we had enough on him to search his place.

You wouldn't find anything if you did, I chip in.

So how is he managing to live?

You don't think he could be dead, do you? Maybe they had a falling out and the other one killed him. That might explain it.

No, he is still alive. I can feel it, I assure them both. *He is licking his wounds. They nearly got caught that night which must have scared him rigid. He'll lie low now until he is ready to kill again.*

We'll find out soon enough. It's the beginning of June in another three weeks, Nigs says, getting up to fetch them another beer and the chocolate cake Fester brought from his wife for dessert.

It is so frustrating. We could clone the accomplice from his DNA but we can't identify him. We have to nail these bastards before they kill again, Fester. Nigs thumps the table with his fist to underline the imperative of this.

He is looking ravishing in navy cords, with a dusky wine coloured, long sleeved, polo shirt. So ravishing I've no idea what Fester is wearing at all even though he is sitting opposite me.

I wish Kate were here. She was good at turning up wild cards. Nigs grins in remembrance of me.

How is it going with her sister, Carrie?

Guys, please, let's just stick to discussing the case, I chide. *How was I good at turning up wild cards, exactly?*

She has started a business with a woman called Denise Boulay. It is Denise this, that, and the other now. But, she happened to mention the other day that this woman didn't want her name on the paperwork. She's a partner, right, but she doesn't want her name legally on the business? Doesn't that strike you as odd? It did me too so I checked her out. The only Denise Boulay I could find is dead. So this woman is obviously using her identity. When I told Carrie, she wasn't pleased one bit about what I'd done. She went berserk and we're talking Katrina. I've never seen anything like it before. It put Kate at full throttle in the shade. I thought I was doing her a favour but she won't hear a word against this Denise.

Women and their girlfriends! It's a no go area, mate. They always prefer to listen to them, rather than us. Get used to it, is my advice.

Well, we're still seeing each other but...I don't know.

You're not sure where it's going?

I care about her. I do. Why wouldn't I. What is there not to care

216

about? She's lovely, she really is - warm, kind, special in every way.

Fester scratches his bald head. *You should listen to yourself, mate. It sounds to me like you're trying to talk yourself into this. We both know you were in love with the cool, unkind, but extremely funny, and feisty Kate. So where exactly does that leave...*

Nigs' eyes flash back at him. *Kate wasn't unkind. How can you say that? She just didn't wear her heart on her sleeve, that's all.*

His friend studies him in silence for a few seconds. *You really are in deep shit, aren't you?*

Easy for you to say. You married guys have it simple.

Yeah, right, a wife and three kiddies is about as simple as it gets!

Carrie's been through so much I don't want to make things any worse for her.

And, how would you do that?

By hurting her, of course. I like her too much to want to do that to her.

That's a novel sentiment on which to base a relationship.

Nigs shrugs, and Fester rolls his eyes to the ceiling.

Just promise me you won't ask her to marry you, or anything daft like that. I know they let you write your own vows these days, but promising to like someone in sickness and in health, till death you do part, because she looks like the one who got away, and you don't want to hurt her feelings, doesn't seem to have the right ring about it to me.

The sign in large liquid-black letters on a shiny white background, brightly illuminated at night, says: *Hamilton and Sons Motors.* I always thought it presumptuous of Phil to involve the boys in a business they may well grow up to have no interest in at all but I have noticed, since the split with Carrie, the *and sons* part has been increasing left out of his advertisements in the local press. Does he feel he is divorcing them too? Or is this an indication of his growing acceptance that his influence over their future must have waned?

I have purposefully chosen to come here on a day when he is off playing golf with his cronies so I can have unlimited and undisturbed access to his computer records. His office is an airless kiosk overlooking the repair shop. It is presentable, largely due to the efforts of the office secretary, Fiona, a new convert to the Jehovah Witnesses, who has just banned the display of sexually provocative calendars here. But, it is still pretty basic, with a large metal desk, some metal stand-alone shelves, and a couple of metal filing cabinets. Not the kind of office to impress potential car buyers, which is why he makes sure he meets these in the lounge area of his salesroom.

The computer on his desk whirs into life, agonisingly, slowly. It is so old I'm amazed it doesn't use the binary code. Finally, I get into his customer database. I tap in the name, Belinda Montgomery, and wait. If I had any breath to hold I would. Nothing comes up. This was not what I was hoping for. Phil has both BMW and Audi concessions. I really thought her car might be here. She said it was a company car though, didn't she? I type in the name of the PR firm where she worked and this time a file comes up, containing the make, model, and number plate of her car, together with its service and repair record. The company address and her home address are also listed. Next, I try Basil Mountford. He is a customer too. He brought his Audi in for a service, a few months back. Gerte's name draws a blank, but what's the betting the garage she happened to call in at, on the

218

night she went missing, was this one? Dead-gorgeous has been here, under my nose, the whole time. But, which one of Phil's employees is he? Five mechanics and two car salesmen, work here. Reluctantly, I'm disbarring Phil himself as a suspect. I've seen Dead-gorgeous. Not his face but the back of his head and the way his body moves. It wasn't Phil. They're both tall, and slim, with blonde hair, but Dead-gorgeous is more muscular. I go to the personnel files. There are no staff photographs in them but the names and job titles refresh my memory. Dead-gorgeous can't be either of the two car salesmen, because they're both dark, and one is too plump, anyway, and the other, too spindly. That leaves the five mechanics: Brad, Baz, Scott, Jeff, and Miles. Miles is Afro Caribbean and Baz is Turkish. Jeff is too bulky, which leaves only Scott and Brad. I skim their two files. There is nothing which catches my eye in Brad's, but in Scott's, I discover that he gained his qualifications in Leicester. It is not much of a link but it is a link. I keep on reading. He has never had a single day off sick. That must make him popular with Phil. There is also a request form from him to take three weeks leave to see his parents, who live in Australia. It is typed, badly. I check the calendar on the wall. The three weeks leave have already started. He will be off until the second week of June.

219

Scott Ramsey lives in a modern house in Thamesmead, white bricked with a round bathroom window to give it a nautical appeal, since it is technically close to the Thames, although actually lost in a concrete maze of estates that run alongside it. The rooms are estate agent *cosy* and stuffed with self-assembly furniture made out of melamine. Like Gordon, he is very clean and likes to keep fit. His spare room is crammed with exercise machines and weight training gear. There is nothing more incriminating here, though.

I plonk myself down on a chair in his kitchen, feeling depressed, and that is when I notice it - the photograph of a woman pinned up on a small notice board by his phone. She is loading supermarket bags into the boot of her car and seems unaware that her photograph is being taken. She is a petite blonde.

It wouldn't mean anything to anyone else. It might not mean anything anyway. But, I can't help wondering whether I am staring at the face of the next woman to be murdered.

The thought unsettles me and suddenly an image of Scott flashes into my mind. I saw him that night - the night I was killed. It was early evening and I was on my way home from work, feeling frazzled and exhausted, as usual.

My God, of course, I remember now, that's where I saw him. The main road through New Cross was jammed with traffic because a bus had broken down, and I didn't have the patience to wait for it to clear. I decided to try and pick my way around the blockage by using the back streets, instead.

It was one of those charcoal grey evenings of early summer. The streets were oily wet and a rain dense sky was threatening to give them another soaking. There was a lot of litter in the gutters, blown there from the fruit and vegetable market a block away. I recognised Scott up ahead, seconds after I turned off the main road. Tall and good looking he was hard to miss. He was getting out of a BMW wearing a pair of blue overalls. I slowed down to

220

say hello. *Nice wheels*, I called to him. Those two words alone must have sealed my fate. They told him I'd noticed Bim's car. He was probably dumping it after abducting her. *I was just delivering it for a client*, he shouted back with a dazzling smile. Well, I was dazzled by it. I didn't realise a thing. *Say, you couldn't do me a favour and run me back to the garage, could you? Save me waiting for a bus, or calling one of the guys out.* I agreed, immediately. *Sure, hop in. I thought you'd have shut up shop by now.* He played me, beautifully. He was drawing me into his web. *The boss is still there. He was trying to get hold of you, earlier. He wanted to ask you something about your sister, I think.* We went on chatting on the way back. I was enjoying his company. It lifted my mood. And, all the time he was planning to harm me. I dropped him on the forecourt of the garage and I went to get out of the car myself, but he stopped me. *You wait there. I'll go and fetch Phil. It is the least I can do after you've been so kind.* He ran towards the garage before I could argue, and headed around the side where I couldn't see him. I'll never know now whether he actually went inside. It's possible the whole place was locked up. He returned a minute later. *Sorry Kate, we've got to go out and pick up a breakdown with the tow truck. Phil wants you to meet him in the George in half an hour. The breakdown isn't far. It won't take long to recover the car. Do you know the George?* I was irritated with Phil for expecting me to wait for him but I didn't want to show that to Scott. *He could just ring me, later.* He shook his head. *He says it is important. It is something to do with Carrie.* Stupidly, I didn't question that Phil would use one of his mechanics as a messenger for something so personal. *Okay, tell him I'll be there but, if he doesn't arrive within twenty minutes of me getting there, I'm off. I've got things to do.* He winked at me. *I'll make sure he's on time. Thanks for the lift, Kate. Bye.* He jogged back to the side entrance, pausing once to give me a wave, still smiling, real friendly like. The bastard!

Phil didn't show up, of course. I waited half an hour in an increasing state of fury and then I left. I tried to ring him on his mobile from the car park but I couldn't get a signal until I walked towards the road. It was ringing when I saw his tow truck coming along the road. I stepped off the kerb to wave to him and whoever was driving ran me down. It was possibly a moment of inspiration. I bet Scott couldn't believe his luck. When the truck speeded up as it approached me, I thought it was a joke and I stood my ground. The Weasel was following behind. They must have been planning to abduct me. I was so taken in by Scott's ruse to get me there, I saved them the trouble.

Sam and I are in his room finishing off a jigsaw together. This one is a map of the British Isles. It was his choice and I suspect a crush on Kerry – whom is apparently helping him with some computer research for a school project - might be behind it. I've never known him to show any interest in geography before. I am glad of the distraction whatever the jigsaw. My mind has been obsessively preoccupied with the woman in the photograph, on Scott Ramsey's notice board, and how I can discover her identity. It seems like an impossible task. And, we have less than three weeks to pull it off, if we are going to save her life.

Dad wants to have us for the weekend, every other week, Sam announces to me, none too happily from the expression on his face.

Don't you want to go? I doubt anyone is going to make you, I reassure him, adding to myself: And, actually they can't because your mother has custody.

Mum says we get to decide each time whether or not we actually go.

Where is the problem then?

Talking with Sam is like extracting molars. I use the lull to surreptitiously search his room for contraband. There is nothing. Mercifully, he seems to have given up shoplifting.

The scouts are going camping, next weekend.

And?

He brushes his blonde hair back from his face. Even at this age he is becoming self conscious about his appearance. I don't think Carrie and I so much as peeked into a mirror until we were eleven. Maybe identical twins don't have to. If I had egg on my face she'd be the first to tell me.

What will Dad think if I go with the scouts?

He'll be pleased for you.

You think?

Well, there's always the hope he has matured since he left. *Just explain it to him. Or get Mummy to, if you don't want to. And, if*

223

there is any difficulty, you tell me, and I'll talk to him.

He can't hear you. He'd need a medium.

A medium?

That's what they're called aren't they?

Yes, that's right. How clever of you. I hadn't thought of that.

He beams at me. *Well, it wouldn't do any good talking to Dad without one.*

Oh, I don't know, I think I could make myself understood.

He laughs. *I really like having you around, Auntie Kate.*

Thank you, Sam! What a lovely thing to say. It gives me an idea too. I want to move back in with Carrie and the boys. My flat hasn't been the same since Jaswinda and Jitendra left. My new lodgers, Jennifer and Bernard, are newlyweds and there is only so much I want to learn about their love life. Either they're going to have to go, or I will. *Maybe you could do me a favour and tell your mum how you feel.*

I've never been to a séance before and it seems odd to be attending my first now I'm dead. I'm feeling nervous. I've seen enough horror films to expect the worst, even though, technically, I am the worst myself. Margaret Dryer isn't the least like the mediums I've seen on celluloid to be fair. She's too ordinary. She talks about what she is attempting to do as though it were the most natural thing in the world. I have to pinch myself to remember she is sitting here so nonchalantly with five dead women.

Nothing might come through, she warns us, rubbing the photograph of our mystery blonde between her two palms, while we watch her, intently. *I don't often work with objects.*

She has lost a little weight since I met her at Bim's memorial. She is wearing a light grey linen trouser suit, well tailored, with a pale violet silk blouse. The cut of her clothes, their pressed appearance, with not one wrinkle, blemish, or snag, rumours an exactness befitting her profession. I can picture her teaching equations and statistics in school. It is a séance I can't picture her conducting, even though that is precisely what she is doing right in front of me.

We're seated at a large and heavy oak table in her breakfast room. The walls are painted a cheery yellow, and green vases, storage glasses, and candle holders decorate the polished wooden mantel of an original Victorian fire grate. In the alcoves, to the left and right of this, two oak dressers are filled with massive serving plates, vegetable dishes, and soup tureens. They are antique; from the days when families were large. They are beautiful too, with a buttery glaze, and a green and yellow flower design - the everyday china of a wealthy farming family, perhaps. It occurs to me that Margaret may have met the owners. She might know everyone who has had a hand in her home since it was built at the turn of the nineteenth century. I can't sense any other spirits here myself, but she can do what I cannot. She can contact those who have already passed into the Light.

This woman is in mortal danger, Margaret announces.

Gerte smiles, tightly, at me. Like we don't know this already, her look says. But, I'm impressed. We told Margaret nothing about the woman in our photograph before we handed it to her.

I have her aunt here. She is waiting for her in the Light. She will come to meet her when she passes.

Gerte asks, at once: *What's her name?*

Milly. Aunt Milly.

No, I mean the young woman, her niece. What's her name?

Michelle.

Michelle what?

Michelle Seymour.

Now, we're getting somewhere.

Where does she live?

She doesn't...She won't, Margaret falters.

We need to know this, I plead. *It's important. This woman's life depends upon it.*

Margaret shakes her head. *She says her niece is going to die soon. It will be over quickly and she will be there to meet her. None of this can be changed.*

Bim asks for all of us: *Why can't it be changed?*

I'm losing her, I'm sorry. She opens her eyes. *She has gone.*

Bim repeats: *Why can't it be changed?*

Margaret shrugs. *She didn't say.*

Damn, Gerte curses. *I knew this wouldn't work.*

But, we all agreed to it, Jackie, who insisted on coming along, despite me telling her she didn't have to, reminds her, sharply.

That shuts Gerte up.

I use the silence to ask Margaret: *Can you try and find someone else who knows this Michelle?*

She closes her eyes, again. Nothing happens for a while. Then, a presence appears on one of the empty chairs around the table. He is a grey-haired man, tall, but with slightly stooped shoulders. His face is yellow, even the whites of his eyes, and his skin is very lined. It is hard to tell how old he is because he looks so ill. Anywhere from his mid-fifties to seventy, I would guess.

Margaret speaks to him. *Will you tell us your name, sir?*

226

He turns two beady grey eyes on her. He might have been handsome once, and even a smile now would hint at this, but his expression is hostile.

Undaunted by his silence, Margaret repeats: *Will you tell us your name, sir?*

I'm Alec Ramsey, he answers, glowering at the rest of us.

Do you have a message for us, Mr Ramsey?

Wait a minute, Bim says. *Are you related to Scott Ramsey? Scott Ramsey the serial...*

...the mechanic, Gerte cuts in.

My beloved son, he says, sadly.

Mr Ramsey do you know anything about Michelle Seymour? Maybe you could help us find her, I try.

He shakes his head, sternly, his lips pursed together as tight as an anus, as he starts to fade from the room.

No, please don't go, I plead with him.

Bitch, I hear him rasp, before he completely disappears.

Well, how does someone as unpleasant as that get to pass over into the Light?

There's no judgement in the Light, Gerte informs me, loftily.

And, how would you know?

Because, I've seen it!

Well, I'm glad I haven't, Bim says, sulkily.

I haven't either, and I don't want to, Jackie adds.

I smile at her. Suddenly I'm pleased she came. She really seems to have mellowed since I first met her.

If there is no judgement in the Light, it is all the more reason to get these killers judged while they are here on earth.

But, if we can't find Michelle, it is over anyway, Kerry points out.

Gerte nods approvingly at her. *And, we all heard what her aunt said. She is going to die and that can't be changed.*

How can we be sure she knows what she's talking about?

She shrugs.

Listen, why don't you and Kerry just go into the Light and leave the rest of us to get on with this by ourselves, Jackie challenges.

Gerte ignores her and turns to Margaret. *Is there any other way you can think of to help us find this woman?*

Bim adds: *The likelihood is she lives in London.*

Margaret blinks back at us with amusement in her dark eyes. *So why don't we try the telephone book.*

She goes to fetch one, while we try not to feel foolish for failing to think of this ourselves. Opening it on the table, she runs a manicured nail down the names beginning with s.

There are ten people called Michelle Seymour in or around London.

That's easy then, we just check them all, Gerte says, sarcastically.

Margaret rises from the table again and this time returns with a writing pad, a pen, and a crystal on a piece of ribbon.

What are you going to do?

I'm going to narrow your search down to one woman and one address, she confidently assures us.

She writes the ten addresses on separate pieces of paper and places them on the table. Then, she holds the crystal pendulum over them. It swings between them, wildly, at first but gradually it begins to settle into a small circular movement over one of the addresses. When the crystal is completely steady, she hands the piece of paper under it to me.

This is where Michelle Seymour lives.

She has everything to live for Michelle Seymour. She is a twenty six year old musician who plays the violin in a small orchestra. They are preparing for a tour of Eastern Europe and she attends a rehearsal, at a studio in Balham, each afternoon. She is dedicated and talented. A bright future should await her but, according to Bim, she is going to die in three days time, on June 4th.

We know we can't save her, Gerte says. *So we have to concentrate on catching the Weasel.*

I nod in agreement but a part of me is asking the same question that Bim did at the séance. Why can't her fate be changed? Would it matter so very much, if it were? We have discovered that she is another customer of Hamilton Motors. Her car had an annual service carried out by none other than Scott Ramsey, on the day before he went on holiday. Phil's super efficient secretary sent her a reminder to book the car in, one a month earlier than that. It wouldn't have been difficult for Scott to obtain a copy of her key when Michelle brought it in. We know he has one because we see him use it to unlock her car, one day, while she is rehearsing. He lifts the bonnet to take a peek inside at the engine but does nothing more. We are elated to have found him, at last. By the time he drops the bonnet, relocks the car, and returns to his own vehicle - a classic Mercedes - Kerry is sitting in the passenger seat waiting him for him to drive away with her. We're back in business.

He takes her to a lock-up between Thamesmead and Woolwich in South London. It is situated in a row of warehouses on a wide expanse of wasteland. To the north lies the Thames, to the east a railway cutting, to the west there is a patchwork of allotments, and to the south an unfinished estate of houses. It couldn't be more deserted if it were in the wilds of the country.

Kerry summons me there in a panic.

He is inside but I don't think I can go in there on my own.

You could stay outside while I go in, if you prefer.

No, I want to see it, but just not on my own.

We pass through the metal double doors together to find ourselves in a large workshop. On one side it is crammed with tools and engine parts, of every size and description, and on the other, there is the shell of an old Rover which Dead-gorgeous appears to be working on. The bonnet is open and he is loosening a bolt with a spanner. Beside this, under a plastic cover, there is another car, an ancient Jaguar but in mint condition.

I was hoping we'd find your Ford Fiesta, I say to Kerry.

Gerte appears behind us. *They probably stripped that down for spare parts the day after they ran you over, just to get rid of it.* She looks around her. *I think this might be the place where I was murdered. It seems familiar.*

We had better search it for evidence then.

At the back of the workshop, hidden under three large jacks, we discover a trap door. It opens onto a short flight of stairs, leading down to a lower floor, which has been converted into a tiny flat. There's a bathroom, a kitchenette, and a living room. The furniture is a muddle of cast offs; among them a threadbare three piece suite, a wartime utility dining table, and four foldaway wooden chairs. On the floor, but not quite covering it wall to wall, there's a large rectangular rusty-coloured nylon carpet.

Is anything coming back to you, Kerry? Is this where they brought your body, before they buried it?

I'm not sure.

She looks scared to me. *Why don't you keep an eye on Dead-gorgeous upstairs in case he decides to make a move? Gerte and I can take a look around here.*

There must be another room through that door, Gerte says, as soon as she has gone.

Passing through it, we find a bedroom with a large double bed covered by a black satin sheet. The walls are painted black too and, in the centre of each of them, an iron candelabra hangs. In the corner of the room, closest to the door, a camera is mounted on a stand, facing in the direction of the bed. A small monitor rests on the matt black chipboard dressing table, alongside it.

They film what they do? Gerte looks shocked.

If they do and there is something here to prove it, we might be able to get them arrested, before they have the chance to abduct Michelle.

I cross the room to the monitor and press the play button. It crackles into life. A clapper board with the title, *Dead Gorgeous 3,* chalked on it, appears on screen. The opening shot of the film is a close up of a white coffin which has been placed on the black satin sheet of the bed. A man, wearing black from head to toe - including a leather mask, of the type Dead-gorgeous used when he broke into Gail Martos' flat - levers open the lid to reveal a young woman, naked but for the blue satin high heels on her feet. He holds a mirror to her mouth. I can only imagine this is to demonstrate that she is actually dead. What he does next is yet more proof. He lifts her from the coffin, laying her beside it on the bed and nails her hands to the headboard. I can see nothing of the man's face or hair but I can tell from the way he is moving, he is Scott Ramsey.

What is that you have there?

Gerte stops it before Bim, who has homed in on us, can see for herself.

What is it?

Neither of us answers her.

Did they record us?

I nod.

Can it be used as evidence?

I don't think so. Not without other proof. He is wearing a mask.

Who is? Can I see?

Gerte and I glance at each other.

It's me, isn't it?

Yes.

And, the Weasel?

Dead-gorgeous.

What does he do?

It is pretty sick, Bim, I tell her.

Am I still alive in it?

No.

Have you watched it?

No, no, Gerte assures her, immediately.

231

Only the beginning, before anything really happens, I correct her.

But, something does happen?

Yes, I think so.

How do you know that?

It was in the post mortem reports.

Gerte turns on me. *If that's true and it's what I think it is, why didn't you tell us?*

I thought you knew. It came out at Karl's trial.

I didn't go every day. I couldn't face it.

Well, it doesn't matter now.

It does to me! How dare those bastards do that to us? They have to pay for it, Kate. We have to get them put in jail where they belong.

Michelle hums one of the pieces she is going to rehearse later that day as she sips a mint tea. Her elfin face and golden curls are still moist from her morning shower. Her flat is a wreck. She has the habit of leaving towels in wet dollops where they fall - on the bathroom floor and in the bedroom, principally - but there's also the odd one to be found on the work surfaces of the American style kitchen, as well on the back of the sofa. It wouldn't be so bad if it were more spacious but, situated up in the eaves of a house in Lewisham, her flat is tiny.

I'd better get back to the lock-up, Kerry says, watching her. *Today is the day. She looks so happy too.*

We all nod, in agreement.

Gerte asks me: *Do you really believe we should try to stop this from happening? What if it changes everything? What if by saving Michelle something else happens? What if Karl dies, or Kerry's dad, or one of your nephews?*

Using a bunch of what ifs to limit what we do in the present, doesn't make much sense to me, otherwise nobody would ever do anything.

I think you're as scared about this, as I am.

But, we're going to do it, anyway, right, Gerte? That's the point.

So tell me again, why we can't just rely on the police to act on the recording of Bim, we delivered to them?

We've run out of time. We can't be sure they will do what we need them to, when we need them to do it. The only way to be sure is to do this, ourselves.

But, they're the only ones who can arrest these men.

And, they will, but we're going to have to help them first.

I'll be off then, Kerry repeats, without moving anywhere.

Let us know if the Weasel shows up, will you?

Sure, she promises, and after another lingering look at Michelle, she is gone.

The rest of us spend the day easing Michelle's passage. It might be all we can do for her. A cup which topples from the table falls onto the tiled floor without breaking. The mobile phone, she has forgotten to charge and place in her handbag, finds it way there fully charged. We nag her into phoning her mother too just in case it is their last opportunity to speak.

She is wearing a floral skirt, with a white blouse, and a pair of sandals. I would have preferred her to have chosen some jeans to put on but at least the skirt is loose and the sandals flat so she can run if the need arises.

She and three of her colleagues are lunching in a Balti House in Balham before their rehearsal. The car journey there with her is nerve wracking. We constantly expect her to be abducted. We know Scott Ramsey is at the lock-up but the Weasel could be anywhere. We scan and rescan the cars around us and the pedestrians passing by, searching for his face. It would be a relief to see him. The strain of having no idea where or when he will show up is far worse.

The restaurant is packed, which can only mean the food must be good, because the interior – tables, benches, cream walls, with several faded posters of India – is unprepossessing. The four musicians, all women, keep up a salacious banter as they eat. It is the type of conversation women only have among themselves because it is gender subversive, born from understanding one another from the inside out, not the other way around.

Is there any male member in this orchestra these four women haven't auditioned, Bim smirks after awhile.

They spend so much time together it is inevitable there'd be affairs. How else would they get to meet anyone?

But, two of these women are married, Kate, Gerte points out.

Not everyone shares your moral scruples, clearly.

Ooh, is that a confession. Do tell, Bim encourages me.

No, sorry. I've never knowingly had sex with a married man.

How disappointing. I have.

So have I, Jackie admits.

If a man is prepared to be unfaithful with you, it is the best proof you can have that he is capable of being unfaithful to you, Gerte informs her.

I never wanted to take him home to meet my mother. It was just

234

mindless sex, Jackie laughs.

Before I met Reece, I had a relationship with a man who kept saying he was going to leave his wife. Everything seemed so good between us I wanted him to, but when he did, he lost his sex appeal in a little under a week. There was a slob in him I'd never met before, because his wife had been the one dealing with that part of him. I suddenly realised to my horror, she was the most important person in my relationship. Without her it didn't work. It was terrible.

Am I the only person here thinking, poor wife?

Do you ever think you might be a little too much in your head, Gerte?

Maybe you're right. I never enjoyed sex enough to want to sleep around.

The rest of us turn to examine her with curiosity.

Jackie breaks the silence. *Wasn't Karl any good at it then?*

We all lean closer.

Well, we met as students and I don't have anyone else to measure him against.

And, size does matter, Jackie quips.

I thought that was a myth.

Width, not length, silly. She points to Michelle's friends. *If those women had had more sex before they'd gotten married, they wouldn't be so rampant now.*

Oh, I don't know. According to my married friends not having sex seems to be the normal matrimonial state, Bim confides. *That's probably why they have to have affairs.*

There are different kinds of love, you know. Some couples might be happy together whether or not they're having sex.

That's exactly what I'm saying, Gerte. That's the whole problem with marriage. As soon as you live in the same space as a man, some kind of incest taboo asserts itself.

Don't tell me you read about that in Vogue, Jackie teases.

Bim starts to laugh: *No, it is a well known geographical fact. You ask the triffid, she'll back me up.*

235

Once Michelle is ensconced inside the studio for her rehearsal, we know she'll be safe for the rest of the afternoon. It is when she comes out to go home, we'll have to worry. We wait for her in a small pub - a dismal place with dark red flocked wallpaper and a sticky worn carpet. Its only saving grace is that it is adjacent to the studio with a good view of both the entrance and Michelle's car.

In the public bar, a couple of regulars are perched on stools, chatting to the landlord. They're the only ones here who are actually alive. The saloon bar, where we are, is teeming with spooks.

Bim leans across to the next table to address a stern faced middle-aged woman who is wearing an old fashioned coat and hat. *Is this some kind of meeting?*

She stares at her uncomprehendingly so she tries again. *Why are you here?*

The woman answers as though she is being asked a trick question. *Waiting for the all clear to sound?*

What's that?

She examines Bim, wearily. *For the air raid.*

What air raid?

Gerte nudges her. *I think she is talking about the war.*

What war?

Gerte rolls her eyes. *The Second World War.*

Bim addresses the woman again with her new information. *Oh, you mean bombs.*

The woman frowns as though she can't work out whether or not she is making fun of her.

Bim whispers to the rest of us. *Do you think we should tell her the war is over?*

I doubt she'd believe us, if we did, I reply. *You know how it was with the Spanish housekeeper. They're not proper spirits.*

Yes, they're more like fragments of energy that have somehow become separated off so they can continue doing whatever it is

236

they do here, even though the rest of them has moved on into the Light, Gerte says.

Bim frowns at her. *I don't see how that can be possible.*

Don't you? I think it might explain reincarnation.

What?

Having more than one life.

I know what it is. I just have no idea what you are talking about.

Don't you believe....

Do you have to yap so loudly, Jackie interrupts. *Our companions are beginning to stare and they don't look very happy to me.*

Neither would you, if you'd waited all these years for an all clear to sound?

They must have been killed really suddenly, don't you think?

Oh, I know about this, Gerte whispers, exaggeratedly. *Part of the underground collapsed during an air raid killing sixty eight people. It was right by here. There is a plaque commemorating them in the ticket hall of the station but it has the wrong body count on it. I read about it in a book. It happened in October 1940. A bomb fell on the road above and one of the underground tunnels - which was full of people sheltering from the bomb raid - partially collapsed. Earth and water from the broken water mains, and sewers above, flooded into what was left of that tunnel, as well as the one running alongside it. It must have been an awful way to die.*

We gaze at the crowd sitting in small groups around us. Nobody is talking, that's what strikes me most about them. Have they been silent all these years, or did they simply run out of things to say to one another? An emotional scale from resignation to bitter resentment is etched on their faces. A few are sleeping and there are two children, sitting side by side on their mother's lap, backed into the shadow of her arms, an expression of terror and shock in their eyes. They loll their heads against her chest like zombies, pale-faced, open-mouthed, but silent as the grave. On the floor, and scattered across some of the tables, are their possessions. Bundles of this and that tied up with string; wicker shopping baskets and leather handbags; a pail and cloths; whatever they were carrying when the siren went off and they took shelter in the underground station. The men are in work clothes. A few wear suits. The women have dresses and coats on. One or two are wearing aprons and a woman, on the table next to us, has curlers in her hair covered by a headscarf. It is almost unbearable to watch them, their sadness is so palpable. I glance at the living sitting in the public bar. Do they feel it too? Do they drink to drown the sorrow of these people, or their own?

What is going on here?

Kerry has appeared beside us.

We think they were killed in an air raid, during the Second World War, Gerte explains.

Why are you whispering?

Jackie thinks we're disturbing them.

Kerry glances at Jackie. I wonder whether like me, she is marvelling at how much she has changed. There was a time when she would have relished the idea of disturbing someone.

Is there any news, Kerry?

Yes, the Weasel is here. Dead-gorgeous has just picked him up from Victoria coach station. He has taken him straight to the lock-up. He is still there now but Dead-gorgeous is on the move. I think he is headed here.

Okay, you get back to him, I tell her. *We mustn't lose him. And, Bim, how would you feel about keeping an eye on the Weasel at the lock-up?*

Anything, if it gets me away from these dead people, she says, without a trace of irony.

Dead-gorgeous gets out of his Mercedes and makes his way nonchalantly to where Michelle's car is parked on the other side of the street. Nobody notices him except us. I find that so extraordinary, that someone can hide their murderous intent with such ease. It makes me wonder about all those men and women I've stood beside on crowded trains and buses: or those who milled about me in the street, or queued with me in the supermarket. How many of them were on their way to kill someone? How many were planning a murder? You never know what's going on inside someone's head. Not until it's too late.

Unlocking the driver's door, Scott bends in to release the bonnet. He lifts and secures it with the metal rod, which - with a little help from Jackie - immediately slips its notch and crashes down on top of his fingers.

That's for hurting Gail, she says, triumphantly.

He rips off his latex glove, and pushes his hand into his mouth, as much to stop himself yelling as to soothe his throbbing fingers. They are still red and awkward with pain, as he puts the glove back on, and reaches into the engine to tinker with it.

We can't see what he is doing but we can guess what the result is going to be.

Glancing around, Kerry asks: *Are there no CCTV cameras here?*

I doubt he'd be here, if there were. He is bound to have checked it out, beforehand.

But, isn't that a camera over there at the garage across the street?

Yes, but it's facing in the wrong direction.

The camera is secured about a metre above the kiosk of the garage. Jackie studies it for a few seconds.

It would be a piece of cake to turn that so it records what he is doing, you know, she announces. *Shall I?*

We nod, gleefully.

She really is incredible. She doesn't even have to approach it to turn it towards us.

Now let's get him to look at it.

She throws a stone across the road.

Scott brings his head up out of the engine. The flicker of puzzlement on his face soon becomes suspicion. His eyes dart up and down the street, nervously, before deciding it was nothing. Closing the bonnet, he removes his gloves and places them in the pocket of his blue overalls. He has just sabotaged Michelle's engine in broad daylight without a single person showing one jot of interest but at least, thanks to Jackie, he has been recorded doing it.

Michelle Seymour leaves the rehearsal studio, at seven o'clock in the evening, clutching her violin case. Getting into her car, she starts the engine without problem and pulls away from the kerb to make her way home. She glances in her mirror as she completes the manoeuvre but she doesn't notice the classic Mercedes, one car behind her, nor the blonde-haired man driving it.

It is a beautiful evening. The showers of the previous few days have left the streets wet but fresh smelling. The puddles glitter in the mellow light of a sun which is beginning to dip below the rising crescent moon. I couldn't think of a less sinister scene than this: sun, splashing cars, late night shoppers, commuters hurrying home from work, and young revellers hitting the bars before dinner. It seems impossible that anyone could harm her.

She is almost home, taking a short-cut to avoid the traffic through the back streets of Catford, past terrace after terrace of bay-windowed artisan cottages, when the car gives a curious shudder. The engine recovers, for several hopeful seconds, but another follows, and another, until there is no power left. She only just manages to pull it out of the flow of traffic before it stalls. Turning into a side street, and realising it is a hill, she coasts down it in the hope she can jump start the engine. She just makes it to the kerb, at the bottom, as the wheels finally lose momentum without the engine coming back into life. Here she sits, wondering what she should do now.

The Mercedes has pulled in behind her. The driver gets out and starts walking towards her car. He knocks on her window, wearing his gloves again.

Kerry, who has driven here with him, passes into the back of Michelle's car with the rest of us, while she is cautiously buzzing down the window, by no more than a fraction, to speak with him.

Smiling broadly at her, he says: *Hi, remember me?*

She screws up her eyes and looks embarrassed. He is familiar to her but she can't quite place him.

While they're distracting each other, I reach down into Michelle's bag behind the passenger seat and take out her mobile phone. Pressing the camera record button on it, I place it on the back seat, at an angle where it should pick up his face.

From the garage? Remember? I'm Scott, the mechanic.

She returns his smile. *Oh yes. I've never been so glad to see anyone in my life.*

He laughs. *I thought you were having trouble, when I saw you pull over.*

Thank you so much for stopping, she gushes, her voice thick with gratitude. She can't believe her luck.

Professional pride. It was only serviced last week, wasn't it? Pop the bonnet for me and I'll take a look.

He sounds so genuine, like he believes what he is saying himself, Kerry says. *How does he do that?*

He is a psychopath, I answer. *They're like human cobras.*

Scott appears to be fiddling with the engine.

Is it anything serious?

He closes the bonnet. *I'm afraid so. It needs surgery.*

Expensive?

You know how it is with cars, he chuckles.

Michelle grimaces.

Don't look so worried. I'll phone for a tow truck and get it brought back to the garage, where I can take a better look at it.

I'm covered by one of the motor organisations for that.

It won't cost you anything, I promise. It's not far anyway. It won't take a minute, and with a bit of luck you'll get the car back by tomorrow evening. It might not even cost that much either, if I can find a second hand part.

Do you think you could? I'm a musician in an orchestra. It looks glam from the outside but it doesn't pay well.

He has got her. The way he enticed her away from using her own breakdown service was so neatly done, it is hard not to be impressed.

He nods. *Understood. I'll do all I can to keep the cost down. Okay?*

Thanks, she beams back at him.

He has acted on Michelle's defences like a sedative. She suspects nothing. Strolling to the back of the vehicle he makes his call.

He must be letting The Weasel know how he's getting on, Jackie says.

Or he is just pretending to make a call, Gerte replies.

Right, that's arranged, he tells Michelle when he comes back. *Now, how are we going to get you home?*

I can get a taxi.

You'll be waiting all night. Not a nice place to be hanging around either.

Maybe I could get a bus.

He looks doubtfully at the violin case on the back seat with us. *They're very crowded at this time of day and that looks too expensive for you to want to knock it about.*

Well, I don't live that far from here. I'll walk. It won't do me any harm.

Do you really think that's a good idea at this time in the evening? Listen, if it isn't far, why don't I give you a lift?

No, please, I wouldn't dream of it. I wasn't fishing for one, really. I can manage perfectly well on my own.

His handsome face fills with concern. *I have a younger sister about your age. I wouldn't want her finding her way home from here on her own. Come on, let me make sure you get back, safely.*

But, what about the car? Won't you have to be here for the tow truck?

It's going to take about twenty minutes to arrive. There's another job. I'll be back in time, don't worry. I wouldn't forgive myself if anything happened to you on your way home from here.

242

Come on, set my mind at rest. Let me get you home, safely, first.

She hesitates, possibly because we're all screaming in her ear: *No, no. Don't listen to him!*

He has made it sound as though everything around her is dangerous, except him. His insistence is hypnotic. If she were able to think clearly for a few seconds, she'd take her own advice and jump on a bus, ring for a cab, or walk home. She'd be able to get on with her life without incident - rather than risking everything by getting into the car of a man she barely knows. But, she's tired and fed up and the idea of someone else taking over is too appealing to resist.

Okay, then, if you're sure you don't mind, it would be a help, she agrees, despite us.

He is such a gentleman, Scott. He helps her out of the car and walks her to the passenger side of his Mercedes. He even holds the door while she goes to climb in, but as she puts one leg into the well and leans forward to shift her weight inside, he pushes the white handkerchief he has in one hand over her mouth.

She doesn't realise what is happening and, by the time she figures it out and starts to struggle with him, she has already been overwhelmed.

Please can we do something to help her now, Kerry pleads.

We all feel the pain in her request. She isn't just seeing this happening to another woman. She is re-experiencing what happened to her.

Michelle isn't our only priority, I explain to her, gently. *We want to save her but we also want to put these killers in jail where they belong. And, to do that, we must let them play this out a little more. She has to see the Weasel, before we can intervene.*

Dead-gorgeous arranges Michelle so it looks as though she has fallen asleep in the passenger seat and fastens her seat belt around her. In the distance, there is a traffic warden and he hurriedly pumps a couple of coins into the meter by his Mercedes. Then, he pulls the hood of the sweatshirt he is wearing under his overalls up over his head before returning to Michelle's car and hopping into the driver's seat. The engine starts, immediately. He has already fixed whatever was wrong with it.

243

Jackie asks: *Why is he bothering to move the car? Why not simply leave it here?*

So that anyone who has seen him here in this road won't connect him with the abduction of Michelle Seymour, whose car will be found in a different road altogether, I reason.

But, isn't there more of a risk that he might leave some evidence by getting into it?

Between the gloves and the overalls - particularly with that hood up - he'll probably be okay. He didn't leave any evidence in Bim's car, or Gerte's, at least. And, even if he does, he has the perfect alibi. He serviced Michelle's car, last week. Who's going to suspect him?

Let's frighten him, Jackie suggests. *If we manage to get him to leave her car, according to your reckoning Kate, there'll be more chance somebody might remember seeing him here with it.*

She looks around at us all to make sure we're in agreement with her and then, before Scott can drive away, she sets off the anti-theft device. It screams out loudly in short yowling bursts.

What the hell is wrong with you, he curses, banging the steering wheel in frustration.

The traffic warden is getting closer and he can't shut the alarm up.

Visibly shaken, he gets out and hovers, for a few seconds, as he thinks about whether he should disconnect the wires in the engine, but he is out of time, the traffic warden is still advancing so he abandons the car where it is.

The Weasel is dressed like a scene of crime officer - in white overalls, a plastic hair cap, latex gloves and plastic shoes - when we arrive at the lock up. Over his mouth and nose, he is wearing a mask. He places a plastic sheet on the ground beside the car and the two men lift Michelle onto the middle of it, wrapping her up like a filo pastry parcel. Then, they carry her inside, passing her down through the open trap door to the lower floor. She is still unconscious but her limbs are stirring, and as they put her on the floor, she emits a faint moan.

The Weasel strokes her hair. *It's all right pretty one, you're home now. I'm going to run you a nice bubble bath. That will help to relax you.*

I'm pushing off for a bit, Gordon, Dead-gorgeous announces.

The Weasel's eyes, the only visible part of his anatomy, darken. *You don't want to watch?*

No, I'd rather wait until...until she's mine. I'll come back about 2am, shall I?

Where are you going? He sounds tetchy.

A club. I'm going to have a few jars, that's all.

On your own?

Of course.

The Weasel hesitates. Is he wondering whether Scott is telling him the truth? They're such an odd couple: Scott Ramsey, tall, charming, and good-looking, and Gordon Richards small, nerdy and nondescript. It doesn't altogether surprise me their alliance carries tension within it.

You've always watched before.

Twice before. But, I've seen it now.

I thought you liked watching. His voice is thin with petulance.

Gordon! For Heaven's sake! I've had enough of watching. Okay? Just leave her on the bed next door when you've done, and I'll come back around two. You can stay and watch me for a change, if you like.

Have it your own way, Gordon concedes. *I'll leave her on the bed, if that is what you want, provided I've finished with her by then.*

Shall I come back at three to be on the safe side?

Okay.

Where are we going to dump this one? Oxley Woods is out, I take it?

I know a place the other side of Bromley which will do.

Right, I'll leave you to it.

It seems strange.

What does?

You not wanting to be here with me, Scott. I thought we were partners.

We are partners. I've just brought her here for you, haven't I? But, your fun isn't mine, and mine isn't yours. He smiles. *I'll be back later.*

You are coming back then?

You bet I am. I've got the camera set up for her. Go and see. That is the main meal for me. I just don't fancy having the first course, tonight.

Help me get her into the bathroom, before you go, the Weasel instructs.

The two men carry her in there, still wrapped in the plastic sheet.

Let's put her inside the bath.

Do you want the plastic sheet off her?

Yes, that is a good idea. He peels it open at the top. *You hold her up, while I pull it from under her.*

Dead-gorgeous clasps her under the arms and lifts her and, as the Weasel drags the plastic sheet away and throws it on the floor, Michelle starts to moan and moves her head from side to side. Her eyes glitter through her eyelashes.

Just the way you like them, Dead-gorgeous comments.

Her sandal, where is it? It's missing!

It must have fallen off.

The Weasel looks through the doorway. *It's probably in the car. Go and get it would you?*

Okay, boss, I'm on my way, Dead-gorgeous laughs.

246

He walks briskly through the living room to the tiny lobby, at the foot of the stairs, bounding up them, as he keeps his eyes trained on the floor for the sandal.

The Weasel picks up the plastic sheet and listening to Scott's tread above, he places it at the foot of the stairs. Then, he goes to the kitchen and rummages around in the drawers. He can't seem to find what he is looking for. He searches the cupboard under the sink next. Poking his head inside, he emerges, holding a hammer.

Dead-gorgeous has found the sandal. It must have fallen off, when they lifted her out of the car. The Weasel hears him slide the door of the lock-up across and secure it, before climbing through the open trap door. The stairs are wide enough and sufficiently evenly spaced to descend, face forwards. Dead-gorgeous is clearly well-practised at doing this, because he strides down easily, two at a time. He looks through the living room into the bathroom, which is empty of the Weasel.

Gordon, where are you? I've found the sandal.

He steps onto the plastic sheet, craning his neck this way and that, but he doesn't glance behind him so he doesn't see his partner standing at the back of the stairs, the hammer in his hand held high.

The Weasel creeps silently out from his hiding place and brings it crashing down, onto Scott's skull with a dull thud. A fan of blood opens on the wall and he pauses to watch as it begins to trickle down the paint work. Scott drops to the floor and when the Weasel turns his attention back to him, he raises the hammer a second time and smashes it down in the same place as before, exposing Scott's brains. He inspects the wound, closely, evidently fascinated by the damage he has done. And, then he studies the hammer head too, smiling with interest at the bloody hair and tissue adhering to it. Finally, he sees the splatter pattern of blood on his white overalls and gasps with excitement.

I'm here, Scott, he answers softly, with a smile on his face. *Where are you?* Bending down he releases Michelle's missing sandal from the dead man's hand. *Thanks for fetching this, Scott. It wouldn't have been the same without it. It looks like you're going to watch me after all. I want you to watch, Scott. In fact, I*

247

insist upon it. But, first I have to change out of my dirty overalls.

Scott Ramsey's spirit rises up from his body, oozing shock and disbelief like blood. He cannot take the scene in. He fades and forms, fades and forms, as he struggles to understand what has happened to him, and the irrevocableness of it. His murderer doesn't pause over his loss. He tosses the hammer onto the plastic sheet with him and drags this out of the way behind the stairs

You murdered me, Scott accuses. *He murdered me,* he repeats to us, as soon as he registers our presence.

He murdered us too! And, you helped him, Gerte responds, angrily.

Not all of you, he quibbles.

Her presence swells like a storm.

I am only being accurate, he tries to mollify her. *I helped him with two of you.*

Three, Kerry corrects. *I was brought here, after he killed me.*

But, I didn't have a hand in abducting you, he wheedles.

You helped him dispose of my body.

Damn and blast! This is Hell isn't it! I'm going to spend eternity with you lot accusing me.

You don't get it do you? One way or another you robbed us of our lives, Bim shouts at him.

And, that bastard has just robbed me of mine. Which of those two things do you think I'm going to be more upset about?

Get away from us, Gerte commands.

He moves away but he doesn't disappear. *Come on, ladies. Be reasonable. I've got nowhere else to go.*

We don't care. Leave us alone.

But, you need me. I can help you get him. That is what you want, isn't it? That is why you're here. Well, I know him better than anyone, he tempts.

We draw ourselves into a huddle, several metres from Scott, so he can't eavesdrop on our discussion about this.

I don't know why we're even considering this, Gerte snaps.

I'll tell you why, because Michelle is still alive. If there is the slightest chance he could help us to save her, we should accept

248

his offer, Jackie reasons.

Bim looks distressed at this proposal. *But, he should go straight to Hell for what he has done.*

I'm pretty certain that's not going to happen so you might as well try and reconcile yourself to it, Gerte counsels, before adding: *which doesn't mean we have to put up with him hanging around us for a second longer.*

But, if it helps us to rescue Michelle, perhaps we should.

He helped the Weasel kill me!

He helped to kill you, and look, you're still here.

I'm dead! What is it you don't understand about that?

As is he! And, you both still exist.

Oh, so there is no offence in murder, is that what the woman who has spent most of her afterlife torturing the man that only jilted her thinks?

Jackie laughs. *And, I am now able to see that nothing matters, simply because spirit endures.*

Bim glowers at her. *You've seen the Light too, haven't you?*

She is not suggesting we give up, just that we accept Dead-gorgeous' help, Kerry points out.

But he is so new in spirit, what can he do?

He is cunning, Jackie says.

And, untrustworthy, Bim counters.

He is also here, whether we want him to be or not, I trump them both.

This is the deciding factor. He stays because we don't know how to banish him and as long as he is around we might as well accept whatever help he can offer us.

Realising our verdict, he asks, enthusiastically: *Right, ladies, what's the plan?*

We are going to rescue Michelle and put the Weasel in prison, I inform him.

The Weasel is Gordon?

Who else? I look through the living room, towards the bathroom. *Where is he?*

Still getting changed, I imagine. He is very particular, our Gordon.

249

Your Gordon, Bim corrects.

One of us should keep an eye on him, while we're trying to get Michelle out of here.

Done, Bim obligingly agrees, before disappearing to find him.

Michelle, Michelle, I whisper in her ear. *You have to stand up.*

She looks about her, bewildered, rather than frightened. It occurs to me she might be wondering whether she is dead.

Michelle, please try and stand up, I tell her again. You must get out of here.

She begins to respond to what she is being told to do. She sits up and puts her soles of her feet down on the bottom of the enamel bath, ready to struggle upwards.

We help her as best we can, prodding and lifting, until we get her standing.

Gingerly, she lifts one leg over the edge of the bath and stumbles out. She is walking like a newly born animal as we coax her out of the bathroom, across the living room, and towards the stairs.

Where are your car keys, Scott?

He motions towards his body.

Well, get them.

With our help, Michelle treads air up the stairs because left to her own devices, she wouldn't be able to coordinate her legs sufficiently well to mount a single one.

How is she going to drive a car?

She's not, Jackie is.

I am?

You're better than any of the rest of us at moving objects around.

Objects, yes, a car might be a different matter.

I managed to turn the steering wheel, in Spain, when the Weasel was driving. If I could do that, you will be able to do a lot more.

Using Scott's keys to open the padlock on the inside of the door, at the front of the lock-up, I push it open.

The cool evening air hits Michelle like a slap in the face and she straightens up a little but she still cannot support herself. For appearances sake, when we open the car, we put her in the driver's seat but she is too groggy to drive. Jackie sits beside her and starts the car up, without difficulty.

The Weasel is coming, Bim announces, joining us. *He heard the lock-up door open.*

She is holding a plastic shopping bag with something inside it.

What have you got there?

She reaches in and pulls out her blue satin shoes, triumphantly.

They'll come in handy, I comment, dryly.

They're evidence, they are, she tells me, in a mock London accent, reminding me scarily of Dick Van Dyke in the film, Mary Poppins.

The Weasel strolls towards us, wearing a clean pair of overalls, as though he believes he has all the time in the world to stop us getting away. He can see Michelle lying back in the driver's seat, scarcely able to focus her eyes, so he must be congratulating himself on her recapture already. If he is curious about how she managed to get Scott's keys and use them to escape, he doesn't show it. His calm acceptance, of whatever he is presented, with never ceases to unnerve me.

Unlock the door, Michelle, he purrs. *You know you can't run away from me, love. Come on, be sensible.* Then, more harshly, he commands her: *Simon says unlock the doors.*

That will work, dick-head, Jackie answers him.

Bim laughs. *Bim says you haven't a prayer.*

Michelle writhes in fear at the sound of his voice. She knows she has to get away but can't marshal her mind and limbs to do more than lie there. The Weasel strolls around the back of the car to the passenger side.

He has the hammer in his hand, Kerry warns. *He is going to smash the window.*

Do you think now would be a good time to get us out of here, I say to Jackie, who like the rest of us has been transfixed by him.

She doesn't pause for a second. She throws the car into gear, makes the accelerator pedal move downwards and we lurch forwards, several metres.

The Weasel jumps clear in confusion. He can't work out why

the car appears to be moving on its own without any input from Michelle.

Moments later, we've left him behind us. It really is that easy. We start to cheer. We have gotten away.

Hey, look at Michelle, Bim exclaims.

We do as we're told. She has fallen asleep in the driver's seat. She looks peaceful.

Can't you see? We've done it! We've changed her destiny. We've saved her life. Death has left her. She's going to live until she's ninety two!

Our plan is to drive her to the nearest hospital, except an argument breaks out over which one would be least likely to give her a fatal infection were she to be admitted. After much discussion, we agree to take her to a police station instead but then there is a difference of opinion over this too. A general worry arises that her story won't be taken seriously, that she'll be dismissed as a crack head. I protest at this cynicism but I'm wasting my time. We're neurotic parents, where Michelle is concerned. We're so delighted to have saved her life we can't bear to hand her over to the care of anyone else.

It is dark outside, a fine drizzle of rain distorting the rays of the street lights, making them spin and sparkle through the car windows like fireworks. I never thought we'd pull this off, I really didn't, and so far nothing terrible has happened to us for doing it. I'm glad. We needed this, all of us. After everything we've been through, we needed to win a round. All we have to do now is to wait for Michelle to tell her story, with a little bit of help from us, and the Weasel is going to jail. As soon as we drop her off, I shall get Carrie to send the police straight to the lock-up so they'll find Scott's body, before Gordon has a chance to dispose of it. They can hold him for that murder, while they investigate the others. When they discover the wig, in Spain, he is all but convicted.

I can see a white van in the rear view mirror, Jackie informs us.

Bim yells in panic: *What do we do? What do we do?*

It might just be a coincidence, Gerte soothes.

We all turn around to get a better look.

252

Sorry ladies, check the number plate. It is him, Scott confirms.
Jackie shrugs. *So what? There is nothing he can do.*

Then, why is he following us?

Do you want me to lose him?

Can you?

What do you think?

Please be careful of the wheels, Scott warns, as she accelerates.
I've only just finished restoring her, he adds, defensively, when
the temperature around him drops to subzero.

Jackie turns onto the dual carriageway, in the direction of
central London. The Mercedes doesn't even break into a sweat, as
we weave in and out of the lanes to get further ahead.

What did I tell you? We've lost him.

I nervously look behind us but she is right. There's no sign of
the white van.

*Turn off at the next exit, Jackie. It will lead us through Catford.
We need to make a decision about what we are going to do with
Michelle. The sooner we get her into protective custody the
better.*

The traffic lights are against us, at the last major intersection,
before Catford. Michelle is slowly becoming more alert. Her eyes
are open, and although she still can't quite grasp what is
happening to her, it can only be a question of time before the drug
completely wears off. I use our enforced stop to persuade the
others we should drive her straight to my old police station where
we will be able to deposit her into the safe hands of Nigs and
Fester. The rest will be up to them and to her.

As the lights change to green, we've already reached the
midway point of the intersection, when I notice something
peculiar. To our left, a battered old Mini is approaching us at
speed. Two teenage boys are in the front but behind them I think I
glimpse a familiar figure.

Somewhere inside me a siren begins to wail. The Mini jumps
the lights and everything slips into slow motion as it lurches
towards the driver's door of the Mercedes. Jackie takes evasive
action to protect Michelle but the car spins, three hundred and
sixty degrees, making the impact unavoidable.

I take in the shock on the faces of those young lads as they lose their lives but Sergeant Ross, sitting in the back of the Mini, is smiling genially at me.

She is not going to live until she's ninety two anymore, is she, Bim?

Surrounded by the deafening din of bending metal, I can't concentrate sufficiently to pick up her answer.

It stops as suddenly as it started and the car is enveloped in an unsettling stillness. We stagger out of the mess of metal: all of us - the teenagers, Michelle, Sergeant Ross, and us.

What have you done to my car?

Nobody answers Scott. We are all staring at Michelle's body lying in the road. Her head and chest are mushy with bloody tissue and there is a thin silver thread running from her physical being to her spiritual one which is hovering next to us, calmly observing the scene.

Let her live, I plead with Sergeant Ross. *Otherwise we've done this for nothing. Please let her live.*

Not my call, Madding, he answers.

Whose is it then?

Hers, he says, quietly.

The two boys have spotted their bodies inside the wreck of the Mini.

What is my dad going to say?

It was your idea to borrow his car.

They're just zit-faced kids. They can't be more than five years older than Sam. Their poor parents! They should be at home, not mangled to death in that car wreckage. They should be in bed, asleep. So why the hell aren't they?

There is no need to worry about any of that now, boys, Sergeant Ross reassures them. *It is time to go.*

They are too young to have any reason to think of bolting. They do as they're told and follow him towards the Light.

I know it is there but I don't dare look, just in case it draws me in too. Michelle's aunt Milly is beside us. She holds out her hand to her niece who takes it and the silver thread linking her to her body dissolves. She too is going into the Light. It is over, then.

All our efforts have come to nothing: fifth gear to reverse in a matter of seconds. I can barely believe it. I notice Scott walking towards the Light without waiting to be asked. I'm about to protest, when I realise Jackie, Gerte, and Kerry are following behind.

What are you doing?

But, they don't even turn to look back at me. How could they just go off, without a word? How could they do that, after everything we've shared?

Sergeant Ross calls to me: *What about you, Madding? Have you had enough yet?*

Not nearly, enough, I answer back, defiantly.

I feel the brightness of the Light. I'm warmed by it. I could so easily be uplifted. And, in the next moment, it is gone.

They didn't even say goodbye, Bim wails, clutching a blue satin shoe.

You've lost one, I tell her; not wanting to acknowledge how betrayed I'm feeling myself.

I put it on her body. They'll know she is one of us that way.

Why didn't you go into the Light?

I started this by asking you to find my body. I'm not going anywhere until it is settled.

I remember Gerte saying something similar once. She was going to see it through to the finish. Perhaps, she thought she had. She chose to make Michelle's death the finish. I still feel I have something to fight on for though and I'm suffused with warmth towards Bim for keeping me company. I'm nothing without a twin.

Why leave only one shoe on her body?

I'm going to take the other one back to the lock up. She hands me Michelle's mobile phone. *Send a message to the police.*

I look at her quizzically. *What shall I say?*

Tell them you witnessed the crash and that Michelle told you the address of the lock-up where she was held by her abductors before she died.

I start to write the text message.

Have you seen him?

I look towards where she's indicating.

A muttering crowd has gathered on the pavement. *No one is going to get out of there alive*, I hear one of them predict. *Has someone called an ambulance?* In the thick of them, the Weasel is standing. He is grinning from ear to ear.

The newspapers regurgitate the story, over and over again, during the following days. Michelle Seymour was the unluckiest of women, they agree. She was abducted, in broad daylight from a busy London street, without anybody noticing, and yet, despite being drugged, incredibly, she managed to get away after overpowering her attacker and setting light to the lock-up, where she was being held. It should have ended happily but, tragically, as she made her escape in her abductor's car, a couple of joy riders - neither of whom was old enough to hold a licence – jumped a red light and ploughed into the side of the car, killing her. The two teenage boys, one of whom had taken his father's Mini, without permission, also died. In another twist, it is revealed that Ms Seymour wasn't killed, instantly. She spoke to an anonymous bystander, before she died, who texted the police from the crash site to say she had named her abductor as being Scott Ramsey - the same man whose body the police later found, burned beyond recognition, at the lock-up. To cap it all, when the police arrived at the scene of Ms Seymour's crash, she was found to be wearing a blue satin high heel belonging to the last victim of the most wanted criminal in the country, the June Killer who has abducted and murdered four other young women. Who else could this be but Scott Ramsey? There is no mention of Gordon Richards. The police have no evidence against him. Even if they could prove the two men knew each other, they would be a world away from securing a conviction against him. Besides, he seems to have taken up residence abroad. The Spanish authorities can deal with him, if he starts up again over there.

Bim and I observe all of these developments in a state of misery. We have failed in the task we set ourselves one year ago. Our dream of bringing the Weasel to justice is cinders and ash. That's why he was smiling when we last saw him. He knew that by setting the lock-up on fire, he'd destroy the evidence against him, and get away with murder. Nothing can mitigate our distress. Our glass is determinedly half empty. The dregs we are left with we toss aside as not worth having. We feel abandoned by Jackie, Gerte and Kerry too. Ironically, to lose them so suddenly, without the opportunity to say goodbye, makes it seem to us as though they've died. That this was the fate they chose, rather than being with us, makes mourning them more difficult. We're too angry.

Afterlife begins again because of Bim. She suddenly throws down a challenge to me, as we're gloomily watching the ten o'clock news.

We're not really going to let that murdering bastard get away with this, are we? We're better than that, aren't we?

Are we?

You know we are.

No, I don't.

We can get this guy, I just know we can. We solved the whole case, didn't we?

Okay, that's working a little...more, more.

We're completely brilliant. Come on, Kate, if we don't believe in us, who will? We can do this. You just have to come up with the right idea.

There is one thing we could do.

What?

It is a little west of acceptable police procedure.

So are we. Will it work?

Depends. Did the Weasel have a gas cooker in his Leicester house?

Craig Barker, the student living in the converted basement of Gordon Richard's house, is applying for jobs. He is due to graduate, this summer, in psychology. He is regretting choosing this subject, however, because whatever he does to market himself to prospective employers is likely to be seen as a test. If he doesn't know how to present himself, successfully, how good at psychology can he be? His anxiety is such that he has decided to use a scatter gun approach to finding a career for himself. It doesn't much matter to him what he does, as long as it makes him lots of money - enough to enjoy a luxurious lifestyle, and attract a lovely looking wife. He needs all the help he can get in this latter department, he feels. He is not an ugly young man so much as ungainly. He lacks confidence. Or is it polish? He isn't entirely sure what, but he lacks something, that much is certain. He has friends. Of course, he does. He has even had a couple of sexually consenting girlfriends. But, he also has the fear, that were he to disappear tomorrow, nobody would notice his absence for a considerable time, if at all. He makes no impression - that is his problem. Yet, this is precisely what he must do, if he is to get himself a job. Pops has offered him a position in his advertising agency, if all else fails, but Craig cannot bear the prospect of that humiliation. His father is an older, if less sandy, version of himself but he is the type of man who could make an impression comatose. Why couldn't Craig have been born to an underachiever? As it is, he will be the first generation of Barkers to be less successful than the one before. The dynasty will change direction with him. He will be the point at which they're forced to learn the painful lesson that social mobility is a lift that goes up, and down. No! He won't let that happen! He has spent two weeks working on his curriculum vitae, wringing every Saturday and summer job he has ever had - all four of them - for evidence of his employability. Then, there are his activities at university. His one year on the student newspaper. His two years in the chess club. And, his six months in the orienteering club, which he only joined so he could imply some kind of physical activity, other than pub crawls and sex, in his letters of application. He has chosen the civil service, four national banks, an entertainment group, and a magazine company which owns a couple of travel titles as the pool in which he is about to go fishing for a career. Whatever he catches will have to make his father proud, and his friends jealous. He has been cooped up in his bedsit, alternately revising for his finals, next month, and sweating about his future, since the Easter break. He was lucky to find this place. It is well decorated and furnished. It is also dry, even in winter, and best of all, cheap. His landlord is a bit weird. Friendly, enough though. Craig has been invited upstairs for a beer and a game of darts, several times. Yet somehow, he is not knowable. Remote. Chilling, he would be tempted to say, if he was the type to allow his fancy to take flight. It is how he feels about the bedsit, really. There is something creepy about it. Perhaps, this is due to it being in a basement. It doesn't get much light and he has always found artificial light in the day time much more spooky than complete darkness at night. Why is that? Is it something from his past? He has often had terrible dreams in this bedsit too. He isn't sure of the cause. It could be an unconscious reaction to studying psychology. Or it could be leaving home, for the first time. The pressure of studying at university is another possibility, he has considered. Curiously, the dreams always end in the same way. He is awakened by a woman's scream.

As he puts the final touches to his C.V. Craig begins to believe he can smell gas. After analysing what it could mean, psychologically, for another hour, his defences cave in, and he circles his tiny bedsit, obsessively, sniffing the gas central heating installation, the gas hot water heater, and his gas cooker. Where is the damn smell coming from? It appears to be at its most intense in one particular area of his bedsit. It is where the staircase, which once joined the basement to the larger part of the house above, used to be. He tests this theory by going outside, galloping up the flight of stairs to his landlord's front door, opening his letterbox, and inhaling, deeply. Hell!

He rings Gordon in Spain on the number he has been given for just such an emergency. He is too young to want to carry the responsibility of handling a domestic crisis by himself. His father takes care of these things at home. But, even after years of watching him doing so Craig is reluctant to have a go himself. It would seem like too much of an oedipal leap, somehow. He prefers to be told what to do. He is expecting to be instructed to ring the gas company, or at the very least to obtain a key to the house, which his landlord will have probably left, locally, with a trusted friend, so the response he actually does receive comes as a surprise to him.

There is no need to do anything, I'm telling you. I am on my way over, myself. I will get the first flight I can and be there in a few hours. Don't do anything until I get there.

Like light a match you mean, Craig jokes, sarcastically, but the line has already gone dead.

He is in a quandary. Gordon is unerringly softly spoken and polite, but there is something in his manner that demands obedience. That much is reassuring. Yet, Craig is the one living below, what is after all, an unexploded bomb. It seems absurd to do nothing; ridiculous and needlessly dangerous. What if half the neighbourhood goes up in smoke and he gets blamed. What would Pops have to say about that? He'd never get a job anywhere.

Pete Dixon has been reading a book about the law of attraction. It explains everything. How his whole life to date has been a disaster. How if he wants to make it better, he needs to practice the power of positive thinking. He is not doing well. It is hard to think pleasant thoughts, while investigating a potentially fatal gas leak. It is harder still when he has to work with Bill Saunders - the laziest twit he has ever laid eyes upon. He has to do everything himself. Bill is only here for the ride. Although, he has a good sense of humour, he mentally adds, trying to redress the balance of his negativity. And, he does stand his round in the pub.

The two coppers, who've been sent to help him, look bored as hell. Although, they may be just deep in thought. No, they keep looking at their watches as if they're anxious to get off for their tea break. The blues and twos all the way to Maggie's café in the parade of shops around the corner, he shouldn't wonder. But, they are probably extremely committed to their jobs the rest of the time.

Better keep people away from the house, he suggests, to give them something positive to do.

They look up and down the empty street and one of them asks him: *Should we tell the neighbours to evacuate?*

Pete smiles, uncertainly. Is he taking the piss or what? Damn, more negativity. That's another load of bad luck on the way. No, he mustn't think that or it will happen. Stop it! He mustn't think that either. He tries to remember how to make himself feel better. This is the key to it all. He has to feel good if he is to attract good experiences to himself. He sets himself the task of thinking of ten good things to say about the situation he is in.

Nice weather, he tells Bill. *Nice weather,* he repeats to himself.

He hadn't expected to get stuck so fast.

Lovely day, he mumbles, feeling useless and trying to calculate what new disaster will befall him because of this.

The gas meter is inside the house so he makes a temporary disconnection outside, while Bill, the two policemen, and the

262

young student who lives downstairs, stand around watching him. A few neighbours have begun to look out of their windows too. They'll soon be out to investigate what's going on, which might at least give the police something to do. In the meantime, he needs to gain entry to the upper part of the house so he can inspect the installation and discover exactly where the leak is. There's still a strong smell of gas emanating from it. But the front door is locked and nobody seems to have a key.

We can have that down in a jiffy, one of the policemen boasts, when he explains the problem. Or should that be, opportunity?

Pete forces a smile onto his lips. Isn't it nice to have such a helpful police force, he silently adds to his list of positives.

The policemen shake their heads as soon as they actually inspect the door. It is solid wood with three good quality locks. They decide not to mess around. They call out a locksmith straight away.

As soon as the front door is opened, Pete leads the way inside. Bill only follows him in because he is told to, but he does offer to carry some of their tools.

On entering the kitchen, Pete spots the cooker knob straight away. Marvellous what a trained eye will see, he adds to his list. Turning the knob to the off position, he opens the windows.

All clear, he shouts outside to the policemen, who lumber in to join him, with the student trailing behind. *Can you believe this guy left his gas cooker turned on, while he went away on holiday?*

But, that doesn't make sense, Craig Barker says, with a perplexed expression. *He has been away for over a week. I would have smelled gas before today, if the knob was the cause.*

The plonker left the gas on, I tell you. There is no mistake. But, it is probably easily done.

Neither of the officers have anything to say on the matter at all. Their attention has been arrested by a pile of newspaper cuttings on the kitchen table.

Pete takes a look too. They're all about those murders: the four young women who were abducted each June by the June Killer. There are some about an attack in Leicester on another woman too. Very negative energy is all this.

In the middle of the sea of newsprint stands an elegant blue satin high heel.

Isn't it unlucky to put shoes on a table?

Nobody answers him. They're staring at the most bizarre thing of all. The strangest thing they've ever seen. It is a plastic cap, with holes punched into it, through which tufts of hair have been drawn, and crudely glued, on the inside. Blonde hair it is. Real human hair, it looks like. Pete scratches his bald pate. How the hell did he attract that?

The Weasel is arrested on suspicion of murder as he lands at East Midlands Airport. He shows no surprise. Not even when, after hours of questioning, he finally figures out what the police have found in his house. The impossibility of it seems curiously apt. It is the hand of destiny. A sign from God, it is over. His mission here is done. There is even something in him which rejoices at this. It is a relief to talk about it too. To tell them everything he has done. To share with them how clever he has been. He has been so secretive all his life, to be known at last feels orgasmic. It is ecstasy and death woven together.

Bim and I watch and listen, dispassionately. I speculate, fleetingly, about whether the others in the Light know that we've got him, or does it truly not matter to them now? It matters to me less than I expected, if I'm honest. I'm glad it is done. It is good to put a full stop to the whole sorry affair. But, I lack the sense of triumph I anticipated. There is no exhilaration, only exhaustion.

The detectives interviewing him exude the same air of torpor. There is something about Gordon which is deadening even when he is not actively engaged in murder. The gruesome detail of what he has done wears away at you. There is only one thing he says which jolts me. He isn't Gordon at all but Simon. Or so he claims. He and his brother traded places at six years old as a joke which nobody else, including their parents, got. That was the joke, they decided, no one knowing. But, when Gordon developed cancer and the hospital appointments started, their trade was fixed. Suddenly, it seemed to them their joke had a terrible consequence. They didn't dare own up to it. Privately, Simon believed this was essential to his survival. His mother had often said she'd never wanted twins. If she'd been able to abort one of them, she would have, she confessed, within his hearing to a friend. He was convinced had she chosen only one of them to survive it would have been Gordon and not him. The cancer was nothing more than this really: the embodiment of his mother's preference. The boy she knew as Simon was dying. Why tell her it was a case of mistaken identity? No, he cloaked himself in his brother's pelt and went on living in his mother's love.

Gordon, or Simon, never seems to lose the pleasure that talking about his crimes brought him in those first heady days of his confession. He talks his way into court, through his trial and conviction, and on into a Secure Mental Hospital. There is a dull patch, for a while, after this, because he doesn't like talking to psychiatrists. He is smarter than they are, naturally, and he detests the silly games they want to play. But, after a few months, he finds a way of transcending their interference with his fun. He has received dozens of requests to write his life story. But, the one he accepts is from a first time writer whom he believes he can control just as he did Scott Ramsey.

Psychology graduate, Craig Barker's bestseller - My Landlord was the June Killer – will be published very soon.

The Weasel claims me as his in his confession. I'm officially a murder victim now. I don't mind. I barely remember what it was like to have physical form. Nor what physical pain is like. Strangely, having been murdered gives me more credibility as a detective in the spirit world too: the earth bound spirit world, that is.

Are you coming with us to the football match, Auntie Kate, Jethro asks, rousing me from my thoughts.

He is tribal with football regalia: unrecognisable as my kith and kin. My favourite nephew!

Define, we, I toss back at him.

What?

Who is going?

Us...Me, Caleb, and Sam.

On your own?

Daddy is taking us.

Daddy?

Yes.

Won't that be nice?

Are you coming then?

No, I think I'll stay here and keep your mum company.

That was a hard choice to make. Since when did Phil start taking the boys to football matches?

Carrie and I wave them off in his Audi, the boys in the back, properly secured, their limbs moving like tentacles.

I ask casually as we walk back into the house: *When did your ex become a father?*

She grins. *You're never going to like him are you?*

No, why do you?

Well, I have to admit, since he walked out on us...

He was pushed out after he tried to kill you, I think.

Whatever. Since he left, he has become a halfway decent father to the boys.

And, that is good?

For them it has to be.
And, for you?
He is okay with me.
Has he met Nigs yet?
No.

There is something in the way she said this that captures my curiosity.

Is everything okay between you two?
It just sort of fizzled out.
Why? I thought I saw a spark there.

She shakes her head. *I look like you is all.*

I try and ignore the feeling of triumph this gives me. How can I be dead, and still want to compete with her?

It was more than that, Carrie, I reassure her, generous in victory.

Was it?
Course, it was.
Maybe. But, it's over now. I've done with men who don't quite want me.

You're sure?
Yeah, I'm going concentrate on myself for awhile.
A period of abstinence?
Something like that.

Does that mean I can move back in? I ask this swiftly, before I have a chance to feel bad for trying to manipulate her. *Not for work. I'll keep my office on for that.*

Our office.

Yes, quite. It is just that I'm fed up of having to share my own flat with lodgers. I'd rather be one here.

She laughs. *Well, if you have to...*

You wouldn't mind if I brought Bim with me too, would you?

She purses her lips. *I thought she was hanging out with Reece.*

Not all the time.

Are you two working on another case?

We're thinking about it.

She doesn't need to know we're already investigating the suave young doctor with a cocaine habit who killed her business

268

partner, Denise, through his negligence.

I don't want the house filled with ghosts though, Kate, she warns. *I have the boys to think of.*

Spirits, I correct.

I decide to ignore the implication that we are somehow bad for my nephews. And, I make no promise to her on numbers either. It is a little late for that anyway.

Maybe we should go, Denise whispers to the others who are standing around the kitchen, listening to our conversation.

Don't be silly, Bim replies, smiling reassuringly at everyone. *As long as Jethro and Caleb go on keeping their mouths shut... for a price,* Denise interjects....*how's she going to know?*

THE END

Thank you for reading my book. If you enjoyed it, please tell your friends.
Lauren White

Lauren White is a former newspaper and radio journalist, who lived in Spain, for ten years, but is now based in the UK. She is currently working on a new crime novel called, The Silence. She hopes to publish another D. I. Ghost Murder Investigation, next year.